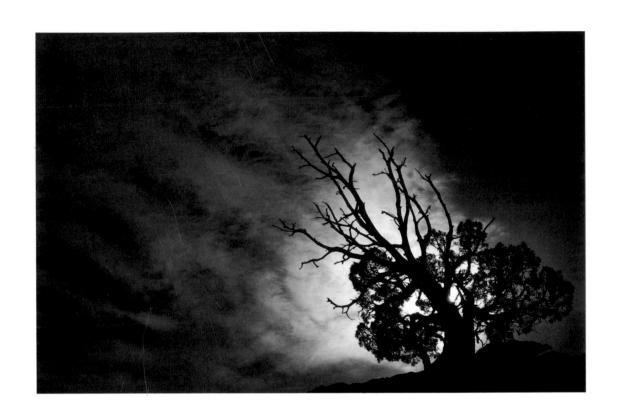

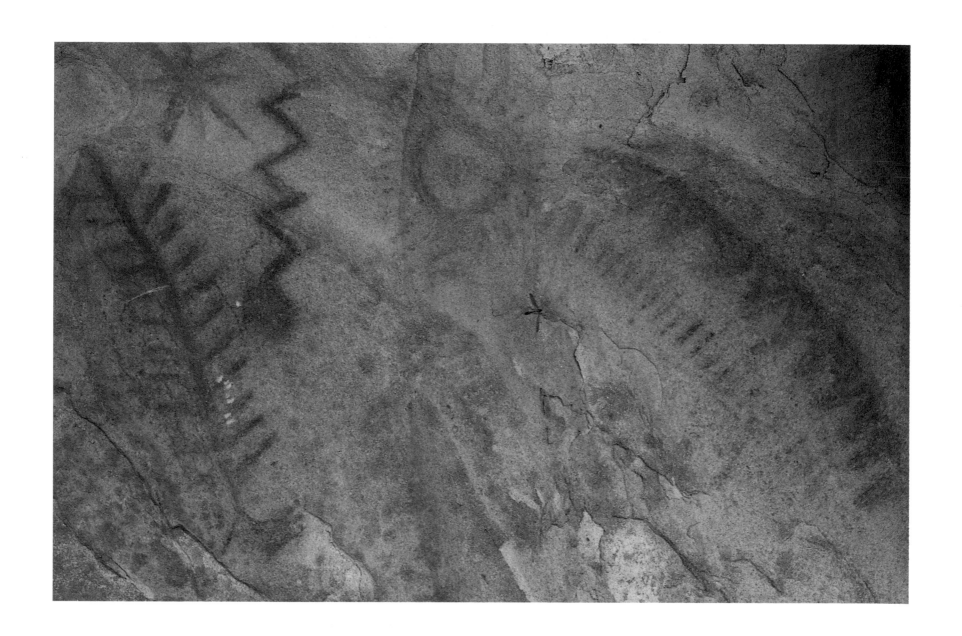

Courtney Milne

# SPIRIT

Sacred Places

# OF THE

in Native North America

# LAND

VIKING

VIKING
Published by the Penguin Group
Penguin Books Canada Ltd, 10 Alcorn Avenue, Toronto, Ontario, Canada M4V 3B2
Penguin Books Ltd, 27 Wrights Lane, London W8 5TZ, England
Viking Penguin, a division of Penguin Books USA Inc., 375 Hudson Street,
New York, New York 10014, U.S.A.
Penguin Books Australia Ltd, Ringwood, Victoria, Australia
Penguin Books (NZ) Ltd, 182-190 Wairau Road, Auckland 10, New Zealand

Penguin Books Ltd, Registered Offices: Harmondsworth, Middlesex, England

First Published 1994

10 9 8 7 6 5 4 3 2 1

Copyright © Courtney Milne 1994

Printed and bound in Italy on acid neutral paper


**Canadian Cataloguing in Publication Data**

Milne, Courtney, 1943-
        Spirit of the land : Sacred Places in Native North America

Includes index.
ISBN 0-670-84985-5

1.      Sacred space - North America - Pictorial works.
2.      Indians of North America - Religion and
        mythology - Popular works.  I.  Title.

E98.R3M5 1993     291.3'5'08997     C93-094708-8

**American Library of Congress Cataloguing in Publication Data Available**

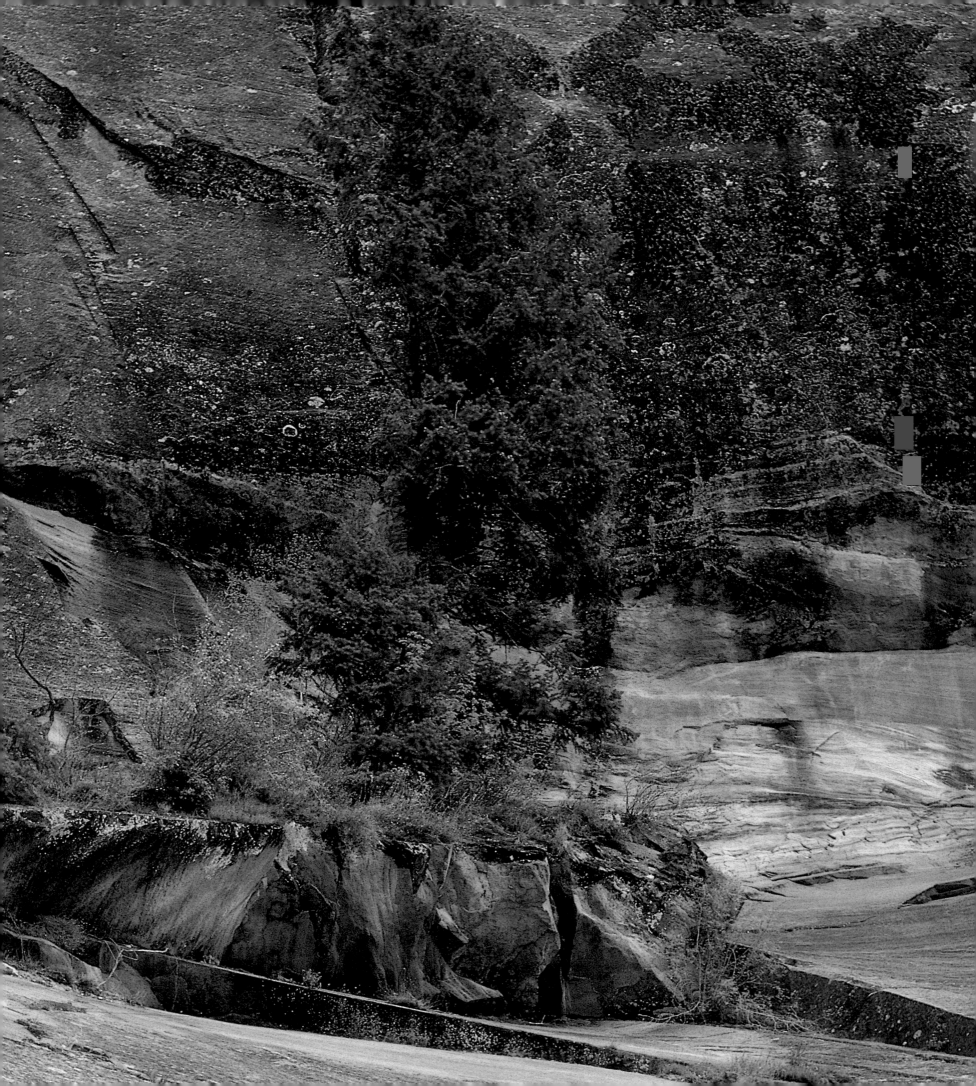

# ACKNOWLEDGMENTS

My first words of thanks go to Sherrill Miller, my mate and partner. Sherrill organized many of the trips and spearheaded the research and writing of the text. So much was she an integral part of the project that when I refer to "us" I mean "Sherrill and me."

I am indebted to many other people, including Dave Courchene Jr. (Leading Earth Man) at Manito Ahbee and Alvin Manitopyes (Sign of the Eagle) for guidance in Anishanabe teachings; Dennis Fast and Kim Belfry for companionship, humour and assistance in Greenland; Chief Henry Midnscum, Tony Neeposh and Jimmy Gurner of the Mistissini Band; Beth Richards and the Mastin family who hosted me at Mnido Mnis; Chief Leona Nahwegahbow of the Whitefish River First Nation; Manitoulin Island artists Shirley Cheechoo and Leland Bell; Father David Nazar of Wikwemikong; Mary Ellen McQuay and Lori Labatt for their help at Nee-ah-gah-rah and cheerleading sessions throughout the project; Ray Redwing at Pipestone for his friendship and support; Michael Stewart of Temple University for valuable background on Ringing Rocks; William Gustin, site manager of Serpent Mound; Sandra Sommerville for showing us the four colours of earth at Bear Butte, for her incredible healing energy, and for her unconditional love; Sandy Spider of Rosebud, South Dakota, for help while we were photographing in the Badlands; Roger Keyes for sharing his joy about life and for steering us to Stone Mountain; and Billy Townsound for providing historical background about that site.

I'd also like to thank Jeff Waugh, my guide through Pahayokee and companion on many photography outings; Dennis Peterson for help at Spiro Mounds; Bob and Ani Stokoe who prompted us to visit Hot Springs, Arkansas; Robert Talltree, Rolling Thunder and the Pikes Peak Library for filling in the missing pieces for Manitou Springs; Mary Jane and Claude Richey and Maureen and Robert Chernick for humour and hospitality in Texas; Rio de la Vista for her hugs and the impetus to visit Pahgasa; Roger la Borde for consultation and spiritual direction; John and Verna, site managers at Three Rivers, for their down-home hospitality; George Tosh whose superb photography of White Sands and the William River inspired me to go there; Ernie Lister for escorting me through Antelope and Peach Canyons, with ladder in hand; Nicholas Mann, Ann Williams and Rahelio for orienting us at Wipuk in Arizona;

Ken Robison and Jay Wiseman for valuable advice on Bryce and Mukuntuweap and for introducing me to Velvia film in the bowels of Antelope Canyon; Marilyn and Larry Frank, cousins who housed us during our stay at Joshua Tree; and Bruce Milne for much needed repairs to my equipment.

I would also like to acknowledge George Butterworth of the Nature Conservancy for help in finding pictographs, and Libby Tolley and Karen Foster, mirthful spirits and kindred artists in the Carizzo Plain; Dr. Roy Salls who directed us to Humqaq and Painted Cave; Virginia Johnson of the Santa Barbara State Parks and the Chumash Council who assisted our access to Painted Cave; Cecily Gregory for continued support and for housing at Bodega Bay; Jane English for showing us the flowers and Missi Gillespie for her wonderful Golden Bough Bookstore at Mount Shasta; Roy Diment for a week of companionship and photography on the west coast; Paul Lazarski, a kindred spirit on many expeditions on Vancouver Island; Carl and Joe Martin of Tofino, B.C., for lending us their dugout canoe to photograph; Jamie Bray for his whale watching excursions; and Roy Vickers whose art continues to inspire me.

Sincere thanks also go to Jim Allen, Ecosummer Expeditions, for touring me to Gwaii Hanaas; Robert Davidson, Haida artist, for helping me find the spirit in the land; Fred Campiou (White Rainbow) for being a model of gentleness and sincerity; Barney Reeves, John Dormaar, Lee Christie and Julian Norris for valuable direction, insights and information on locations in southern Alberta; Graham Wilson for his research on St. Elias and for touring me through the Yukon; Edwin J. Weyiouanna for his evocative carving; Stan Rowe, Peter Jonker and Adam Kosowan for their leadership at the Athabasca Sand Dunes; Cree guides August Mercredi and Paul and Eileen Adam, for the hearty meals and stories around the campfire; David Meyer and Ernie Walker of the University of Saskatchewan; Frank Yeast and family who gave me a home and access to the dunes for my many excursions to the Great Sandhills; Wes Fineday, artist and storyteller, for his touching portrayal of Wanuskewin; Jeremy Morgan, Pat McCloskey and Janice Acoose for inspiration, and Harley Michailuck and Mary Weiler who shared quality time with me at Wanuskewin; Andy DeBray, Delvin Kennedy and the St. Mary Hoop Dancers of Saskatoon for bringing

to life the meaning of the circle; Ian Brace of the Royal Saskatchewan Museum for his scholarly work on medicine wheels; and Elvin McArthur of the Pheasant Rump Reserve for access to Moose Mountain Medicine Wheel.

Special words of thanks are owed to Hanna and Maurice Strong for getting us to the Earth Summit; Chief Leon Shenendoah and Chief Oren Lyons for sharing their wisdom with others; Charles Lawrence, Jackie Gusaas, Ken Budd, Marj Benson, Alan Tremayne, John Cuthand, Henry and Sarah Comerford, Father Lawrence and Sister Miriam, Adele Curtis, Ken Norman, Iva Anderson, Melanie Elliot, Bruce Acton, Tana Dineen, Sheryl and Morrie Sacks, Carollyne Sinclaire and Patricia Langer, for their sharing; Loreen Wilsdon, Sherry Morris, Gladys McArthur and Lyle Bradley for keeping the home fires burning; Jim Berenholtz for continuing guidance, wisdom and stimulation; Monte Hummel and his staff at World Wildlife Fund, Canada; Paul Spencer Sochaczewski at Worldwide Fund for Nature in Geneva; Maryann Gula and Cunard Steamship Lines for getting us to new locations; and the helpful management and staff at the National Parks, Monuments and Forests in the United States, and the National and Provincial Parks in Canada.

On the production side, I'd like to thank Danny Weselowski of Pro-Color Lab in Saskatoon for assistance with the computer-manipulated composites; Randy Hills of Chromographics Inc. in Saskatoon for making the slide sandwiches; John Melnyk and the staff of Gibson Photo in Saskatoon for continued excellence in film developing; Bob Stahl who taught me the cardinal truth: "f-8, and be there!"; Hans Ohlig of Amplis Foto, Toronto for keeping me updated on new product lines; Larry Frank of Nikon, Canada for his continued support.

Finally, thank you to John Lee for a superb book design incorporating new ways for me to look at my work; Brian Maracle for a powerful and sensitively written foreword and his many helpful comments on the text; Jim Loates for designing the map; and lastly, Jackie Kaiser at Penguin Books for a masterful job leading the team.

This book is dedicated to
Natalie Rostad, Lynn Branson, and JoAnne Bird
Three soul sisters whose artworks embrace the spirit of the land

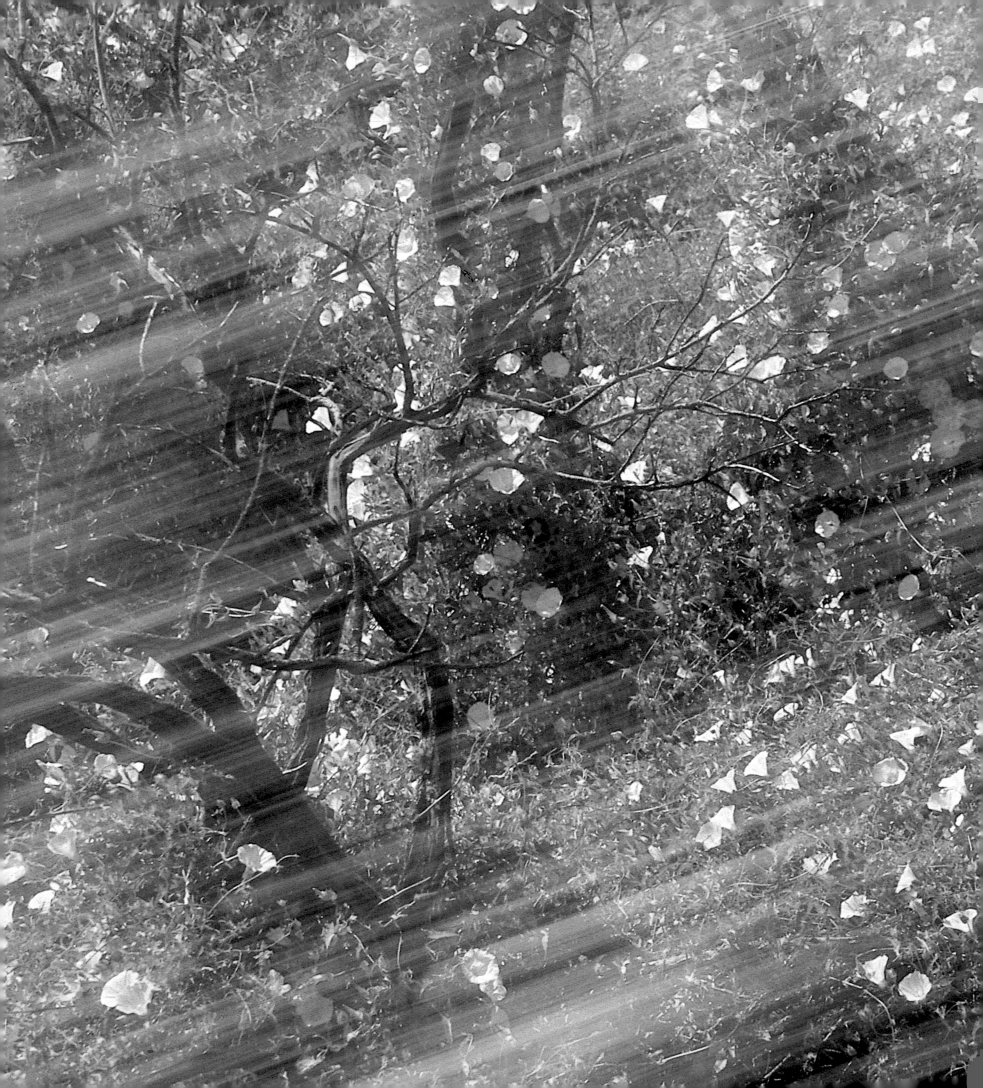

# CONTENTS

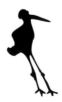

# FOREWORD

OUR ANCESTORS, THE ANCIENT ONES, left many testaments to their existence. The signs of their being – serpent mounds, rock paintings, medicine wheels, petroglyphs, inukshuks, totem poles – have withstood the grinding pressure of time and are scattered all across Great Turtle Island.

The ancient works endure but the people who made them no longer exist. As their descendants we may have retained much of their language, culture and traditions but we are not the same people. Despite the passage of untold generations, however, the meaning of many of these works still lives within our hearts.

These monuments fuse us with our ancestral past. Because they help us to understand where we come from, they also help us to understand who we are. These works give meaning to our lives. They enrich our ceremonies, religions and cultures. They provide guidelines for behaviour and inspiration for the future.

But the meaning of some of these monuments has been lost. Enveloped in mystery, they taunt us with frustratingly unanswerable questions: *Who made it? How was it used? What does it mean?*

People who have a strong link to the past do not mourn the loss of meaning from such creations. We simply accept that these works are the silent remnants of another people, another time.

But there is one thing about these ancient creations that should concern all of us – Aboriginal people and newcomers alike. At the core of each of these works is a statement that expresses the relationship that human beings have with each other, with the land and with their God. And it is clear from these markers of the past that the ancients of Great Turtle Island treated the land, each other and the Creator with reverence and respect.

The monuments the ancients left for us should therefore make us wonder: *What will the monuments we leave for our descendants say about the way we treat each other? What will they say about the way we treat the land? And what will they say about our relationship with our Creator?*

Clearly, it will be a long time before the humans on Great Turtle Island come to one mind about how to treat each other and how to relate to God. But if we are to leave monuments that awe and inspire future generations, then we will have to begin showing respect for one thing that most of the people here have come to take for granted – the land.

Great Turtle Island is scarred in many places because of greed and lack of respect. The forces of nature will help the land recover from the damage because the spirit of the land endures. It may not be the same, but the land will survive.

Few people today have the same relationship with the land that the original inhabitants did. Most of the people living here now are urban creatures, living in an environment they have shaped to their liking. Not only do they not live as part of the natural world, they rarely seek it out and avoid it whenever they can.

At best, most people regard "the land" as little more than an interesting subject for a television documentary. At worst, they regard it as a commodity – something to be shaped, tamed, exploited and controlled for profit and pleasure, for comfort and convenience.

To the Aboriginal people of Great Turtle Island, though, land is more than real estate and nature is more than an annoyance to heat or air condition.

My people, the Iroquois – like probably all the other Aboriginal people – know from our teachings that we were created from the earth itself and specifically placed on this one corner of Great Turtle Island by the Creator. Our very being stems from this one fact: we were born of this earth and to this earth.

Furthermore, the Creator gave our people, and our people only, the knowledge of how to survive on this land, knowledge that we shared with those who came later. The Creator also gave us the instructions on how we should respect the land and how we should give thanks.

From all this, we believe in the deepest part of our soul that this land was divinely and expressly made for us by the hand of God.

It should come as no surprise, then, to learn that we regard the land – all of it – as sacred: every rock, every tree, every river, every blade of grass. All of creation – the four-legged, the swimming and the flying creatures, all of the plant life, the winds, the thunderers – everything from the most seemingly insignificant insect to the mightiest mountain is sacred, because it was made and placed here by the Creator.

And because all things are sacred, all places are sacred. The places we thank the Creator. The places the spirits live. The places we celebrate our ceremonies. The places we seek visions. The places we bury our dead. The places we name our children. The places we get our food. The places we gather our medicines. The places we

greet the morning sun. The places we welcome the spring. The places we seek out for healing, contemplation and rejuvenation. All of the land on Great Turtle Island is hallowed ground because all of our activities are part of the sacred cycle of life.

One other thing must be understood: these sacred places are not nameless. They carry the names that we have given them in our ancestral language. These names give meaning to us and to our lives.

We shared these names with the newcomers just as we shared this land. We are now surrounded by the Aboriginal names of countless cities, rivers, lakes, parks, states and provinces – from Chicago and Chicoutimi to Wichita and Winnipeg. But after countless repetitions by people who don't know their meaning, these once-descriptive names have been stripped of their power, their magic and their beauty. Even the meaning of this country named Canada is known to just a few of the millions who call it home.

Five centuries after the newcomers arrived and began making their mark upon the land, we must ask ourselves: *What kind of testaments are we leaving for our descendants?*

Much of what we leave will last a thousand years, but there is little of which we can be proud. Most of the remnants of our being will testify to the lack of respect that the people now living on Great Turtle Island have for the land and the Creator.

But there are testaments being made of which we can be proud. Of those few, this book is one. This book is the kind of marker we should leave for the future – one that is wholeheartedly concerned with a relationship to the land and to the Creator, one that is based on reverence and respect.

There is much to be done if we are ever to create monuments for future generations that recapture the awe and wonder that are the hallmarks of the works of the ancient ones. We can start by learning the meaning of the Aboriginal ghost names that surround us, because the names of these places were divinely inspired. To learn and appreciate their true meaning will help to create much-needed respect for the land and the works of creation. We need to see the land for what it is – sacred in all its parts. And most of all, we need to develop and nurture a special relationship with the Creator that acknowledges the gifts of creation that have been bestowed upon us.

*Akewenna'okon na' ne'e kenh iken.* So I have said.

*Brian Maracle*
*Six Nations Grand River Territory*
*January 1994*

Brian Maracle, a member of the Mohawk Nation, is an award-winning journalist and the author of *Crazywater: Native Voices on Addiction and Recovery*. During the 1970s he worked for native organizations at the local, provincial and national levels. He is a former host of the CBC Radio programme, *Our Native Land*, and a former reporter for *The Globe and Mail*. Brian Maracle lives on the Six Nations Grand River Territory near Brantford, Ontario.

11

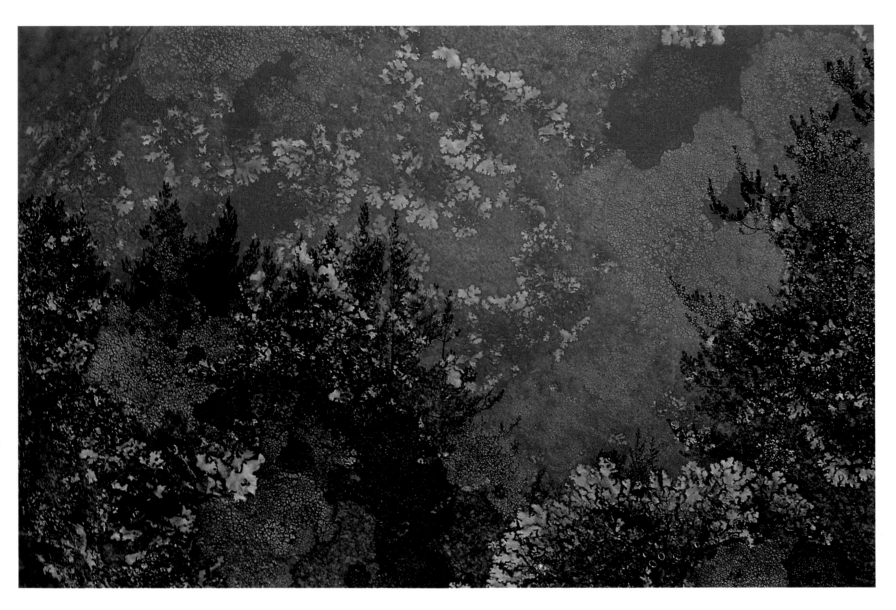

# INTRODUCTION

AT THE DAWN OF THE 1990 AUTUMN EQUINOX, I
climbed into the bucket of a hydraulic lift
and was hoisted forty feet into the air beside
the Big Horn Medicine Wheel in northern
Wyoming. I felt a powerful energy there at the ten-
thousand-foot summit of Medicine Mountain. It
seemed to me that the Big Horn Wheel linked the
distant plains with the heavens.

Though little is known for certain about its origins,
the wheel is believed to be more than two thousand
years old. The Crow, Arapaho, and Shoshone peoples
of this area all have oral histories about sacred ceremonies held here, and present-day prayer offerings can be
found on a fence erected to protect the wheel. I did not
know it at the time, but the Big Horn Wheel would

figure prominently in my life in the coming years. The
sense of mystery and awe I felt then has never left me.

In June, 1992, I participated in the Wisdom Keeper's
Convocation, part of the non-governmental events at
the Earth Summit in Rio de Janeiro, Brazil. While in
Rio, I witnessed the signing of the Charter of the
Indigenous People of the World, and was involved in
lighting a ceremonial fire, a symbolic focus of spiritual
energy from around the world. Soon after, I was presented with the idea of photographing sacred places in
Native North America. This immediately appealed to me
because I have long felt a kinship with Native spiritual
values.

I remembered my experience at Big Horn, and won-
dered where the twenty-eight spokes radiating from the
central cairn might lead. A framework began to emerge.
I decided to use the Big Horn Wheel as the starting
point of my photographic journey, following each
spoke across the continent in search of sacred landscapes.

The photographs in *Spirit of the Land* include specific sites that First Nations identify as holy, as well as
other natural landforms that capture the mystical essence of the earth. Twenty years of photographing the
land have drawn me ever closer to the life-giving cycles
and rhythms of nature; I have long enjoyed discovering
faces in tree bark and driftwood, and seeing animal or
human figures in the land before me. The photographs
in this book have been selected to convey my impres-
sions of how it felt to be at these places. I have sometimes used special photographic techniques in an

These soils were found a short distance from each
other at Bear Butte, South Dakota. The prayer flags
also display the four colours – red, yellow, black
and white – honouring the four cardinal directions,
according to Lakota tradition.

attempt to portray the spirit of the place – for me, small vignettes of nature are often more evocative than overall images of the physical landscape.

Today, despite centuries of oppression, this land's original inhabitants are finding new strength in their own traditions. The banning of such ceremonies as the Sundance, the Ghost Dance, and the Potlatch, combined with the degradation of sacred lands through mining and development, are tragic events in the history of this continent. It is a testament to the enduring spiritual power of Native cultures that these traditions are now experiencing a resurgence.

For many North American Native people, the circle represents the cycle of life. On the circle, there is no beginning and no end. This symbol of infinity and interconnectedness is seen in the sweat lodge, the bowl of the sacred pipe, the sacred hoop, and the medicine wheel. Some Native writers describe the medicine wheel as a microcosm of life, its circular pathway encompassing all aspects of the world within the four cardinal directions. Each of these directions represents a stage of life, within which specific lessons are learned. East is the place of birth and new beginnings; South, of youth, strength and idealism; West, of emotional growth and self-knowledge; and North, of wisdom and life's fulfillment. Corresponding to these directions are the four seasons – spring in the East, summer in the South, autumn in the West, and winter in the North – and the elements of earth, wind, water, and fire. The four related colours, according to the Lakota, are red, yellow, black, and white, which also reflect the main races of the world. At Bear Butte, a hallowed mountain in South Dakota, the same four colours are seen in prayer flags tied to tree branches, and distinct soils of the same colours are found within a short walk of each other.

Although there are many similarities among Native spiritual traditions, there are also, of course, distinct variations. While it was impossible to address all of these within the scope of this book, it is important that these differences be respected, and to this end I have, wherever possible, tried to include information about local traditions. Oral histories may vary, but the truth embodied in each telling endures.

*Spirit of the Land* is divided into four sections, each representing a cardinal direction. We begin our journey to the East of the Big Horn Medicine Wheel, visiting sites that fall in the paths leading to that section of the wheel, and continue to the South, West, and North, so that the photographs of these time-honoured places can be experienced within the context of the wheel that inspired the journey. My hope is that encountering these photographs will allow people to connect with the world as it was when all the land was revered, when all the elements were honoured for their power, when wilderness provided spiritual as well as physical nourishment, and when all humankind respected the sacred nature of their surroundings. I think it is fitting to begin our journey with a prayer I found on a signpost at Bear Butte.

Courtney Milne

Grandora, Saskatchewan
January 1994

15

# *Prayer to the Four Winds*

*Great Spirit, I invoke the peace pipe in reverence and gratitude*
*of thy vast creation, of which I am a part. To the life-giving of thy servant,*
*the sun and all heavenly bodies, the blue sky, the great everlasting rocks,*
*the magnificent mountains with their fragrant forests, pure streams*
*and the animal kingdom. We thank thee for all these gifts.*

*To the North and its guard, the White Eagle*
*Keep us pure and clean of mind, thoughts as white as*
*Thy blanket, the snow. Make us hardy.*

*To the East and thy sentry, the Red Eagle*
*Grant us light that we may see our faults*
*And have better understanding with everyone.*

*To the South, and thy sentinel, Brown Eagle*
*The beautiful one, grant us warmth of heart,*
*Love and kindness to all.*

*To the West and the Thunder Bird*
*Who flies over the universe hidden in a cloak of*
*Rain clouds and cleanses the world of filth,*
*Cleanse our bodies and souls of all evil things.*

*To Mother Earth we come from thee and will return to thee,*
*Keep us in plenty that our days may be long with thee,*

*Great Spirit we thank thee and appreciate*
*all these wonderful gifts to us.*
*Have pity on us.*

18

*Big Horn Medicine Wheel, Medicine Mountain,*
*Wyoming, September 1990*

Shishmaref **181**

Illutalik **26**

St. Elias **178**

Sitka **172**

Gwaii Hanaas **166**

William River **186**

Eskimo Point **196**

Gitchi Manitou
Ouitch-chouap **30**

Shining Mountains **176**

Wanuskewin **192**

Strait of
Juan de Fuca **158**

The Great Sandhills **190**

Head-Smashed-In **174**    Badlands **184**

Manito Ahbee **22**

Moose Mountain **198**

Mnido Mnis **32**

Pictograph Caves **182**

Nee-ah-gah-rah **40**

Crater Lake **156**

Yellowstone **152**

Mateo Tepee **50**    Pipestone **42**

Ringing Rocks **46**

Mount Shasta **146**

Bear Butte **14**
Mako Sica **53**

Red Rock Ridge **44**

Serpent Mound **48**

Bodega Bay **144**

Navajo Mountain **94**

Manitou Springs/
Garden of the Gods **74**

Pinnacles **140**

Bryce Canyon **120**

Mukuntuweap **124**    Pahgasa **84**

Spiro Mounds **66**

Stone Mountain **56**

Painted Rock **132**

Peach Canyon **114**    Mesa Verde **99**

Antelope Canyon **108**    Chaco Canyon **100**

Rock Eagle **58**

Humqaq **138**

Wipuk **116**

Canyon de Chelly/
Betatakin **94**

Hot Springs **68**

Painted Cave **136**

Twentynine Palms **128**    Three Rivers **86**

White Sands **90**

Enchanted Rock **80**

Pahayokee **62**

# Spirit of the Land

## COURTNEY MILNE'S JOURNEY

Numbers following names refer to page numbers.

# EAST

*To the East and Thy sentry, the Red Eagle*
*Grant us light that we may see our faults*
*And have better understanding with everyone*

*Petroform, Bannock Point Petroform Site,*
*Whiteshell Provincial Park, Manitoba,*
*May 1993*

*right: Composite of moon, trees and human*
*effigy (see Photographer's Notes, p.202),*
*Bannock Point Petroform Site, Whiteshell*
*Provincial Park, Manitoba,*
*May 1993*

# Manito Ahbee

## *Place of Beginning*

22 This journey starts at the beginning place, Manito Ahbee, located in what is now Whiteshell Provincial Park, Manitoba. It is revered as a teaching and healing place by the Three Fires Confederacy, a society formed in the sixteenth century by the people who call themselves Anishanabe (meaning "Original People") from the Odawa, Potawatomi and Ojibway nations. Since the 1960s, a movement has been underway to revive the Three Fires Confederacy and its spiritual tradition, which is dedicated to the pursuit of sacred knowledge about the universe that will provide the Anishanabe with a spiritual balance. It is this Grand Medicine Society of Medewewin that has rekindled the creation story of the Anishanabe people, who now number more than 250,000 throughout North America.

Here at Manito Ahbee, it is said the Original Man was lowered by rope from the sky to become the first inhabitant of Turtle Island, so named because, after the Great Flood, the Earth was formed on the back of a turtle. It is here that Original Man received from the Great Spirit the following seven sacred teachings: wisdom, love, respect, bravery, honesty, humility and truth – the principles to guide the Anishanabe in caring for the earth and for each other. These teachings have been recorded in the stone shapes of animal figures and geometric designs called petroforms, which are unique to Manito Ahbee.

The age of the petroforms is not known, but the Anishanabe believe they were built by spirits as a physical reminder of their sacred instructions. One form of a turtle and snake is said to interpret the afterlife journey of the spirit. Some are used ceremonially by medicine people during tobacco offerings and healing rituals. At Bannock Point, one of two major sites in the area of Manito Ahbee, a human effigy lies face up, arms and legs outstretched. According to the Medewewin, an Anishanabe asked Waynaboozhoo (also known as Nanabush, or in Cree as Wesake Jack) to grant him everlasting life. Waynaboozhoo, who was both spirit and man, both trickster and guide, complied by turning him forever into a stone effigy.

Today Manito Ahbee is revered by the Anishanabe as a gateway to higher understanding, as a site of origin that is connected to other spiritual centres on our planet. It will stand for eternity as a place to teach, to heal and to pray.

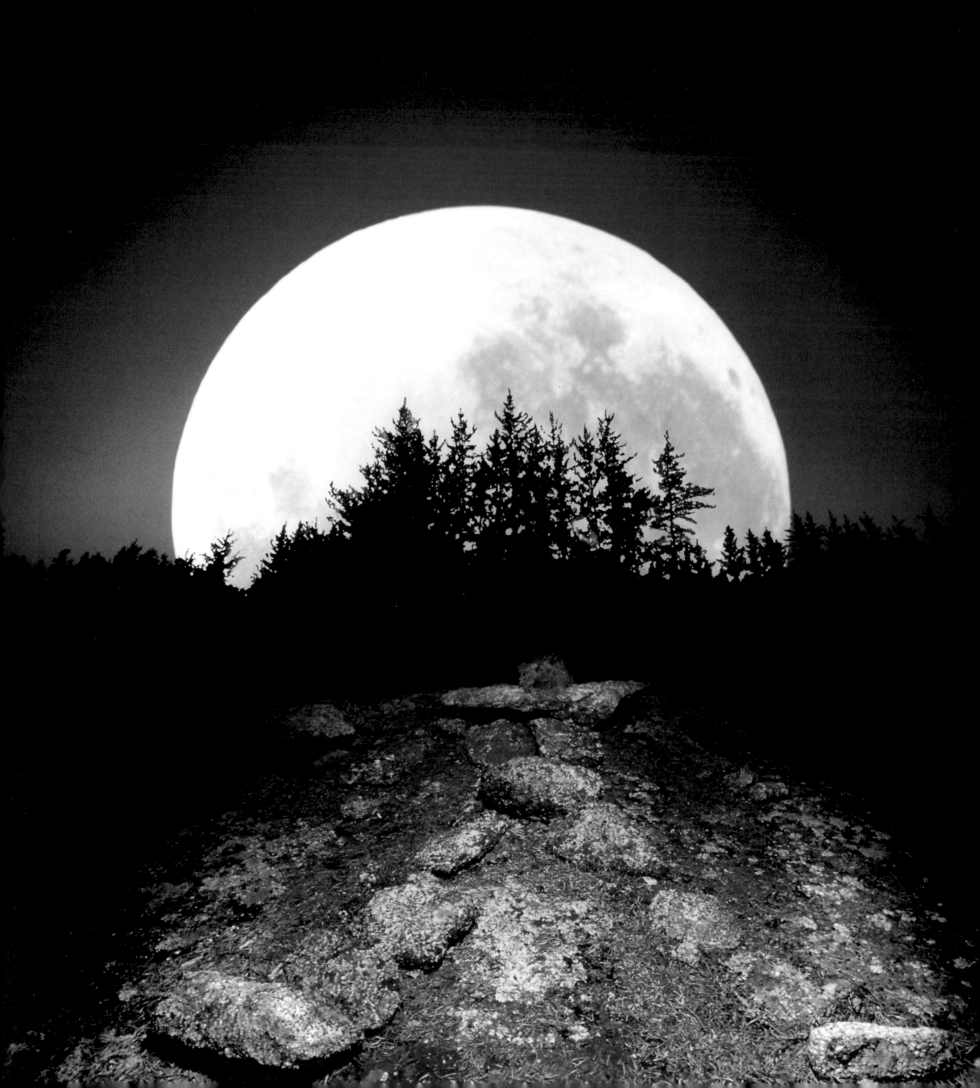

*Mineral stain, Bannock Point Petroform Site, Whiteshell Provincial Park, Manitoba, May 1993*

*below: Snake petroform, Bannock Point Petroform Site, Whiteshell Provincial Park, Manitoba, May 1993*

*right: Predawn light, Whiteshell Provincial Park, Manitoba, May 1993*

24

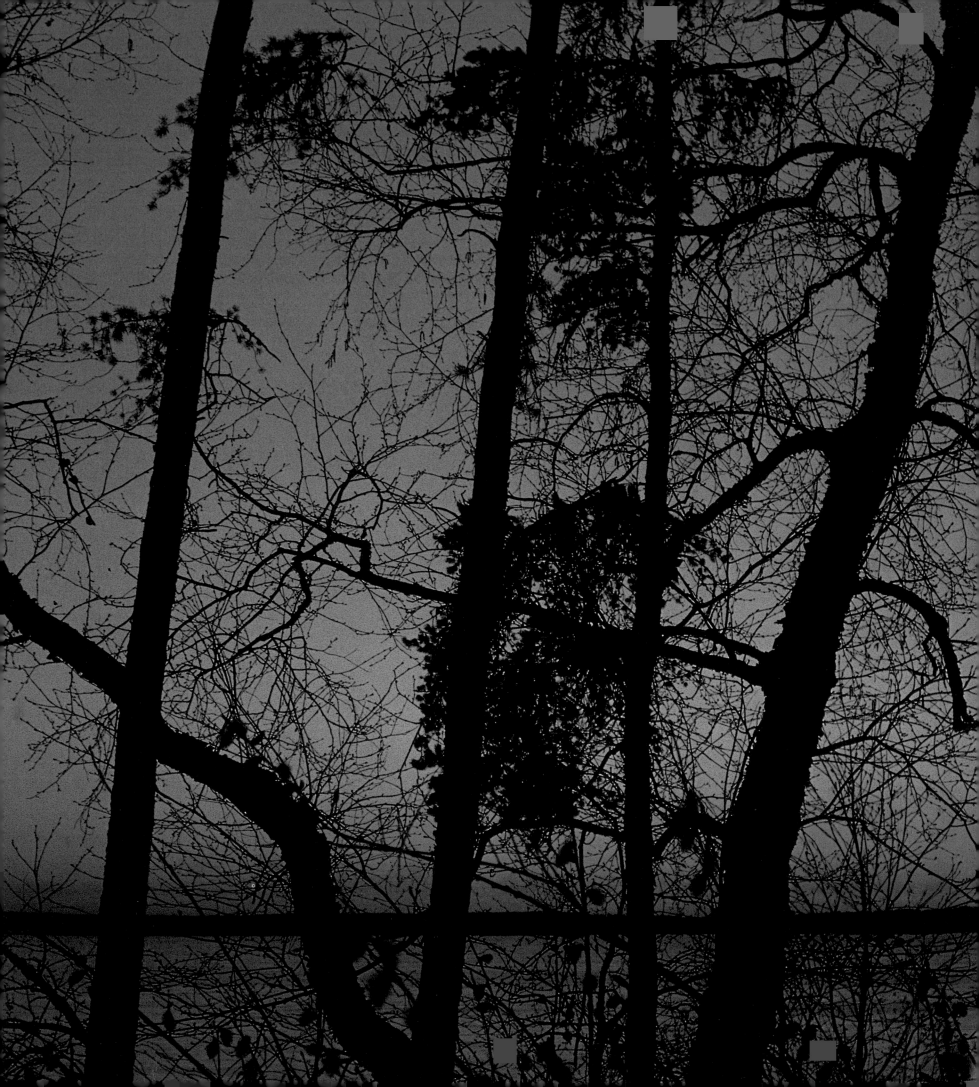

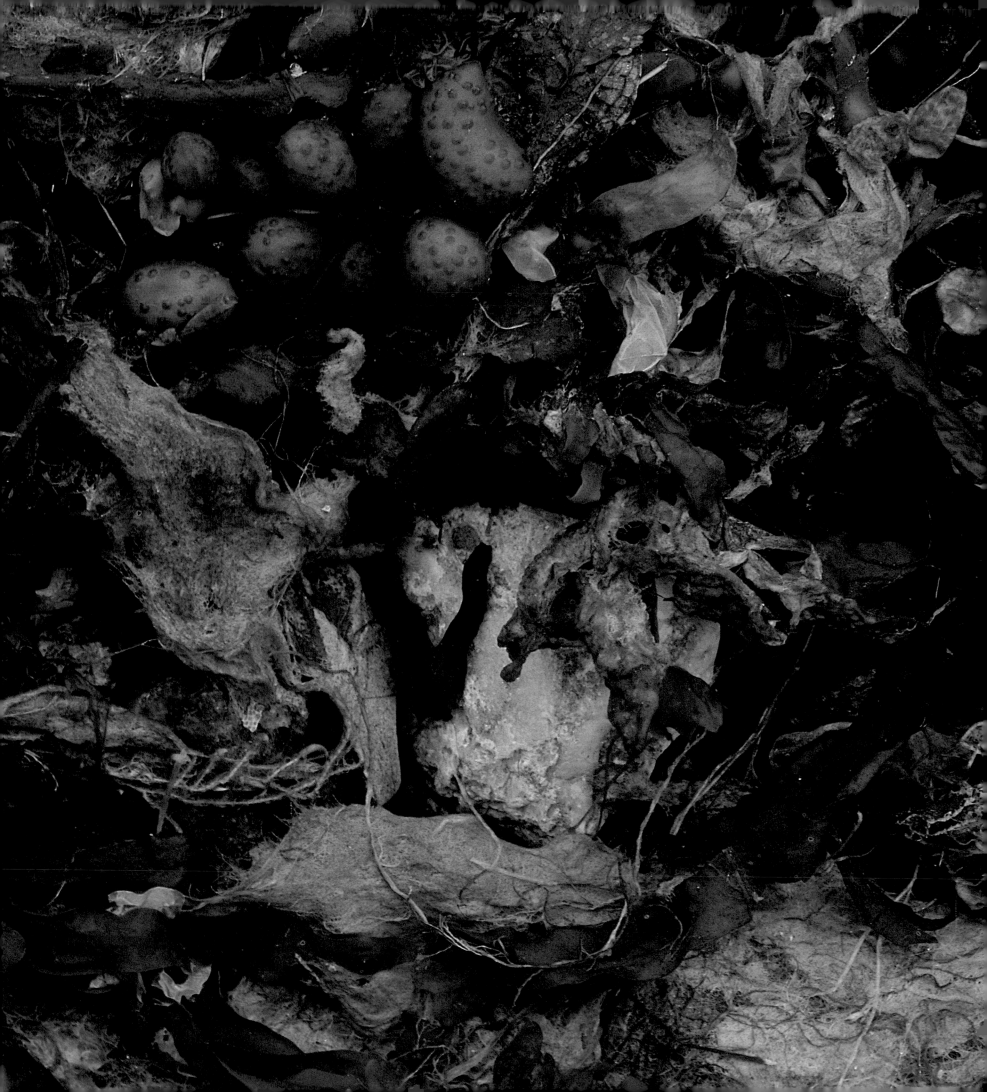

*Dried kelp on beach, Illutalik,*
*Greenland, July 1992*

*right: Reflected light on shore ice,*
*Illutalik, Greenland, July, 1992*

# Illutalik

## *Corridor to the Underworld*

## 27

The ancient Inuit village of Illutalik is located on the southern tip of Greenland. The first Eskimo settlements in this area are some of the oldest in the eastern Arctic, dating from as early as 2500 BC, when various cultural waves of people who crossed the land bridge from Asia to Alaska moved south and east, becoming the ancestors of the Inuit in Greenland today.

In Inuit culture, the land and sea are occupied by spirits who interact with them daily. Because traditional survival is dependent on hunting and communal living, social equilibrium is achieved by honouring many taboos. Otherwise, it is believed, the animals will not appear willingly to the hunter. Misfortune comes from breaking taboos, and public confessions and shamanic rituals are required to cleanse the community. For example, when game is scarce, the shaman might go into a trance state, during which his soul journeys under the sea to the home of the all-powerful goddess, Sedna, the Keeper of the Animals; here he would comb her hair, untangling the vermin of broken taboos, thus ensuring a plentiful hunt.

Another spirit, the mighty Sila, talks to humans through all the forces and forms of nature – storms, snow, rain and sunlight – and sends messages to children at play. When all is well, Sila sends no message, provided people act with reverence toward life.

The jagged icebergs and rocky shoreline are reminiscent of another Inuit story, which tells of the soul's archetypical journey through clashing rocks and shifting islands of ice, finally reaching the safety of the sacred country of ancestral deities.

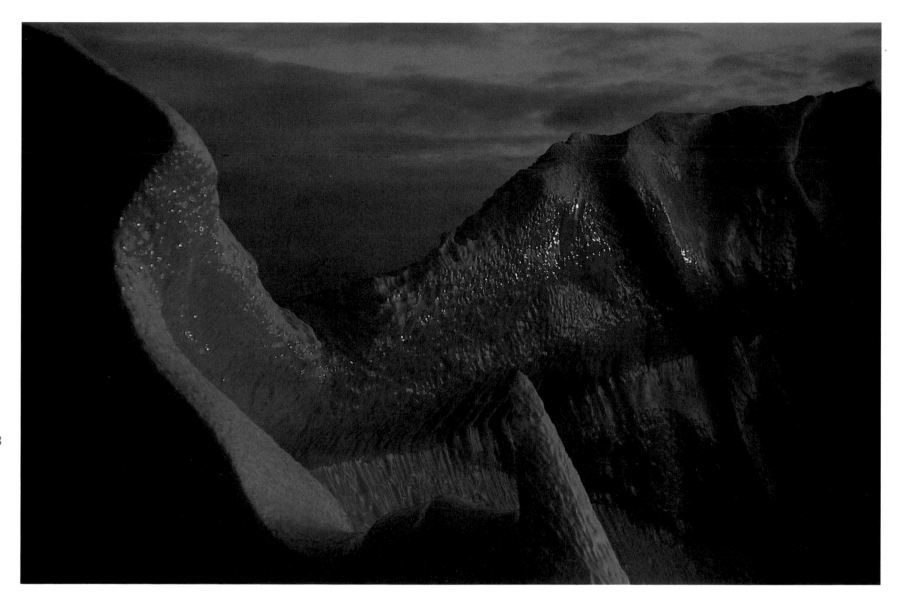

28

*Floating icebergs, Illutalik,
Greenland, July 1992*

29

*Melting snow on wall of white quartzite cave,*
*La Colline Blanche, Mistissini, Quebec,*
*October 1993*

*right: First snow on landscape,*
*Mistissini, Quebec, October 1993*

# Gitchi Manitou Ouitch-chouap

## *House of the Great Spirit*

30    An early October blizzard threatened as my guide, Jimmy Gurner, a Cree from Mistissini Lake in northern Quebec, paddled to the end of Yadogami Bay. We poled through the shallow reeds, and pulled the boat ashore to explore La Colline Blanche, a huge out-cropping of white quartzite along the south-ern shore of the Témiscamie River. To the local Mistissini Cree, this rock is known as Whapuushakanukw (pronounced wa-bush), meaning "House of the Rabbit." About 3,900 feet long, and almost 1,500 feet high, it is mainly covered with trees except for a distinctly white talus slope high on the northwest side.

Near the summit is a remarkable cave, its walls of smooth white marble polished by the action of violent glacial streams. Known as Gitchi Manitou Ouitch-chouap, or "House of the Great Spirit," it was to this place of protection and beauty that Cree hunters would come, praying to the Spirit of the Caribou or Moose for the gift of a good hunt. One Mistissini story says that the Memequash once resided here; these hairy-faced dwarfs lived in cliffs and paddled their stone canoes down the river to make rock paintings and to raid Indian fishnets.

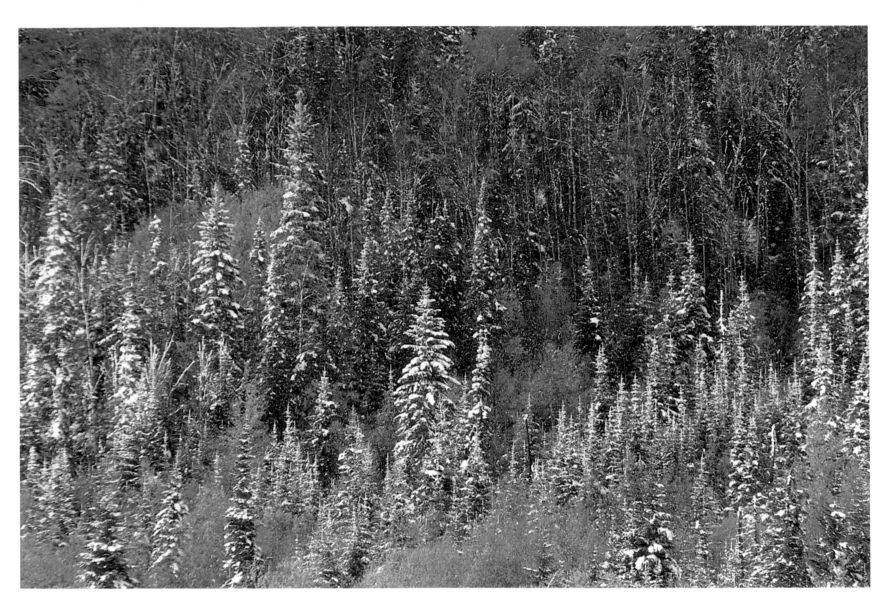

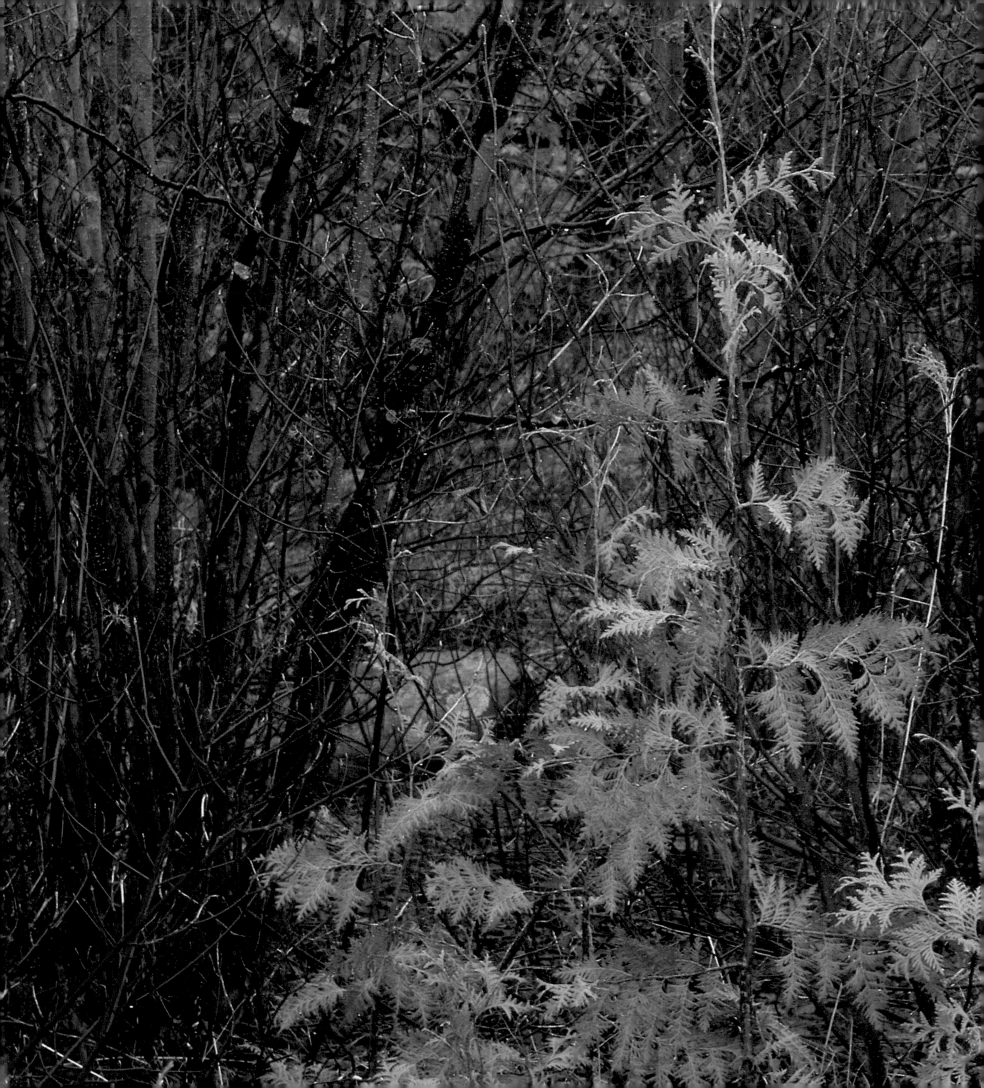

*Spring colours, Manitoulin Island,*
*Ontario, April 1993*

*right: Alder branch in stream at*
*Bridal Veil Falls, Manitoulin Island,*
*Ontario, April 1993*

# Mnido Mnis

## *Island of the Great Spirit*

Manitoulin is the world's largest freshwater island, rising up between Lake Huron and Georgian Bay in Ontario. Based on translations from the Ojibway, Odawa (Ottawa) and Potawatami languages, Manitou means "spirit," or "the Great Spirit," also known as Gitchi Manitou, and Manitoulin or Manitouminiss (Mnido Mnis) means Isle of the Manitou or "Spirit Island."

The story of Manitoulin's creation is rich in sacred significance. Gitchi Manitou had a dream, a vision of all that is good, and a mandate to fulfil his dream. He began by making the four elements – fire, earth, water and wind. From these he created the universe – the sun, moon, planets and the stars, bequeathing special powers to the land, the rivers, the lakes, the animals and the forest. Then he created humans, and bestowed on them the greatest gift of all – the ability to dream.

The Anishanabe Three Fires Confederacy says that all of Manitoulin is sacred, its spiritual stories recorded in the landscape. It is told that even today, Gitchi Manitou dwells on a tiny island in one of the large lakes on Manitoulin Island. Manitowaning Bay, known as "the den of the Great Spirit," is where Gitchi Manitou sometimes comes to travel through an underground secret passage in order to reach South Bay. Lake Mindemoya is where Nanabush, the trickster also known as Waynaboozhoo, stumbled as he was carrying his grandmother, and stopped nearby to rub the magic alder bushes on his cuts and bruises. The alders turned red from his blood and remain that colour to this day.

33

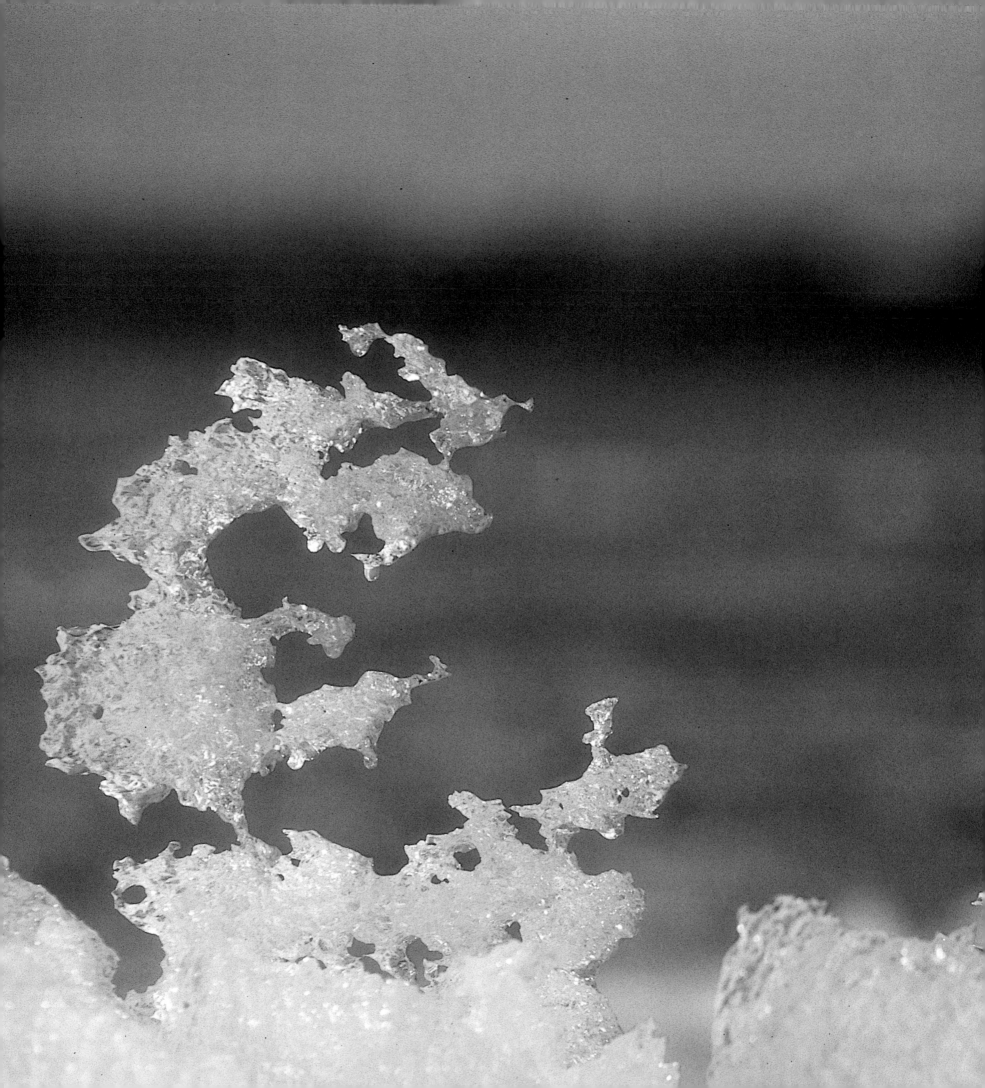

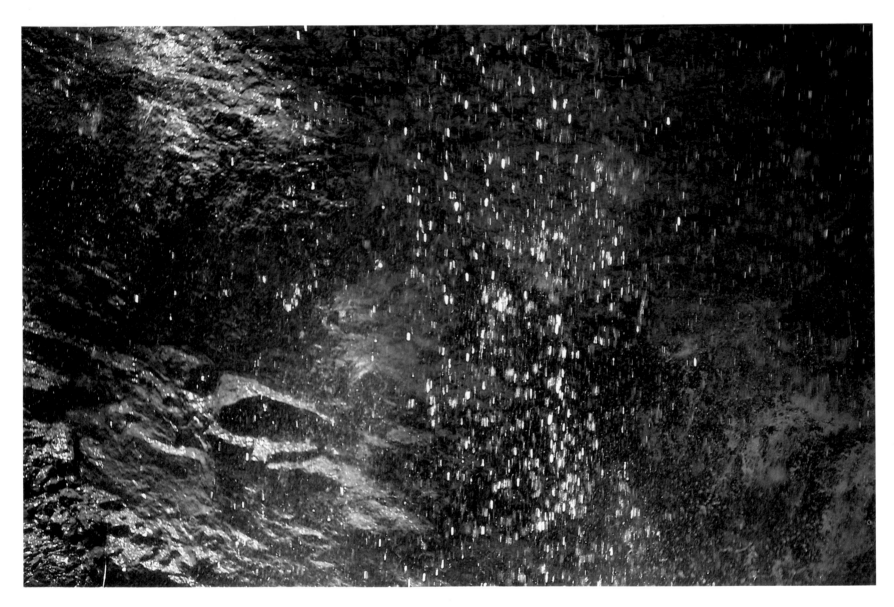

*left: "Balance," detail of melting pack ice*
*on shore, Manitoulin Island, April 1993*

*Sunlight on Bridal Veil Falls, Manitoulin*
*Island, Ontario, April 1993*

36

*Predawn light with receding ice on Lake Manitou, Manitoulin Island, Ontario, April 1993*

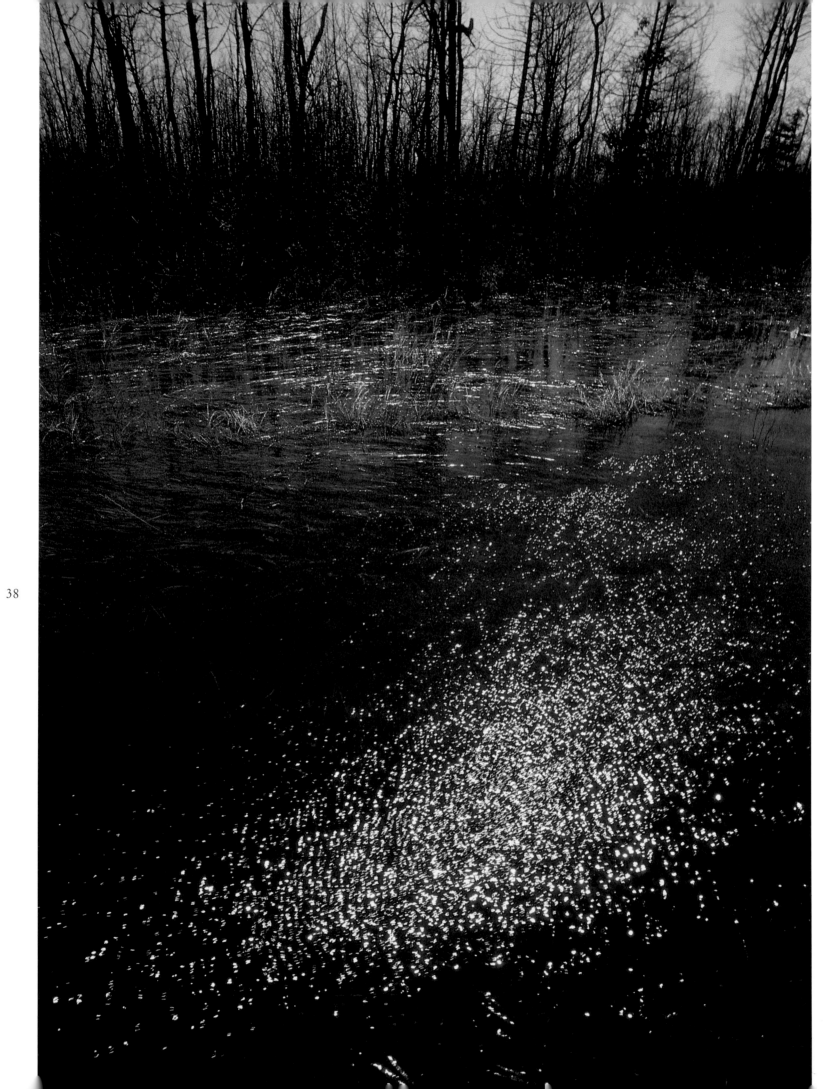

38

39

*left: Wind on pond, Manitoulin Island,*
*Ontario, April 1993*

*above: Ice flow on pond, Manitoulin Island,*
*Ontario, April 1993*

*Snow puffs on bushes, Horseshoe Falls, Niagara Falls, Ontario, April 1993*

*right: Snow on deadfall, Niagara Falls, Ontario, April 1993*

# Nee-ah-gah-rah

## *Place Where Thunder Strikes*

40    Niagara Falls is by far the best-known cascade in North America, with five million visitors a year. Iroquoian people such as the Seneca and Huron call it Nee-ah-gah-rah, meaning "Thundering Waters." Stories say the sound of the falls is the roar of the spirit living in the waters, who needed to be appeased every year with the sacrifice of a maiden in a canoe adorned with fruits and flowers. In 1679, French explorers tried to stop Chief Eagle Eye from sacrificing his daughter Lela-wala. To ensure the ritual's completion, the chief and his daughter set out in separate canoes and both plunged to their deaths, transformed into spirits of strength and goodness that can still be felt today. The lure of the abyss is still strong; it is not uncommon to see daredevils, driven by fame, and desperate people, driven to suicide, challenging the fast-flowing waters over the falls.

For both the Huron and Seneca people, the spirit of Lake Ontario is a serpent whose voice can be heard the loudest in the roar of the plunging waters, which is also known as "the place where thunder strikes." It is here that, according to Seneca legend, the Good Spirit who lives in the Cave of the Winds sent a thunderbolt to kill the serpent, causing the monster to thrash with such force that a broad basin was scooped out, forming the now famous "horseshoe" of Niagara Falls.

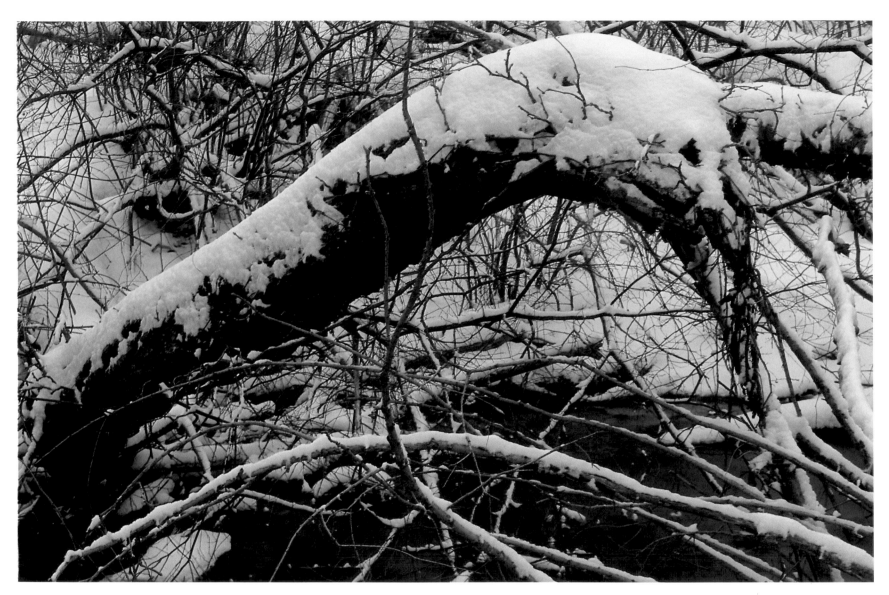

*Detail of catlinite cliff, Pipestone National Monument, Pipestone, Minnesota, June 1993*

# Pipestone

*Quarry of Peace*

42  An ancient catlinite quarry in the southwest corner of Minnesota is the site of a thousand years of sacred pipe carving by the Ojibway, Lakota, Cheyenne and Blackfoot tribes, among others. Both history and legend refer to Pipestone as a holy ground where warring nations would put down their arms and smoke the pipe together, united in reverence for the Great Spirit. Today almost all the pipes used in ceremony by North America's Native people come from the quarries at Pipestone, though much of the remaining rock is hidden under ten to thirteen feet of quartzite.

The stories about Pipestone are as rich and colourful as the cliffs themselves. One Lakota story speaks of the deep crimson stone as the hardened blood of those crushed in a great flood. Another of Lakota origin, says that the first pipe was brought to the ancestors by White Buffalo Calf Woman, a messenger from the Great Spirit, thus forming a link between those on Earth and the spirit world. She taught them that the pipe – the bowl engraved with a buffalo calf – joins land and sky, and its smoke carries messages to the Great Spirit. She showed them how to pray with the pipe, how to decorate themselves when praying to Mother Earth, and above all else, to use it as a peace pipe to be smoked before all ceremonies. She taught them the seven sacred rites, including the Inipi (the cleansing sweat lodge), the Wiwanyaq Wachipi (the sundance of thanksgiving) and the Ishuata Awicalowan (the ceremony to prepare a girl for womanhood). In this last ritual, the girl is honoured like a towering tree; she is a source of strength, and like the Mother Earth, will bear children, raising them in a spiritual way.

Today, Pipestone remains a meeting place revered by many First Nations people.

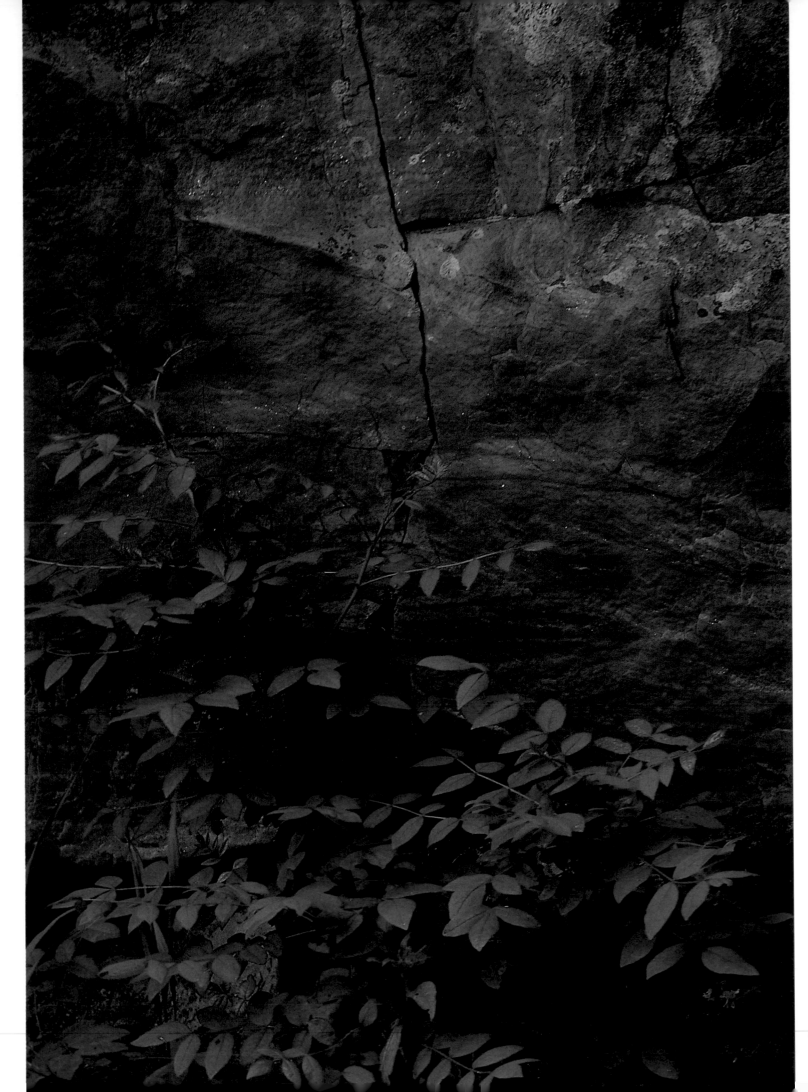

*Petroglyphs in sunset light, Jeffers Petroglyph Site, Jeffers, Minnesota, June 1991*

*right: Butterfly and lichen on quartzite, Jeffers Petroglyph Site, Jeffers, Minnesota, June 1991*

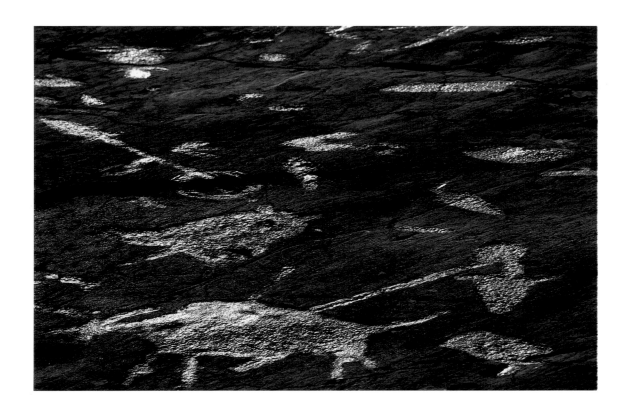

# Red Rock Ridge

## *Place of Ancient Carvings*

While there are petroglyphs at many sites throughout North America, there are few locations with as diverse a collection as the two thousand carvings at Jeffers Petroglyphs site on Red Rock Ridge, a short distance to the east of Pipestone in southwestern Minnesota. Little is actually known either about the origin or the meaning of these quartzite etchings, though many of the figures are thought to have spiritual significance.

Petroglyph art is believed to have served many purposes: it played a role in sacred ceremonies, it helped people remember events and it recorded important occurrences. Some designs appear to be clan symbols, while others identify the best places to hunt, the location and strength of an enemy or a favoured migration route.

Of the 203 clusters of carvings at Jeffers, some may be as old as 3000 BC; these portray magic hunting rituals, with depictions of ancient spears. Others date from AD 900, and even as recently as 1750, when the Siouan-speaking peoples first used the horse in this area. The bison is a dominant figure, known to possess a particular magic for the Plains Indians. The serpent appears with frequency; to many native cultures it is a symbol of potent life energy and universal knowledge.

On a twenty-three-mile ridge above ancient game trails following the Little Cottonwood River, this thousand-foot mural of ancient artwork is one of the most extensive petroglyph sites in North America, and an enchanting place to explore, especially when the figures transform to gold in the low light of a clear evening.

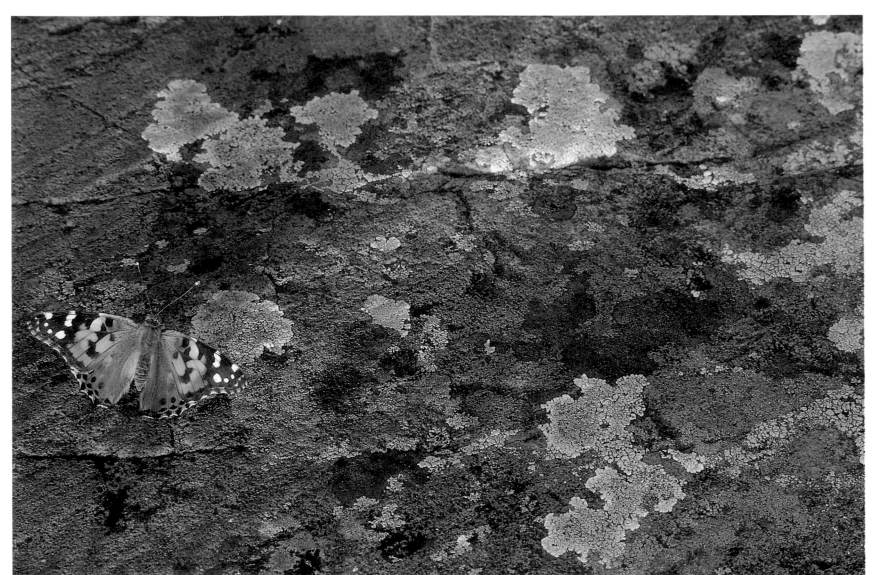

45

*Rock detail, Ringing Rocks State Park,*
*Pennsylvania, June 1991*

*right: Boulders and trees, Ringing Rocks State*
*Park, Pennsylvania, June 1991*

# Ringing Rocks

*Harmony of the Earth*

Nestled in a grove of woods near Upper Black Eddy on the Delaware River lies a clearing strewn with boulders that have a special history. Although the glaciers did not reach this far, a unique paraglacial climate that lasted here until about 7000 BC produced periods of freezing and thawing. This allowed volcanic intrusions to heat and crack the bedrock, leaving rivers of rock.

This area of what is now Pennsylvania was originally inhabited by the Unami- and Munsee-speaking people who lived in small agricultural and hunting villages. Although much remains unknown about their beliefs, the Unami name meant "original person," and their stories speak of a Cannibal Monster and of the Thunderers, winged spirits who protect the world from the enemy, Great Horned Serpent. Other benevolent beings were the Little People, who lived in the woods, as well as "our Older Brother the

Sun" and "our Mother the Earth."

The descendants of these people were the Delaware tribes, named in the seventeenth century to honour the region's first English governor, Lord de la Warr. With European settlement, the Delaware people were driven west to Oklahoma and north to Canada, where they have since been absorbed by the Indian peoples in those areas.

The uncanny sense of mystery and spirit that pervades this place is heightened by the unique musical quality of its rocks. The bowl-shaped indentations in this malleable shale are the result of decades of visitors attempting to hear the ringing; when struck with a hammer or small stone, the boulders resound, their crystalline nature producing characteristic tones. The note from each rock is so distinct that I felt certain I could have constructed, with a little diligence, a complete musical scale.

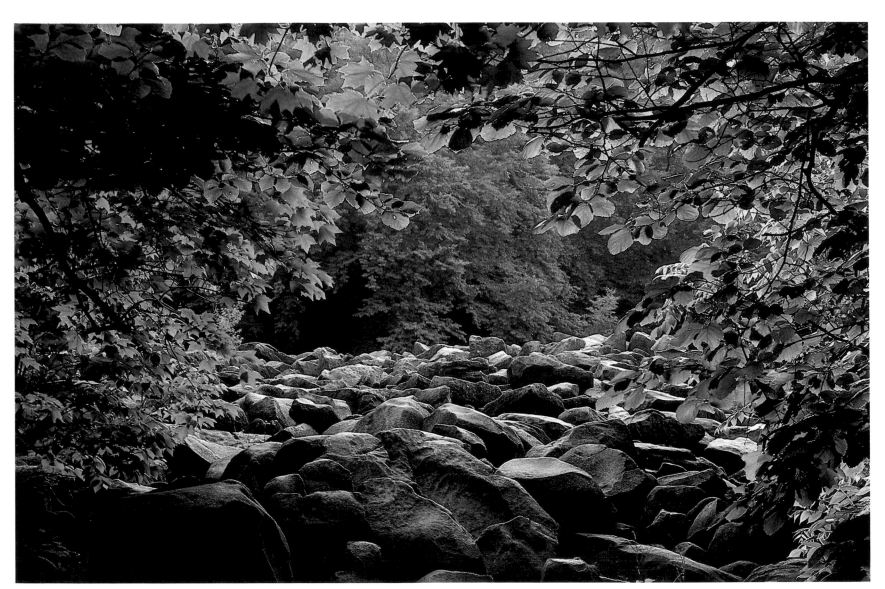

*Detail of coils, Serpent Mound,*
*Serpent Mound State Memorial, Ohio,*
*October 1990*

*right: Aerial view of Serpent Mound,*
*Serpent Mound State Memorial, Ohio,*
*October 1990*

# Serpent Mound

## *Effigy of Unseen Power*

48  Serpent Mound is an enormous earthen snake that would measure more than a quarter of a mile uncoiled. Poised in a grove of trees on a ridge that parallels Ohio Brush Creek near Locust Grove, Ohio, this is the largest serpent effigy in the world. Serpent Mound is believed to have been created sometime between 1000 BC and AD 400 by people anthropologists call the Adena or the succeeding Hopewell; the latter of which evolved into the Mississippian culture. All three of these Eastern Woodlands people, ancestors of present-day North American Indians, built ceremonial and burial mounds. Although thousands of burial mounds exist in North America, predominantly in the Mississippi and Ohio River valleys, and many of the later ones featured extensive temple complexes and walled cities, the Serpent Mound emerges as a particularly fascinating site. Its unique shape and the fact

that no human remains were unearthed here imbue it with a sense of continuous mystery.

The serpent plays an important role in many cultures. In the ancient Quechua language of South America, the western hemisphere is called "Amaruka," or "land of the serpent." Many Toltec and Mayan temples in Mexico are adorned with snake carvings, indicating a place of wisdom. To the Hindus, the serpent means enlightenment; to the Christians, forbidden knowledge; to the Greeks, it was the life force symbol on the physician's staff; and to the Chinese metaphysicians practising the art of Feng Shui (geomancy, or the ancient science of earth energies), the serpent force is the energy that circulates not only in the human body but also through the earth. It may be significant that this Serpent Mound is near a creek; perhaps these early builders believed, as do modern geomancers, that the presence

of water increases the electromagnetic forces in the earth.

To many North American Indian people, the serpent is a manifestation of the life energy force and of unseen power. Some anthropologists believe that Serpent Mound represents a solar eclipse, with the egg shape symbolizing the sun about to be swallowed by the snake. We may never know for certain what the ancient valley dwellers intended to portray.

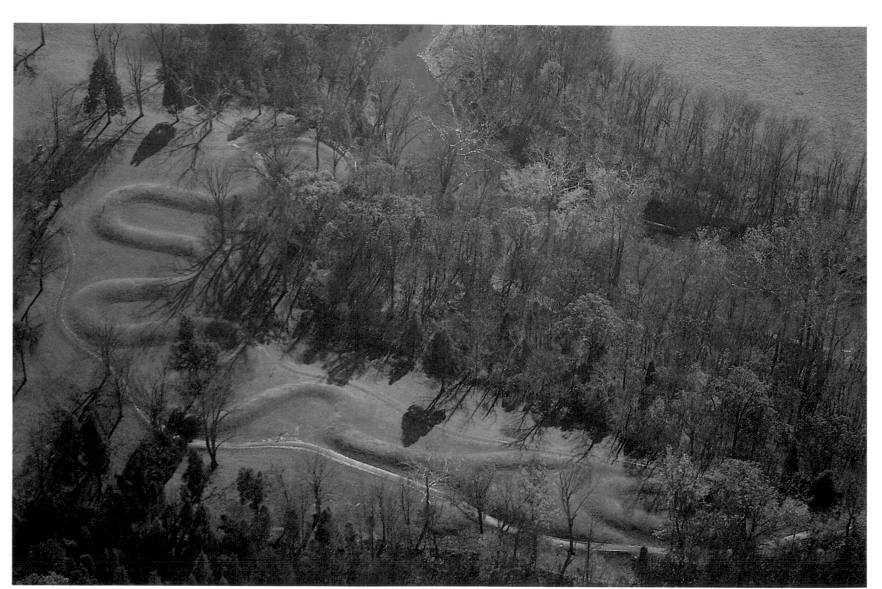

*Composite of Big Dipper and tower,*
*Devil's Tower National Monument,*
*Wyoming, February 1993*

*right: West face of tower, Devil's Tower*
*National Monument, Wyoming,*
*February 1993*

# Mateo Tepee

*Tower of Deliverance*

50 Known today as Devil's Tower in eastern Wyoming, Mateo Tepee is the teardrop-shaped core of an ancient volcano that rises 867 feet from its base. There are several stories about the origin of this monumental landmark; all of them involve a giant bear. One Kiowa account tells of a young boy playing with his sisters, when he is suddenly struck dumb and transformed into a ferocious bear, growing sharp claws and long hair on his body. The boy-bear drops on all fours and chases his seven sisters who climb onto a tree stump and cry for help. The Great Spirit responds to their cries by turning the tree into a tower and placing them beyond their pursuer's reach. The vertical striations now seen on the sides of the tower are the claw marks of the giant bear. The stranded sisters can still be seen on a clear night, transformed into the seven stars of the big dipper.

The Lakota version of the story of what they call "Bear Rock" tells about two boys who get lost while looking for their ball. After walking westward for three days, they suddenly see Mato, the giant grizzly, who chases them. They call out for the Great Spirit to save them. A tremendous earthquake suddenly raises the boys up a thousand feet; although Mato is enormous and digs his claws into the rock, he is unable to reach them. Finally Mato retreats, but the boys remain stranded on the top of the tower. It has been suggested that perhaps it was a giant wanblee, or eagle, who rescues them.

Lame Deer, a Lakota medicine man born in the late 1890s on the Rosebud Reservation in South Dakota, liked to tell the story of a great flood that covers the land and drowns everyone except a beautiful girl who is rescued by Galeshka, a spotted eagle who picks her up with his enormous claws. He takes her to the only land not submerged by the flood, the tip of a rocky tower – perhaps Mateo Tepee – and makes her his wife. She gives birth to twins who become the founders of the great Lakota nation. Lame Deer ends his epic account by saying that all people are descendants of the eagle, the wisest of birds and the messenger of the Great Spirit; thus the eagle plume is worn as a symbol of this spiritual relationship.

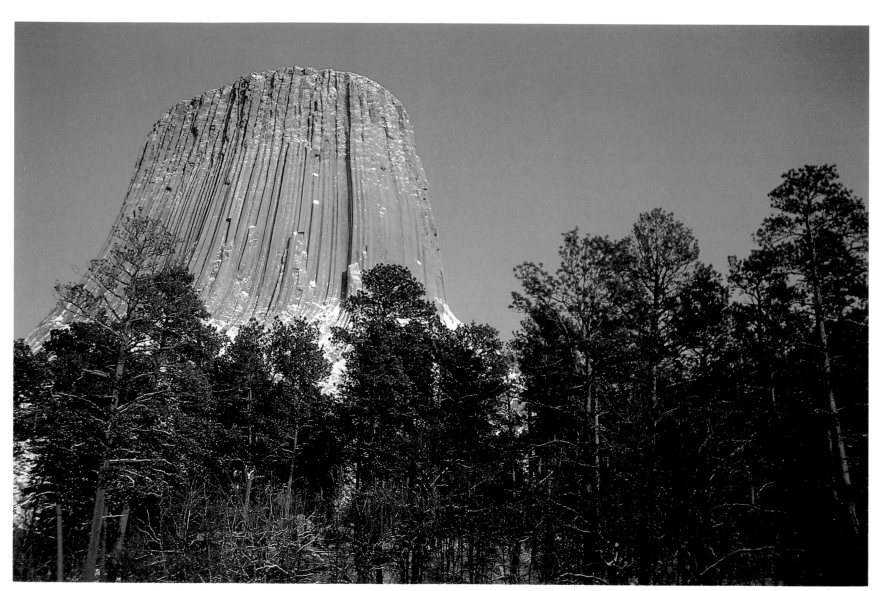

*Eastern ridge, Bear Butte, Black Hills, South Dakota, February 1993*

# Bear Butte

## *Shrine of Vision*

52    The Black Hills, or Paha Sapa of South Dakota, are a sacred shelter and spiritual centre known to the Lakota as Wamakaognaka E'cante, meaning "heart of everything that is." Cheyenne and Lakota stories speak of a time before any hills existed here, when humans and fellow creatures preyed indiscriminately on each other. Man summoned all to a race in the path of a great circle, where everyone participated in a frenzy. This commotion disturbed the spirits. As the path wore the earth away, it began to sink, and the land within the circle rose up to form a mountainous bulge that burst. Many were killed, including the monster Uncegila, whose bones can be found on the ridges of the Badlands. The Black Hills, at the centre of this cataclysm, are a reminder to humans that their strength is insignificant compared to the awesome power of the earth spirits.

Bear Butte is perhaps the best known landmark of the hills; it is considered the centre of the universe by the Plains Indians. Known to the Lakota as Mato Pah, it was a place of prayer and vision quest for ancestors of the Kiowa, Mandan, Arikara, Crow, Lakota and Cheyenne. Lakota oral tradition says it was formed from the titanic struggle between a huge bear and Uncegila. Both shed blood, until finally the strong and fierce bear – symbol of power and vitality – conceded defeat and collapsed. The land convulsed, covering his body with earth. Now he hibernates here forever, the keeper of dreams.

The great Lakota chief, Crazy Horse, came to Bear Butte many times throughout his life. In one vision, he was directed up a bright white path on the eastern ridge toward an arrow-shaped cave where his body was imbedded with seven small stones that gave him messages from the Great Spirit, Wakan Tanka, and sent out sparks when he performed healing ceremonies. The eastern meadow is designated as his Teaching Hill, where he spoke to many councils who gathered to receive his direction and wisdom.

The Cheyenne call Bear Butte Noahvose, meaning the place of Maheo, the Above Spirit. It is here that their great prophet, Sweet Medicine, waited four years before he received the four sacred arrows from the Great Spirit. The sacred arrows contain Maheo's teachings, including the four taboos – murder, theft, adultery and incest. Sweet Medicine took the sacred bundle of arrows and used their powers to show his people a spiritual way to live.

*Sage Creek Wilderness Area,*
*Badlands National Park,*
*South Dakota, February 1993*

# Mako Sica

## *Badlands of the White River*

Called Mako Sica by the Lakota, the Badlands have been a hunting ground for more than twelve thousand years. First used by ancient mammoth hunters, this tortuous land was later occupied by the Arikara people, and then the Lakota whose principal hunt was the bison. Today, much of what is Badlands National Park lies on the Pine Ridge Reservation, home of the Oglala Sioux nation, which oversees the administration of the park.

Once covered by a vast inland sea, the Badlands harbour many fossil remains associated in Lakota lore with Uncegila, the great female water monster who emerged out of the primordial sea. It is here that the legendary Uncegila flooded the land, bringing devastation to the people and angering Wakinyan, the frightful and awe-inspiring Thunderbird, who worried that there would be no people to pray to him nor to dream of his great powers. So Wakinyan created a violent storm, flapping his wings to produce thunderbolts that dried up the flood and destroyed the vengeful Uncegila; her red crystal heart shattered, but her bones remain scattered in the Badlands as a testament to the power of the spirits.

Lakota elder John Lame Deer adds a variation to the story. While looking for lost horses, he grew fearful. He could feel the ground shaking, as though Uncegila were wriggling beneath him, her bones protruding from a ridge of red and yellow rocks. Taking refuge from a storm, Lame Deer heard Wakinyan giving him encouragement. Later he was unable to find the ridge again, or the horses. It is said that this is a good place to hide; the last Ghost Dancers took refuge here in 1890, when the Ghost Dance was banned by the U.S. government.

53

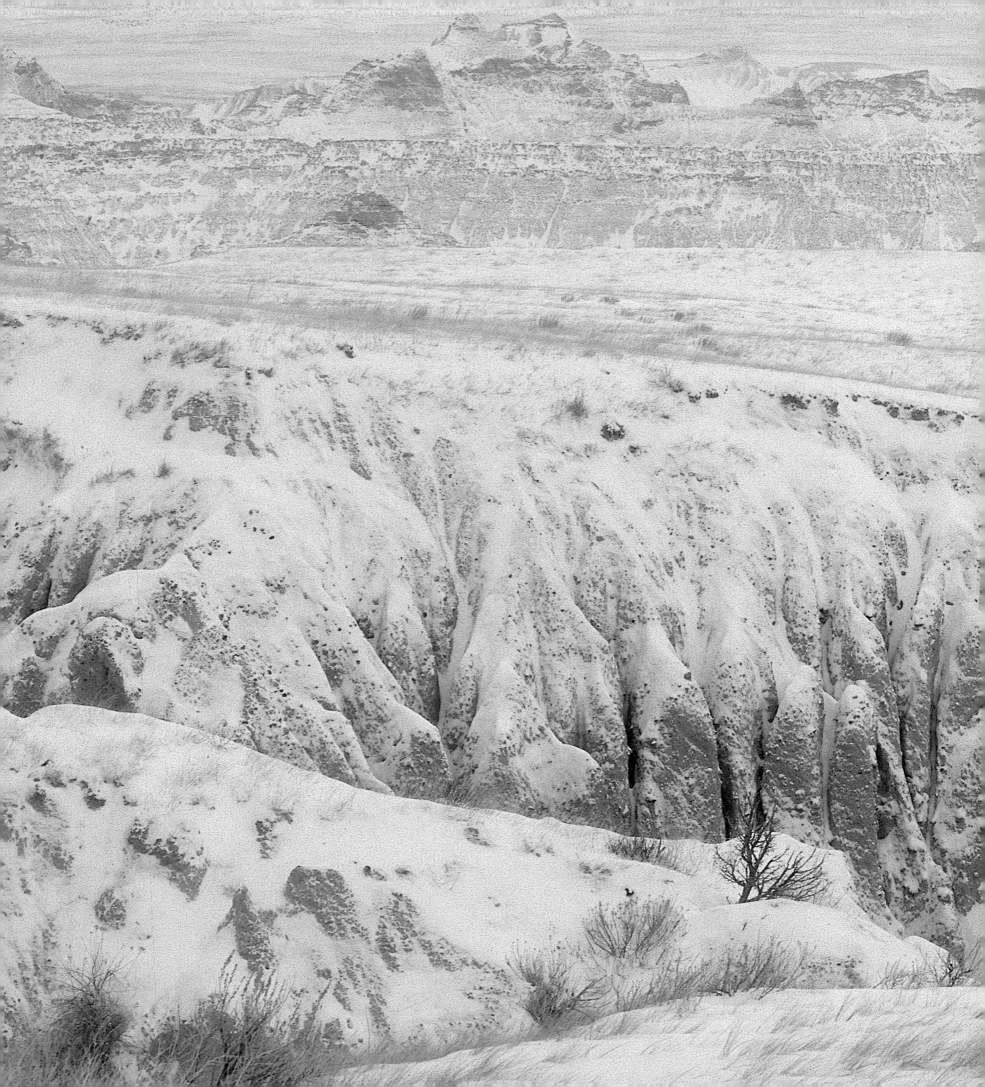

55

*left: Sage Creek Wilderness Area, Badlands
National Park, South Dakota, February 1993*

*above: Mule deer, Badlands National Park,
South Dakota, February 1993*

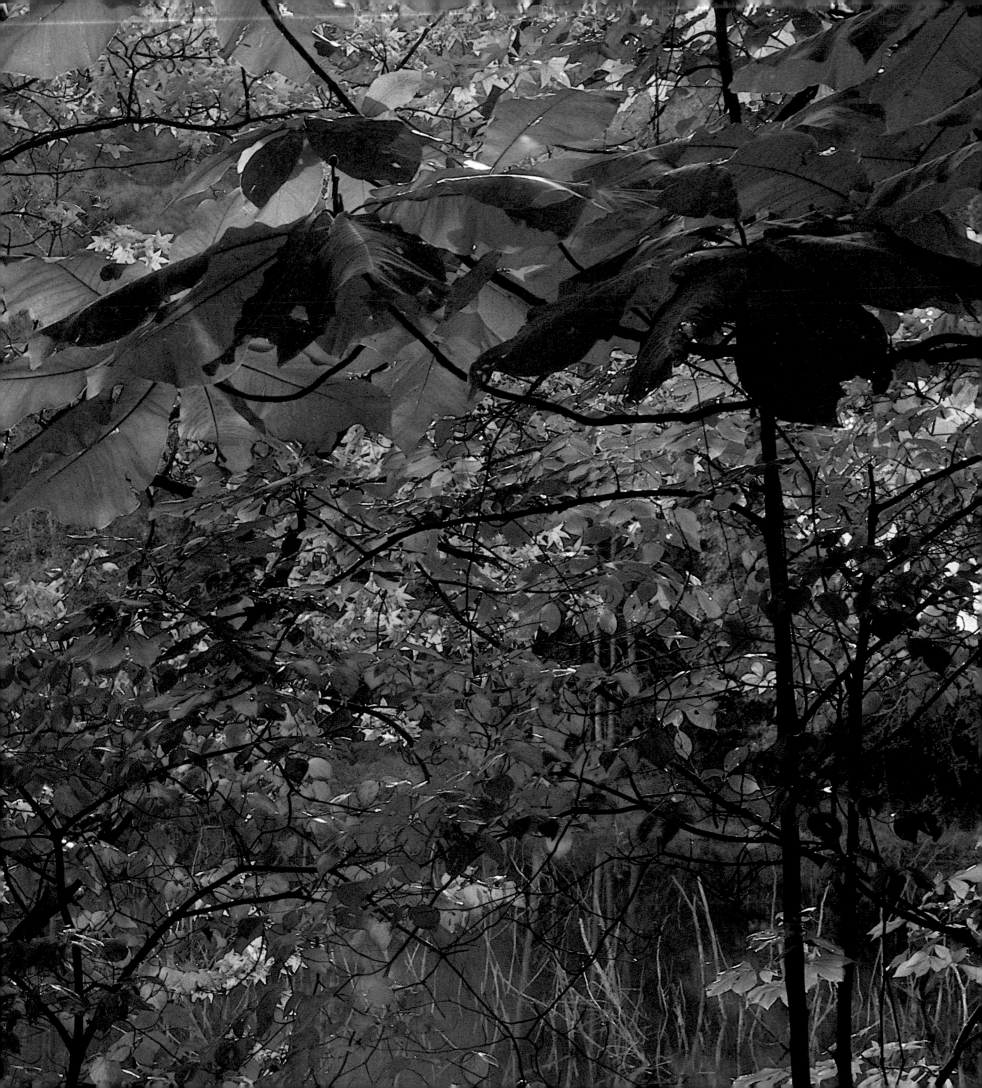

*left: Autumn foliage, Stone Mountain Park, Georgia, October 1993*

*North face of Stone Mountain, Stone Mountain Park, Georgia, October 1993*

# Stone Mountain

## *Legend of the Great Serpent*

Stone Mountain Park is situated on 3,200 acres, sixteen miles east of Atlanta, Georgia. Rising four hundred feet from the base, Stone Mountain is the largest exposed granite outcropping in the world.

The monolith sits like a large grey bison, quietly protecting the adjacent forest reserve inhabited by indigenous cougar, elk and bison. But Stone Mountain also harbours stories of its mysterious past, such as the 1873 report about the remnants of a large stone wall that zigzagged like a snake along the west side, halfway up the mountain. Its pattern was similar to other serpentine walls found in Georgia, including one on nearby Fort Mountain, which measures eleven hundred feet in length and two to eight feet in height. It is believed that the now-dismantled snake wall on Stone Mountain was built by the Adena culture as an effigy of the Great Serpent, about the same time as Serpent Mound in Ohio.

The Cherokee and Creek people of this area have many stories about a supernatural serpent. One variation refers to food taboos and tells of two old men who were out hunting. One ate a fish from a pool at the top of a tree and was suddenly turned into a talking snake, who then called a meeting of all his kin from the Deer Clan. At the appointed time, he appeared to them in a powerful torrent of water that swept them away, turning everyone into water snakes. The story concludes that water snakes are transformed humans, bearing horns of many different colours.

*Autumn colour, Rock Eagle 4-H Club Center,*
*Eatonton, Georgia, October 1993*

*right: Rock Eagle effigy in dawn mist,*
*Rock Eagle 4-H Club Center, Eatonton,*
*Georgia, October 1993*

# Rock Eagle

## *Mystery of the*
## *Stone Mound Culture*

58   Rock Eagle, an enormous bird effigy with a 120-foot wing span, is located near Eatonton, Georgia. Constructed entirely from white quartz boulders, it is believed that it was built five thousand years ago, making it older than the Great Pyramid of Egypt. The Mississippian people, ancestors of the native people who live here today, constructed many burial and effigy mounds in this area between AD 1000 and 1500, and may be descended from the people who built Rock Eagle.

Little is known for sure about this effigy, although it is thought by some to have been a guardian spirit for the Eagle Clan and used by them as a ceremonial centre. In many Native traditions, animals are seen as spiritual messengers that instruct through dreams or trances. The eagle is often symbolic of a shaman's journey to communicate with the spirit world.

The Creek and Cherokee people who currently live in the area say their ancestors found the Rock Eagle as it is today, and they have no knowledge of its use. It seems clear that it was a site of great spiritual importance, since the large rocks used in its construction were brought from a great distance without the benefit of wheeled transportation or horses.

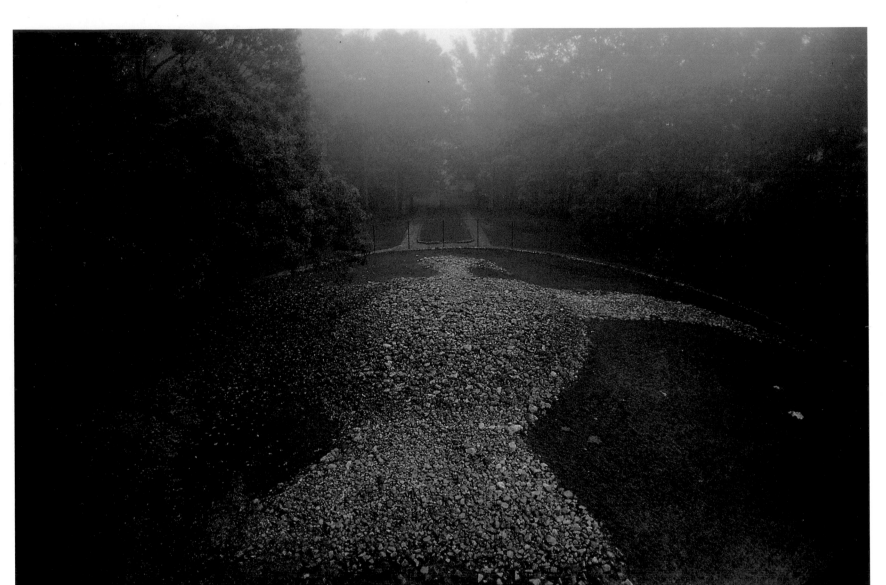

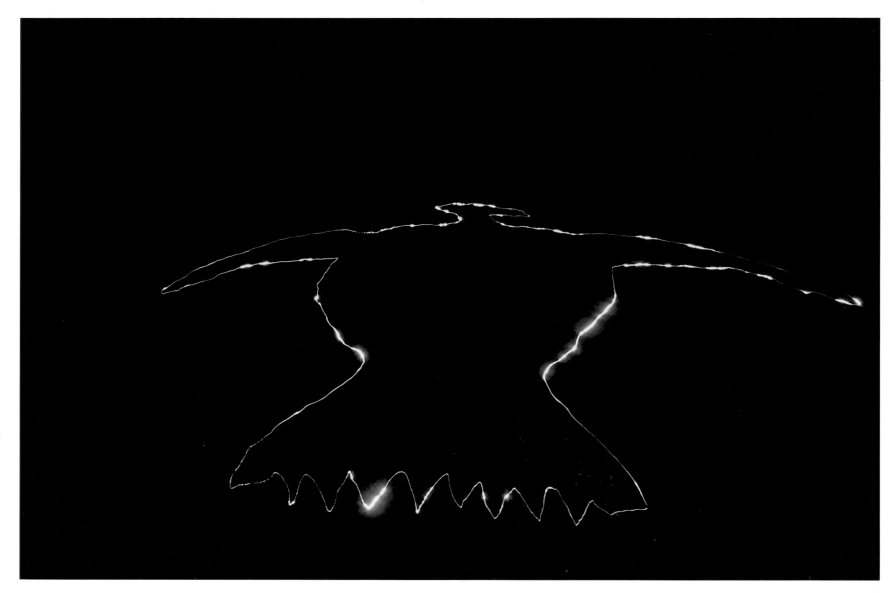

*Flashlight tracing at night, Rock Eagle effigy,*
*Rock Eagle 4-H Club Center, Eatonton,*
*Georgia, October 1993*

# SOUTH

To the South, and thy sentinel, Brown Eagle
The beautiful one, grant us warmth of heart,
Love and kindness to all.

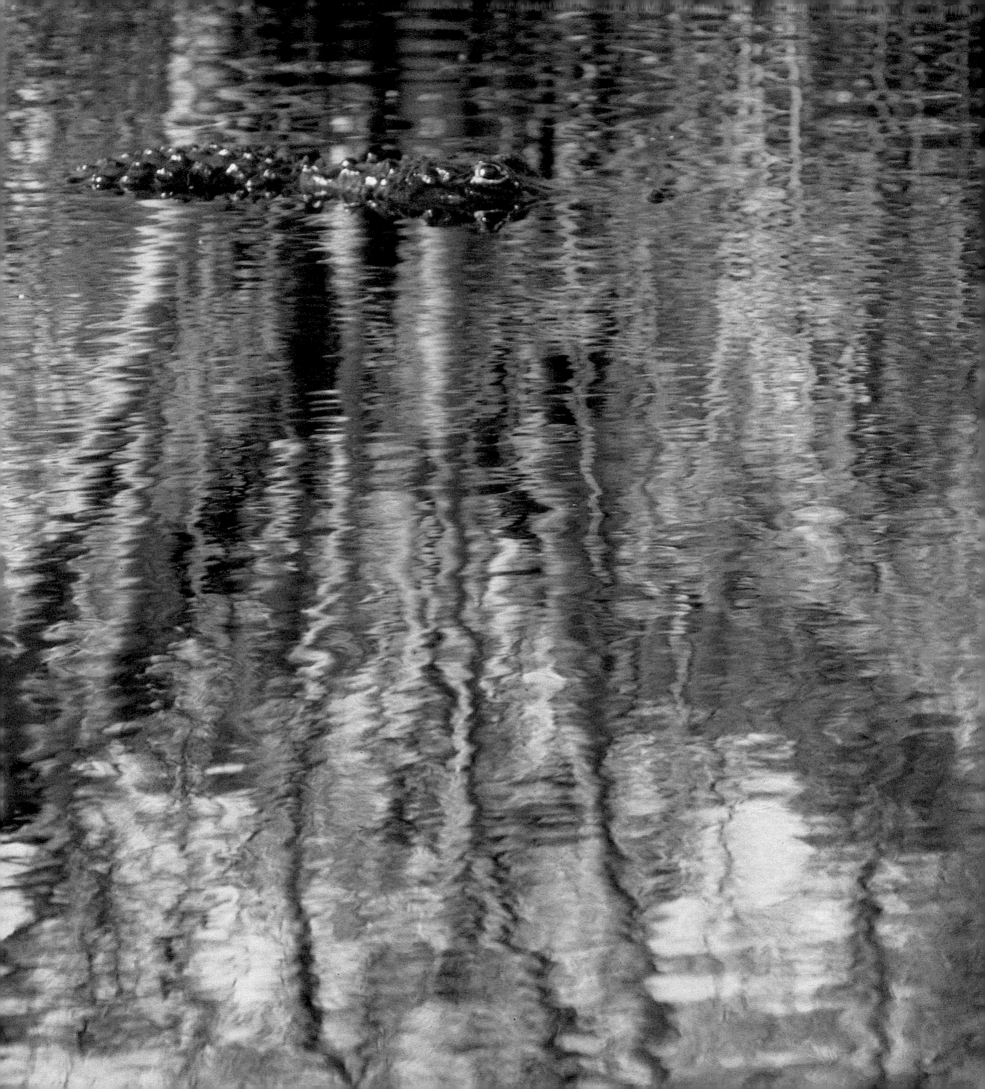

left: *Alligator and reflection, Anhinga Trail,
Everglades National Park, Florida,
January 1985*

*Silt in stream, Pearl Bay, Everglades
National Park, Florida, January 1985*

# Pahayokee

## *River of Grassy Waters*

Prior to the arrival of Europeans, the swamps of Florida were inhabited for more than two thousand years by the Tequesta and Calusa Indians who called them Pahayokee (pay-HIGH-oh-geh), "the grassy waters." To the Spanish explorers who arrived here in the late fifteenth century, this was a mysterious place they called "lagoon of the Holy Spirit." Only since the 1820s have these eight million acres of water, mangrove, cypress, sawgrass and rushes been called "the Everglades," so named by British newcomers who thought the shiny green marshland went on forever. Today it is known to be a broad, shallow river that flows at an almost imperceptible rate from Lake Okeechobee southward to the sea.

The Seminole, a splinter group of the Creek Confederacy consisting of Cherokee, Chocktaw, Chickasaw and Creek tribes, resisted European influences. While many of their people perished when they were forced to travel along the infamous Trail of Tears to reservations in Oklahoma, a group of two hundred Seminole took refuge in the Everglades, where they shared the safety and isolation of the swamp with slaves fleeing Georgia and Alabama in 1819 when the Everglades was opened to slave traders. According to Seminole tradition, the Milky Way was created by the Breathmaker who blew toward the sky to make a pathway to the City of the West where good souls go after death. It is said that Rain and Rainbow (or "stop-the-rain" – which it does) live along this path, and that the Big Dipper is the boat that carries the good souls away, while bad ones stay in the ground where they are buried.

In the unique ecosystem of plant and animal life that is the Everglades, the alligator is a kind of living fossil, little changed from its primeval predecessors. The alligator is regarded as a predator now, but the area's original inhabitants revered its role as provider. Ancient stories refer to a special collaboration between alligators and humans; in one Choctaw story, a stranded animal asks for assistance and returns the favour of his human helper by pointing out good deer-hunting spots.

I made the images of red mangrove leaves (overleaf) from a canoe. The leaves rotting in the shallow depths are being restored to the earth's food chain, attesting to the interdependency and constant renewal of life in this challenging landscape.

63

*Mangrove reflection, Pearl Bay, Everglades*
*National Park, Florida, January 1985*

65

*Decaying mangrove leaves, Pearl Bay,*
*Everglades National Park, Florida,*
*January 1985*

*Composite of light refraction through
quartz crystal and silhouette of Craig Mound,
Spiro Mounds State Park, Oklahoma,
February 1993*

*Ice deposit on trees, sunset light, Ozark National Forest, Arkansas, February 1993*

# Spiro Mounds

## *Site of Ancient Burial*

In what is now the northeast corner of Oklahoma, a group of large burial mounds gives testimony to the area's original inhabitants, the Wichita and Caddoan tribes. This thousand-year-old site, now called Spiro Mounds, was a major ceremonial and trade centre. It controlled movement on the Arkansas River from the western plains to villages in the southeast woodlands until about 1350, when it is speculated that climatic changes brought a devastating drought, driving people to the southern plains to hunt buffalo.

Archaeological remnants give evidence of ceremonial activities based on ritual, militarism and the unique burial practices of the Southern Cult, a tradition of religious beliefs, symbols and priestly leadership. When a tribal leader died, the body was allowed to decompose so that the bones could be buried in a communal underground chamber. There the honoured bones were surrounded by ceremonial pipes, shell masks, copper-covered earspools, engraved pottery, axes, baskets, knives and copper plates embossed with intricate designs.

From time to time, eerie blue lights have been reported over Craig Mound, the largest multiple burial mound on this site, where excavations have revealed 189 burial units with evidence of at least nine successive layers of building. Scientists have suggested that the lights may be the result of interaction between the large number of copper objects found in the mound and natural gas radiating from the surface. Many quartz crystals have also been found buried at Spiro, perhaps used by shamans to look into the future.

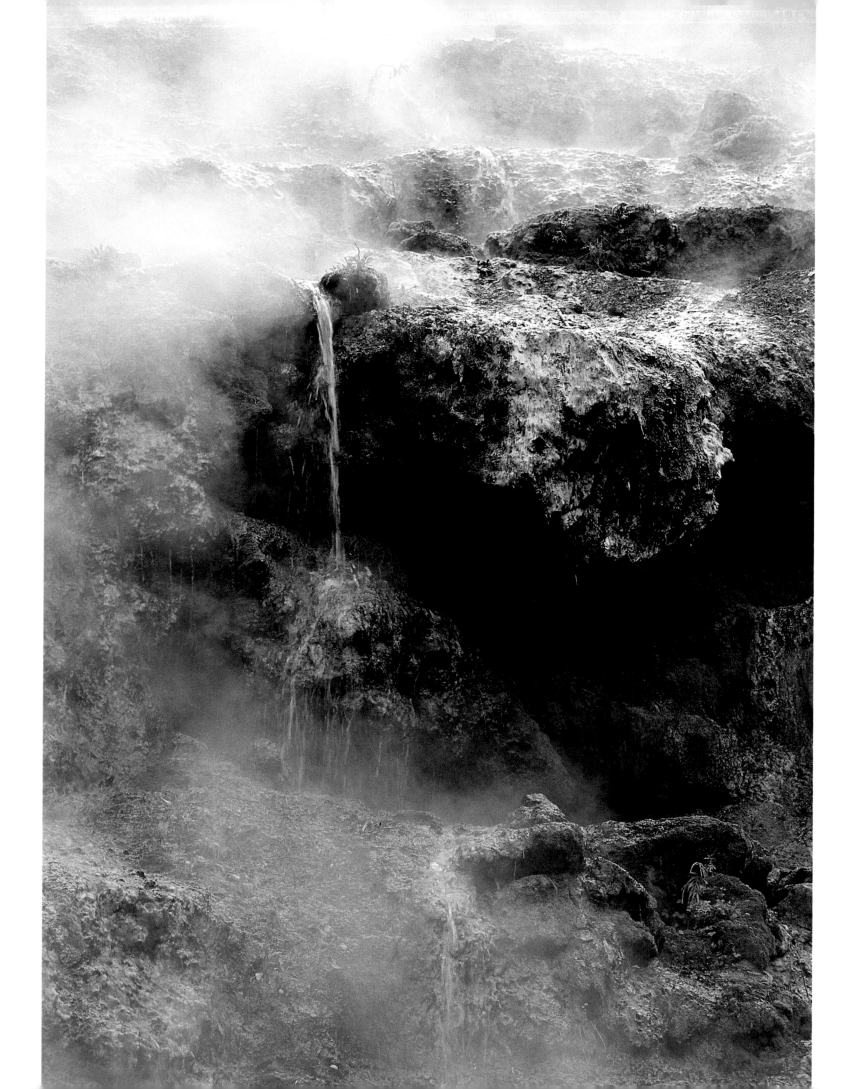

left: *Hot Water Cascade, Hot Springs National Park, Arkansas, March 1993*

*Lichen detail, east slope of Hot Springs Mountain, Hot Springs National Park, Arkansas, March 1993*

# Hot Springs

## *Valley of the Vapours*

The medicinal waters of Hot Springs, located in the Ouchita Mountain Range in Arkansas, are heated to 143 degrees Farenheit by hot rock deep within the earth. These healing waters have taken four thousand years to form before reaching the surface, where they gush at a rate of 850,000 gallons a day to numerous springs seeping through a fracture zone on the western edge of Hot Springs Mountain. Like so many of North America's sacred sites, Hot Springs is known to have been neutral ground where a number of tribes came to hunt, trade and bathe in the naturally sterile therapeutic mineral waters.

Indian people have dwelt here for ten thousand years. The Tunicas of the Caddo Nation, whose ancestors were mound builders, were successful agriculturists, planting maize and squash in the nearby flat prairie soils, and hunted an abundance of game in the surrounding forests. European exploration from the east pushed other tribes into the area, including the Quapaw and Cherokee people.

According to a Tunica creation story, they originated here in the thermal springs. The vapours were said to be the breath of the Great Spirit who favoured the hot springs and the surrounding mountains as a retreat. Another story tells of a dragon named Mogmothon who brought sickness, hunger and devastation to the people of this land. A council of Indian Nations met and prayed to the Great Spirit to help them; their prayer was answered, and the beast was hurled into a cave, but even when buried by the mountain, the dragon could still shake the ground and cause thunderstorms. As a sign of his power and goodness, the Great Spirit brought forth the healing waters to remind his people to live in peace and to maintain this beloved spot as a neutral place to partake in life- and health-giving activities.

In addition to the therapeutic mineral waters, Hot Springs is noted for the intricately patterned lichen and moss and the exquisitely coloured rock in its vicinity. A large deposit of dense rock called chert is at nearby Indian Mountain. The thick accumulations of chert, known as novaculite, have been quarried here for centuries by native peoples and carved for tools, arrowpoints and spearheads. Later, Europeans fashioned whetstones. This unique geological area also produces some of the finest white crystal rocks on the continent, often used as healing stones by shamans past and present.

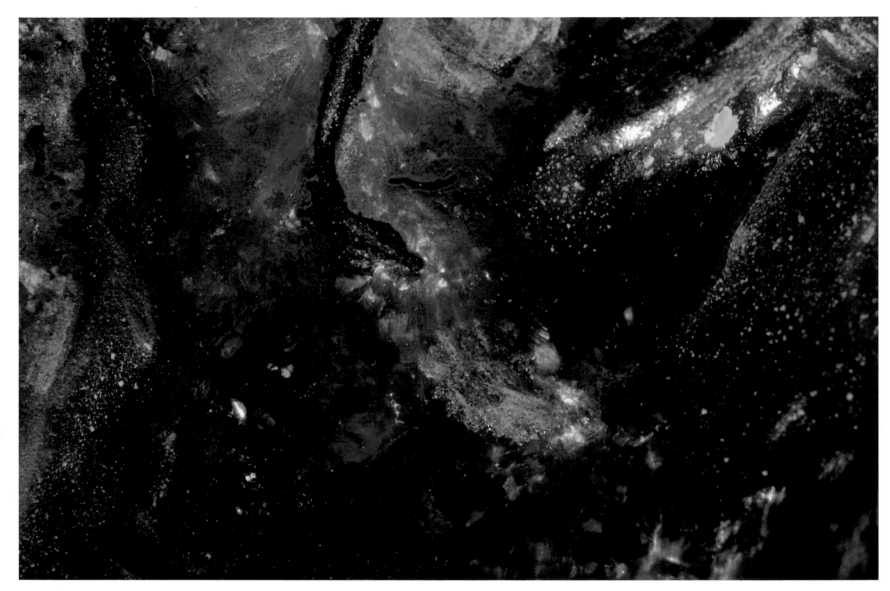

*Detail of refracted light in quartz crystal,*
*quartz mine, Arkansas, March 1993*

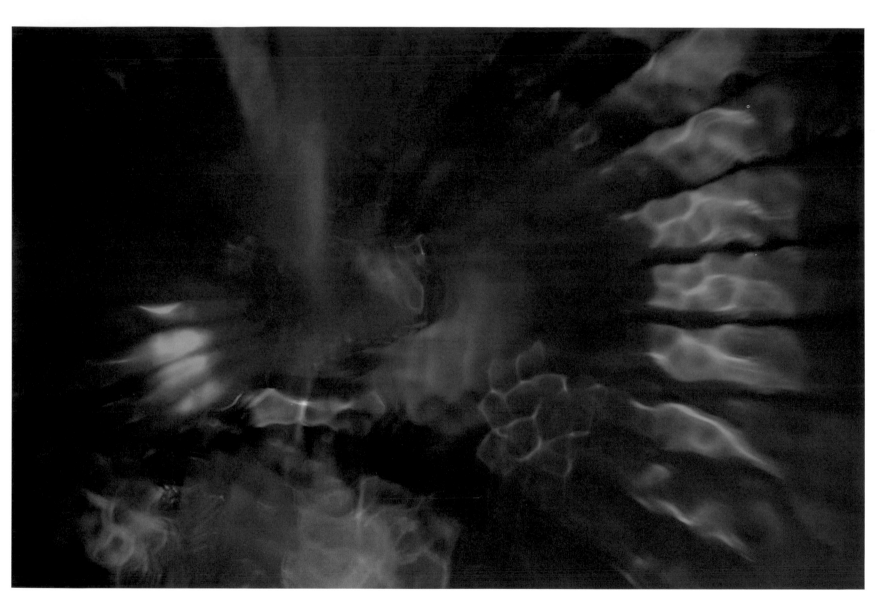

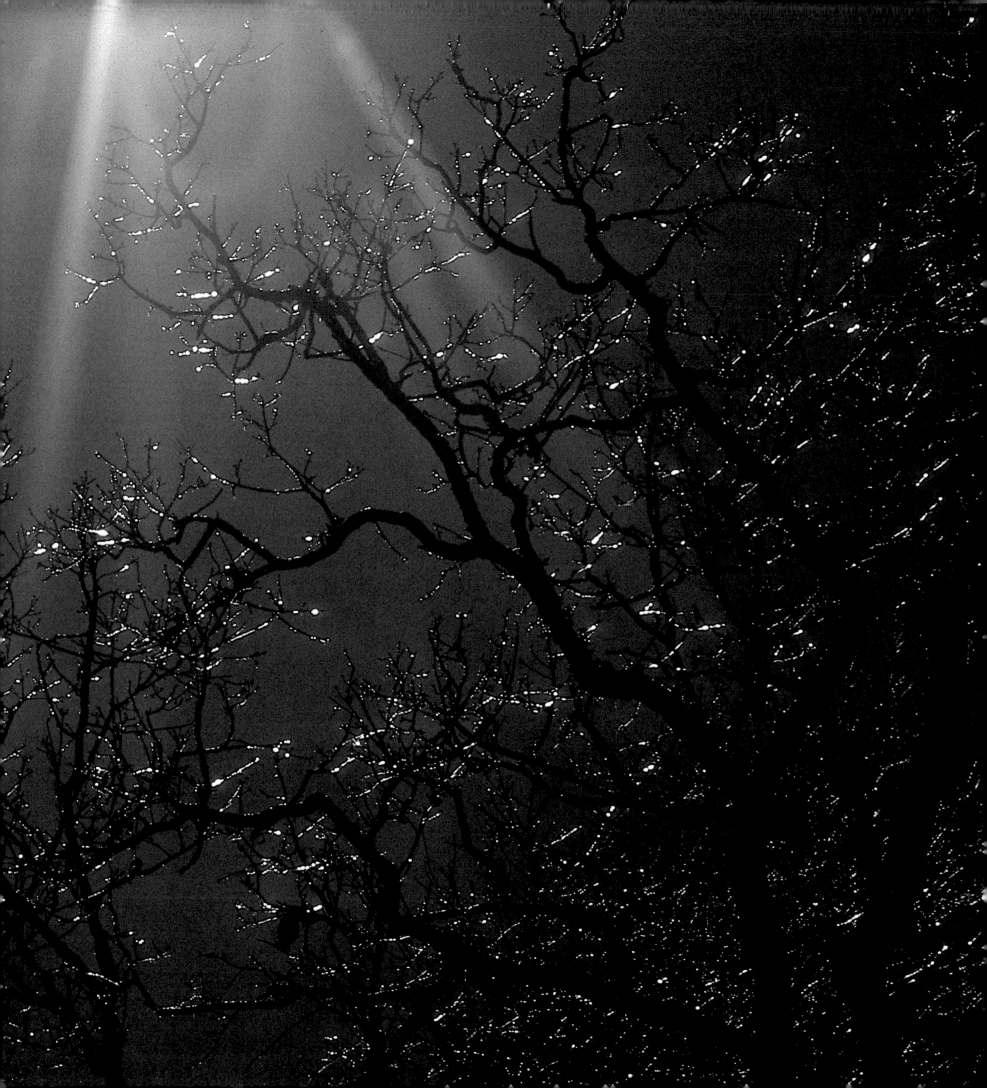

*Ice deposit on trees, Ozark National Forest,*
*Arkansas, February 1993*

*Gateway Rock, Garden of the Gods, Manitou Springs, Colorado, March 1993*

*right: Detail of opening, Iron Springs, Manitou Springs, Colorado, March 1993*

# Manitou Springs

## *Place of Gathering*

74    Nestled in a valley on the eastern edge of Pikes Peak in present-day Colorado, Manitou Springs is a network of twenty-six mineral fountains. The Ute Indians, whose culture dates back ten thousand years and continues to thrive, used the mountain trail now known as the Ute Pass to travel from Colorado Springs to their wintering camps on the western plains.

According to Ute stories, the natural effervescence of these waters is the result of Manitou breathing into them, so the waters were named in honour of the Great Spirit. As with other places of healing, these springs were shared with all tribes who came in peace, including the Navajo, Shoshone, Cheyenne and Arapaho. For some, the springs were the scene of an annual pilgrimage, where spiritual offerings were left with the hope of health and good hunting.

Other remnants of native history are seen in the Anasazi cliff dwellings built between AD 1100 and 1300 in the hills above Manitou Springs and the nearby Cave of the Winds. Stories from the Jicarilla Apache, who lived in these mountains as early as AD 1000, tell how the moaning created by wind swirling at the front of the cavern sounded like the voice of the Great Spirit who lived there. In order to avoid disturbing and angering the Great Spirit, no one entered the cave.

By the late 1800s, the Native tribes in this area were forced to move to reservations in the Four Corners region, where the states of Utah, Arizona, New Mexico and Colorado intersect. Pikes Peak swarmed with settlers and gold mines, while the springs became a tourist attraction. Today, all the springs are capped and most are piped to the surface in the form

of fountains. While the natural ambience is lost, local people say that the spiritual magnetism of this area still exists. At present, Native people from about thirty different tribes such as the Lakota, Cherokee, Apache and Ute live in and around Manitou Springs.

Adjacent to Manitou Springs is a fourteen-hundred-acre park now called the Garden of the Gods, but known to native people as "the Old Red Lands." Here several tribes would gather amidst the elegant spires, jagged pinnacles and spirit faces in the rock. For the Ute, it was also a sacred place where elders climbed the cliffs and wedged themselves into crevices until they passed over to the other world. Then their bodies were removed to the nearby burial ground.

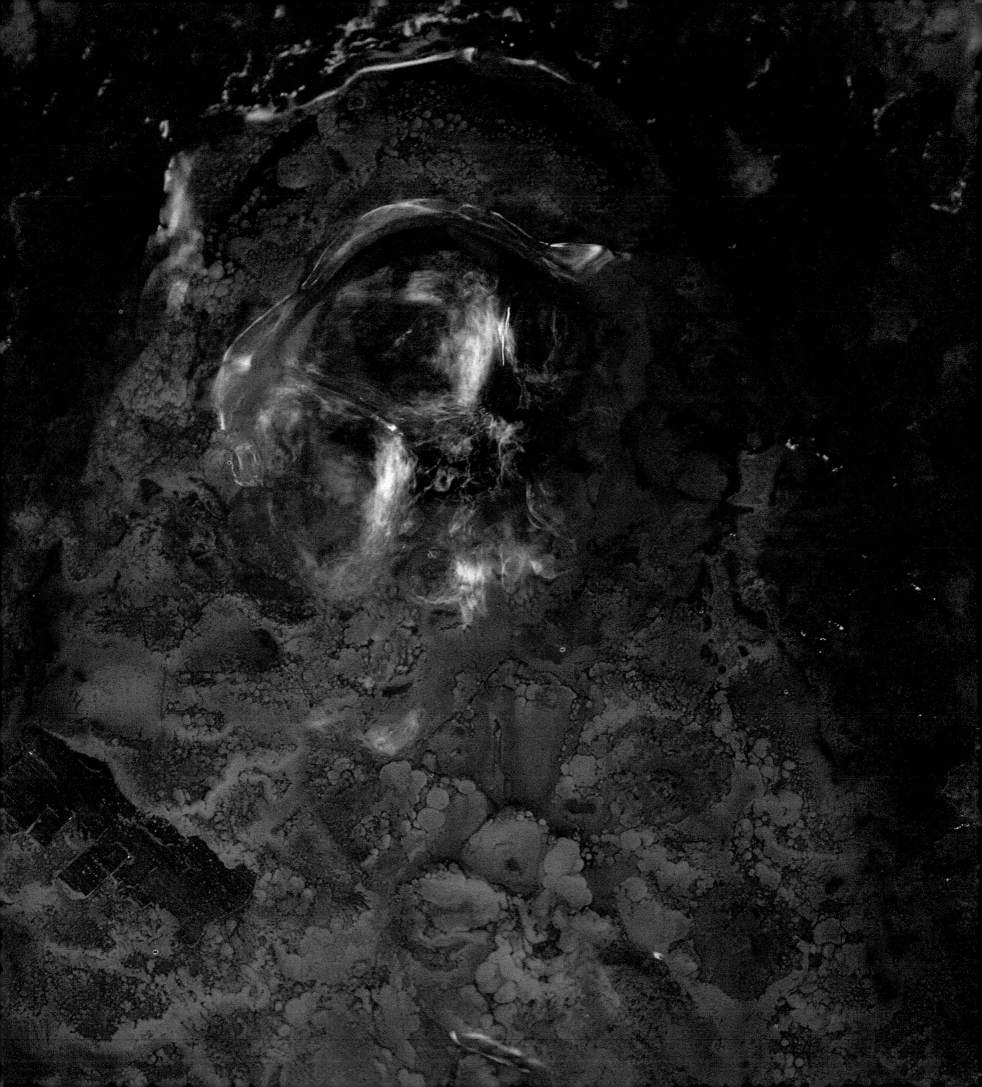

*Detail of west face, Cathedral Rock,*
*Garden of the Gods, Manitou Springs,*
*Colorado, March 1993*

*White Rock, North Gateway and Pikes*
*Peak(distance), Garden of the Gods,*
*Manitou Springs, Colorado, March 1993*

*Silhouette of unidentified rock, Garden of the Gods, Manitou Springs, Colorado, March 1993*

*right: Pikes Peak (distance) and North Gateway, Garden of the Gods, Manitou Springs, Colorado, March 1993*

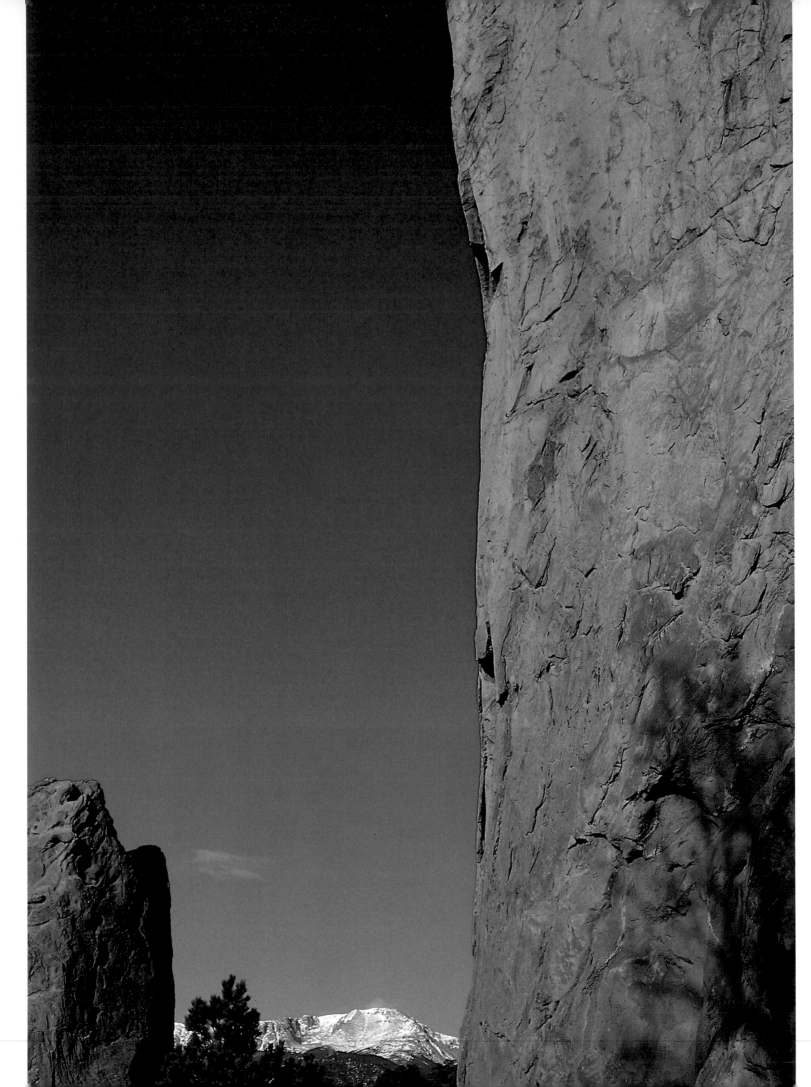

*Enchanted Rock, west face, post-sunset light,*
*Enchanted Rock State Natural Area,*
*Texas, March 1993*

*far right: Granite slabs on Little Rock,*
*Enchanted Rock State Natural Area,*
*Texas, March 1993*

# Enchanted Rock

## *Dome of the Supernatural*

80  By day, Enchanted Rock lures the hiker to explore the valleys, creeks, fissures, caves and oblong slabs of rock draped on the exterior of this pink granite dome. By night, it taunts visitors with its mysterious cracking sounds and deep crimson glow.

Ancient peoples have lived in this area of central Texas for eleven thousand years, from the nomadic spear throwers who hunted the woolly mammoth to the later (AD 900-1700) hunting and gathering nations who used the bow and arrow to bring down bison. Their descendants, the nomadic Tonkawa, had a great respect for death; they buried their dead with the head facing west, believing that the spirit departs in that direction in the form of an owl or wolf. The strange sounds emitted from within Enchanted Rock were attributed to the dead, and the Tonkawa thought that if the spirits haunted a place, those nearby could be tainted and die.

Today there are some who see Enchanted Rock as a doorway to the other side of existence. Shamans and medicine people still come here to practise their art and to connect with the spirit world. Enchanted Rock's legacy includes a stirring account of an Apache elder who instructs a youth to listen to the spirit here – not to his brothers – because what is learned from the mountain will endure forever.

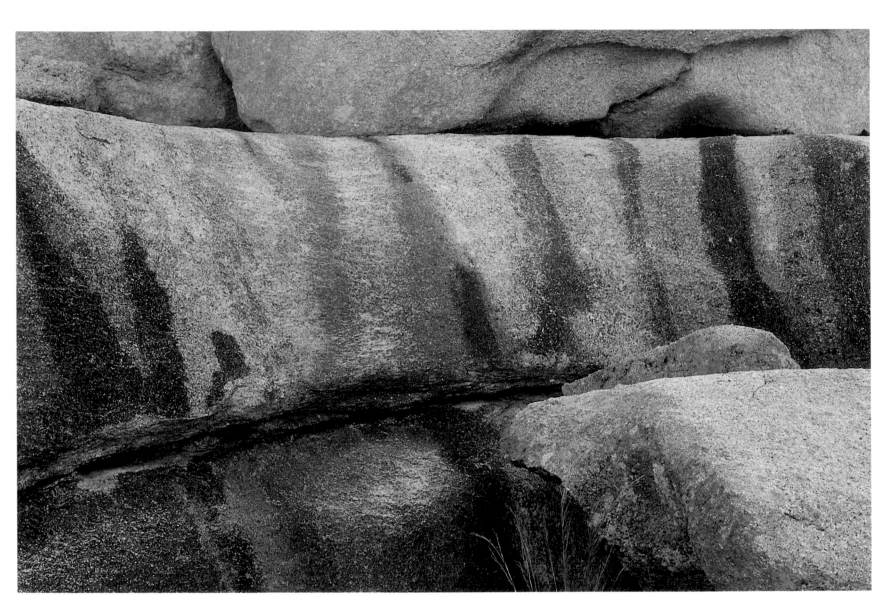

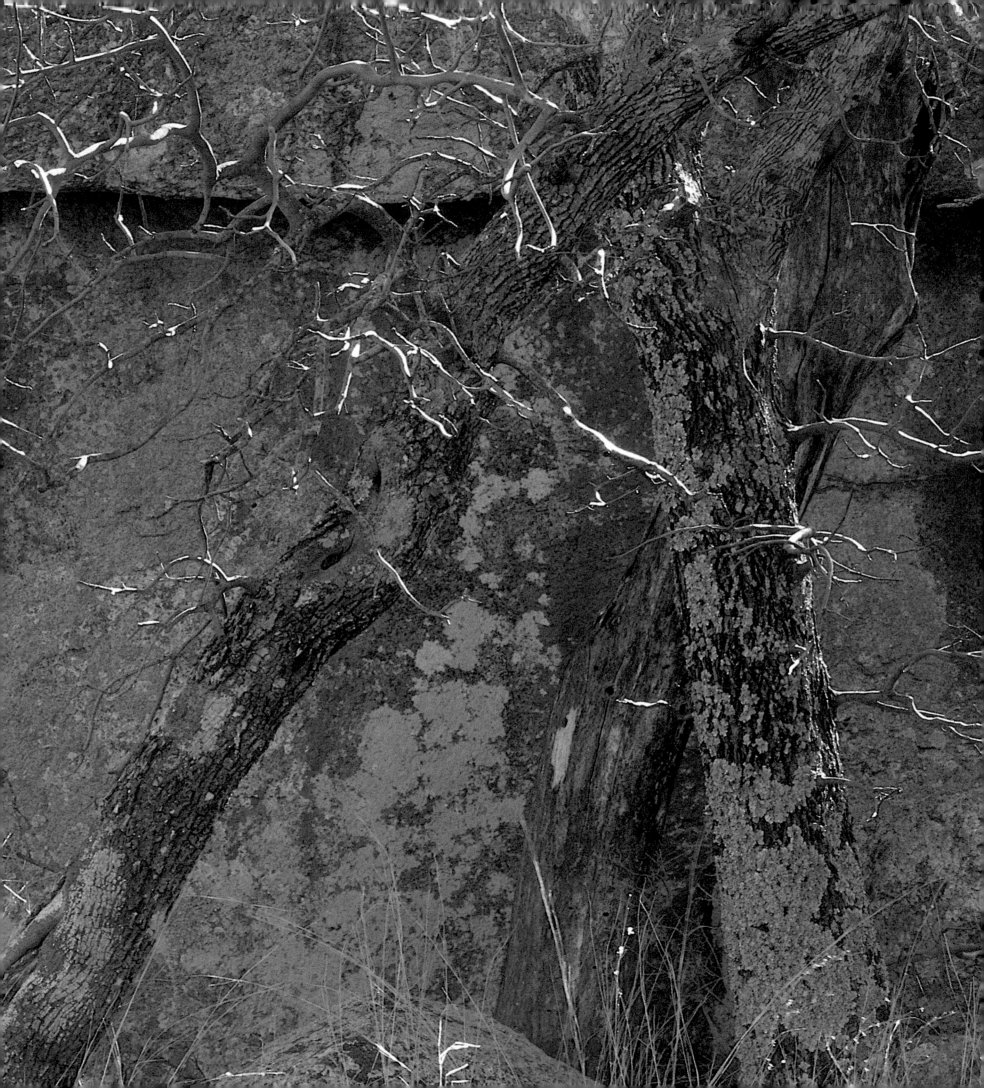

83

left: *Rock detail near Scenic Overlook,*
*Enchanted Rock State Natural Area,*
*Texas, March 1993*

*Granite domes near Scenic Overlook,*
*Enchanted Rock State Natural Area,*
*Texas, March 1993*

*Thermal springs and San Juan River,*
*Pagosa Springs, Colorado, April 1992*

*right: "Pagosa Landscape," detail of travertine*
*residue on side of fountain, Pagosa Springs,*
*Colorado, April 1992*

# Pahgasa

## *Warm Sands of the Tewa*

84    Pagosa Springs, Colorado, gets its name from the Ute word Pahgasa, meaning "boiling waters." A Ute story recalls a time of plague, when even the medicine people failed to stop the deaths. A tribal council built a giant bonfire, then danced and beseeched the gods for help. They slept, and when they awoke the bonfire was replaced with a pool of boiling water, a gift from the Great Spirit who healed them of their sickness. Today it is known that Pagosa has been holy ground for many thousands of years, a special place where warring tribes co-existed in peace.

To the Tewa Pueblo people of Arizona, Pagosa Springs was known as Warm Sands, a place of winter pilgrimage. A story is told of two Tewa Pueblo men who, driving north on their way to a sundance, stopped and knelt on the sand, and were overcome by memories of distant ancestors. They had never been here before, yet felt a powerful homecoming.

Although much of the site's natural atmosphere has been destroyed, colourful mineral encrustations called travertine can be seen in a fountain in the town square and flowing down the nearby banks of the San Juan River.

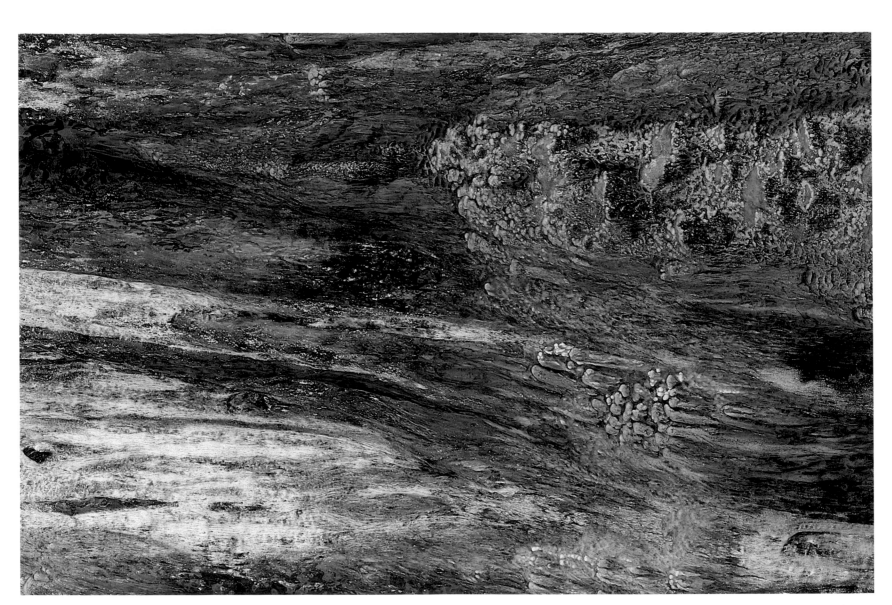

85

*Petroglyph of Bighorn sheep, Three Rivers
Petroglyph Site, Three Rivers, New Mexico,
March 1993*

*right: Petroglyph at Three Rivers Petroglyph
Site, Three Rivers, New Mexico, March 1993*

# Three Rivers

## *Petroglyphs of Mystery*

86  No rivers are seen now at the site of Three Rivers Petroglyphs, north of Tularosa, New Mexico, but there remains an abundance of superbly carved figures in the rock outcroppings. It is one of the largest collections of petroglyphs in North America, with nearly twenty thousand carvings of birds, insects, animals, hands, masks, human figures, suns, moons, stars, crosses, circles, geometric designs and anthropomorphic beings.

Archaeologists believe the carvings were made more than six hundred years ago by people they call the Jornada branch of the Mogollon culture, descendants of those who inhabited New Mexico from about 5000 BC. Some of the figures seem to depict the type of game that roamed this fertile valley in abundance, while others may record great events in people's lives. What the majority of the carvings have in

common is a mystical quality. One symbol in particular – a cross within a circle with varying numbers of distinct dots around the circumference – occurs repeatedly. While the cross within a circle is a prominent southwestern symbol for the Hopi Sky God, the version with the dots rarely appears at other North American sites. It is, however, seen in diverse forms throughout Mesoamerica as a symbol of the god Quetzalcoatl, and some believe these petroglyphs provide evidence that links three great cultures – the Mexican, the Mogollon and the Pueblo.

Images of faces and masks abound at Three Rivers. One of the most prominent is a large face with almond-shaped eyes and an inverted mouth full of jaguar-shaped teeth. These teeth are drawn in a fringelike design similar to the Tlaloc masks on the Temple of Quetzalcoatl at

Teotihuacan, Mexico. Tlaloc was an important deity, "he who makes things grow," and as one of the most ancient gods of Mesoamerica, he lived on the mountain surrounded by clouds, where he controlled the all-important rains. Here at Three Rivers, the Tlaloc-inspired carving faces the twelve-thousand foot Sierra Blanca, towering over the valley to the east. To the Mescalero Apache, who continue to reside in this area, this is a sacred mountain; here the Apache believe the mountain spirits live, offering power to the shaman and providing songs and other sacred knowledge to the people.

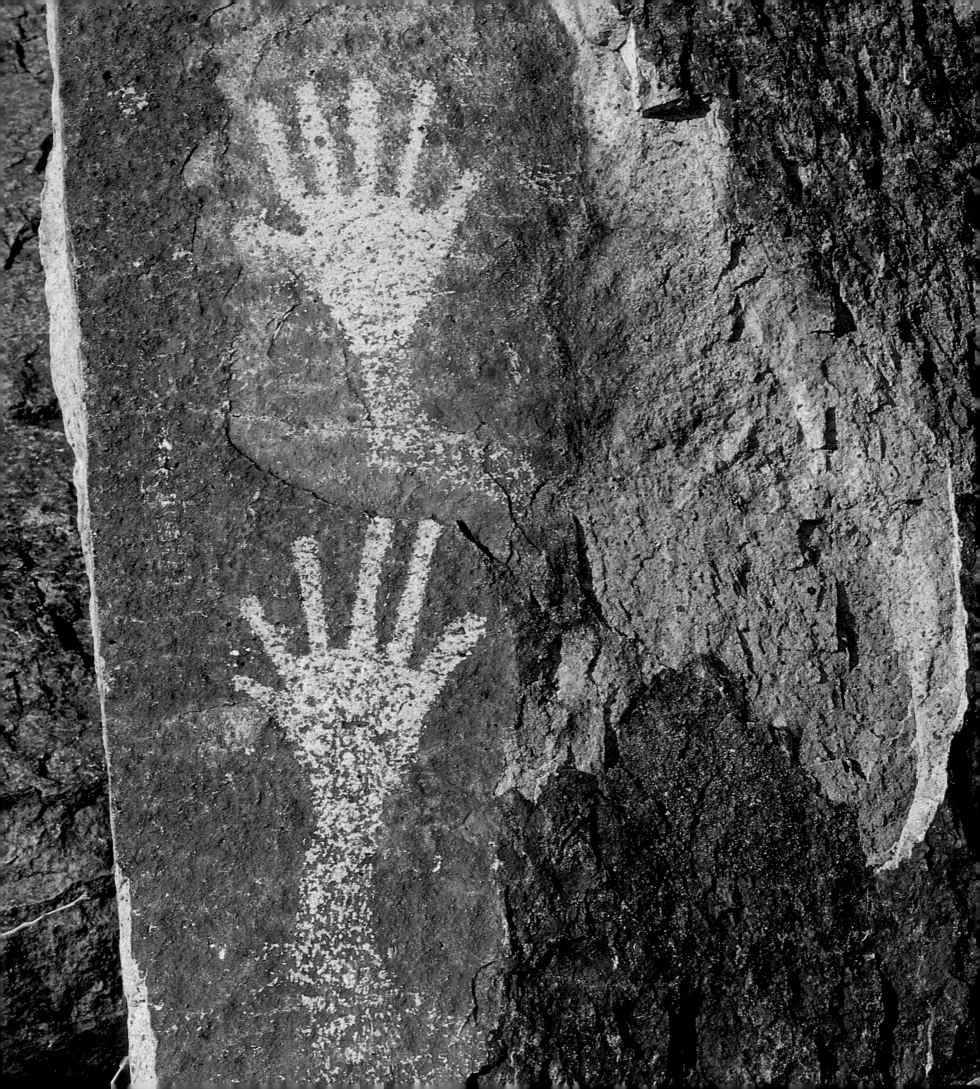

88

*Detail of petroglyph resembling "Quetzalcoatl"*
*symbol, Three Rivers Petroglyph Site,*
*Three Rivers, New Mexico, March 1993*

89

*Petroglyph resembling Tlaloc mask and Sierra Blanca, Three Rivers Petroglyph Site, Three Rivers, New Mexico, March 1993*

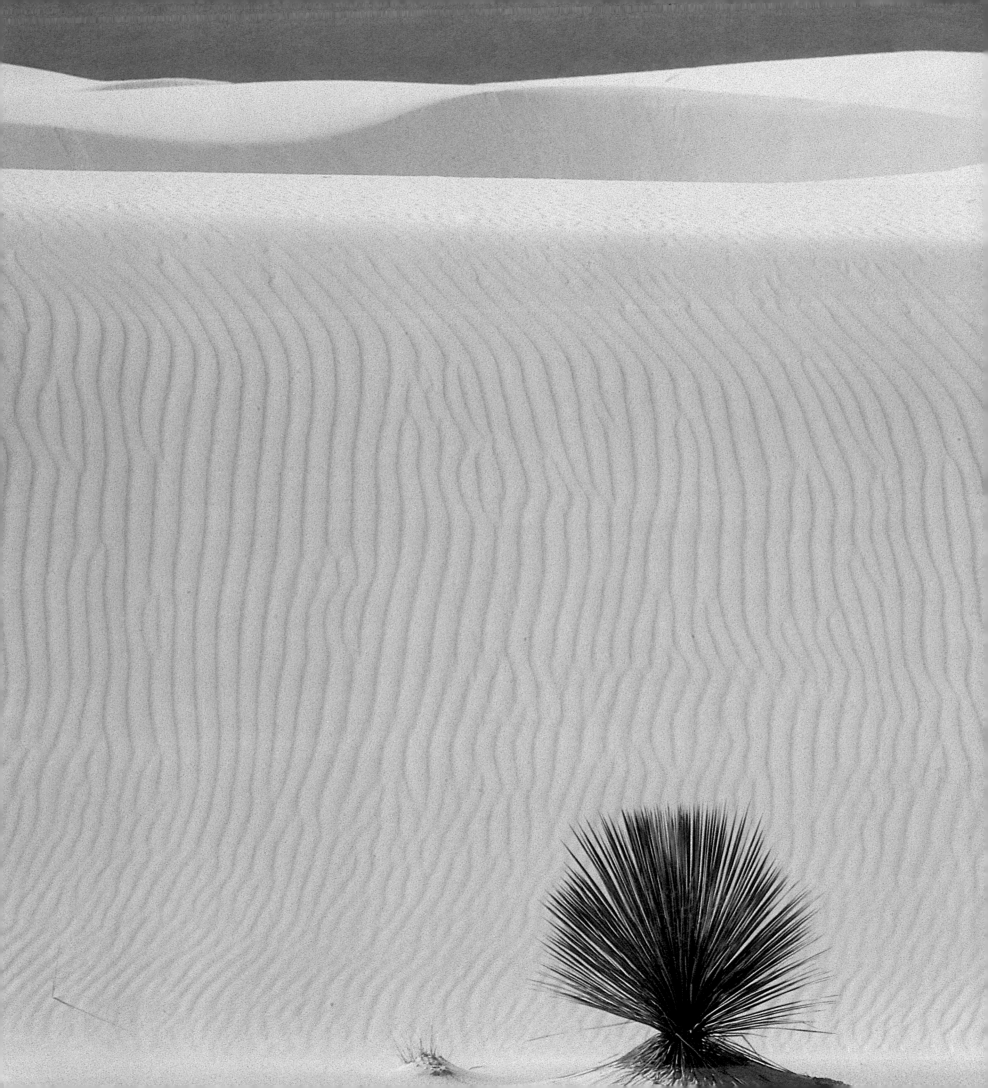

*left: Gypsum dunes, White Sands National Monument, New Mexico, March 1993*

*"Horned Serpent," cloud and sun, White Sands National Monument, New Mexico, March 1993*

# White Sands

## *Sea of Alabaster*

From the highest trail at Three Rivers one can see fifty miles southwest to the chalk white sliver of White Sands, New Mexico. Contrasting starkly against the flat prairie and the jagged foothills of the San Andreas Mountains, the dunes of this "alabaster sea" shift ceaselessly over an area of nearly three hundred square miles. Because it is so bright and easily identifiable, White Sands has served as a reference point for thousands of years – for stone-age hunters following the big-horned bison and for space-age astronauts who can spot the white sand sea from their space capsule. Composed of particles from an elegant crystalline form of gypsum called selenite, the sand has been produced for twenty-five thousand years by the annual drying of Lake Lucero, the lowest point in the entire Tularosa Basin, and once an inland sea.

According to an Apache creation story, the Giver of Life told of a coming deluge and directed White Painted Woman to an abalone shell. She took refuge in the floating shell until the waters receded and the shell came to rest at White Sands, where she gave birth to two children, Son of the Sun and Child of the Water. Also known as Changing Woman, she is the greatest cultural hero of the Apache, who have lived in this area since the 1400s. She teaches how to rid the world of evil, and she never ages, continually renewed to a youthful appearance in the same way that these sands are continually re-created.

These seemingly inhospitable dunes are also home to a Pueblo Indian story of romance and mystery. A Spaniard named Hernando de Luna accompanied the infamous Spanish conquistador Coronado on a northward expedition to conquer New Mexico a half-century after the arrival of Columbus. Hernando brought with him his bride-to-be, Manuela. On the edge of the Great White Sands, a party of fierce Apache warriors ambushed Coronado's scouts, among whom was de Luna, who was never seen again. It is said that even today the ghost of the bereaved Manuela, called Pavla Blanca, can be seen following the sunset, her white wedding robes blowing like sand in the wind.

Perhaps it is best that I did not see Pavla Blanca on my journey across the dunes. According to legend, to see her once is good luck, twice is bad luck, and three times brings death.

*Gypsum dunes, White Sands National Monument, New Mexico, March 1993*

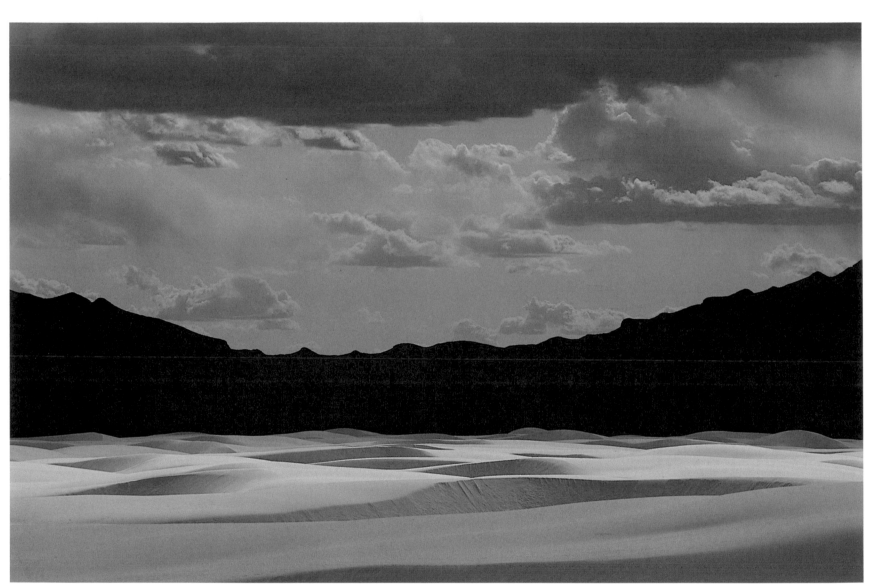

# Canyon de Chelly

## *Teachings of the "Holy Beings"*

Canyon de Chelly in northeastern Arizona was home to the Anasazi, who flourished here between AD 800 and 1050. The story of these early people, known by the Navajo word meaning "Ancient Ones," is still being revealed. The name de Chelly comes from the Spanish pronunciation of the Navajo word meaning "where the water comes out of the rock," referring to the mouth of the canyon where the life-giving waters of the Chinle Wash originate.

This is one of the most important ceremonial sites of the Navajo, who found refuge and sustenance here in the mid-eighteenth century, escaping from warring tribes to the east. According to Navajo stories passed orally from generation to generation, this is where the Holy Beings taught them how to live, and where medicine rituals are performed to restore harmony to mind and spirit.

A colossal landmark of the natural world combines with a compelling history at Spider Rock, a thousand-foot-high twin column of sandstone. Sacred to both Hopi and Navajo, it is the home of Spider Woman. She spins a web that captures and devours misbehaving children who are reported to her by Speaking Rock across the canyon. The white rocks on top of the tower are said to be the sun-bleached bones of the victims.

The most extensive Anasazi cliff dwellings here are the White House Ruins, which are accessible by a foot trail down the rim of the steep cliff and across the waters of Chinle Wash. Not far from the White House is an unusual grouping of pictographs – a fish, two white crosses and a reddish-coloured maze. Reminiscent of symbols showing the four cardinal directions, these crosses are found at several sites in Canyon de Chelly. They are thought to depict panels of stars or "planetariums" and are sacred to the Navajo. Among other pictographs in the canyon are depictions of Kokopelli, the Hopi humpbacked flute player that is a symbol of fertility.

Betatakin, meaning "Ledge House" in Navajo, is another prominent Anasazi site, that lies in Navajo National Monument, northwest of Canyon de Chelly. Like the White House ruins, it is a harmonious blend of architecture and nature. The cliff dwellings here have been constructed on a narrow ledge protected by an enormous rocky overhang, giving the appearance of an amphitheatre, its vaulted ceiling rising eight hundred feet above the valley floor. A Hopi creation story tells of their emergence from a corrupt Third World into the present Fourth World, where the guardian spirit, Maasaw, revealed their destiny to live out the Creator's plan and to look to the valleys, rocks and woods to find his footprints. It is said the Hopi ancestors stopped here at Betatakin during their long migration to Tuwanasavi, the Centre of the Universe. Their journey took them sixty miles farther south, where they now maintain a traditional lifestyle in a network of villages on the Three Mesas.

*View from south rim, Canyon de Chelly National Monument, Arizona, September 1990*

*right: Spider Rock, Canyon de Chelly National Monument, Arizona, September 1990*

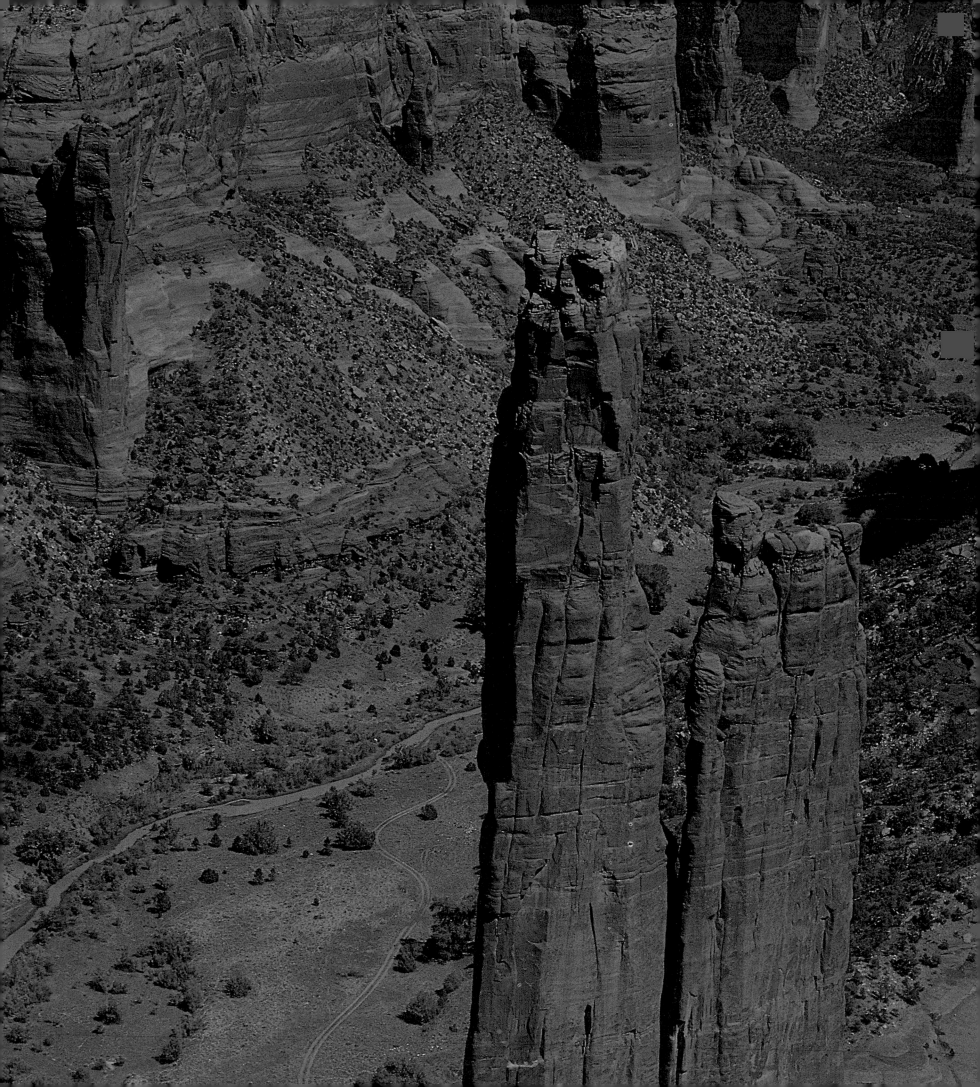

97

*left: Reflection in Chinle Wash,*
*Canyon de Chelly National Monument,*
*Arizona, September 1990*

*Detail of sandstone cliff at White House Ruins,*
*Canyon de Chelly National Monument,*
*Arizona, September 1990*

*Cliff dwellings at Betatakin, Navajo National Monument, Arizona, September 1990*

*Double exposure of Cliff Palace
and cliff face, Mesa Verde National
Park, Colorado, April 1992*

# Mesa Verde

## *Cliff Palace of Antiquity*

From the high plateau country of southwestern Colorado, one can see many sacred landscapes. To the north, the La Plata Mountains mark the boundary of the Navajo Nation; to the south, the "Rock of Wings," known as Shiprock or Tse Bit'a'i, is the home of the Winged Monsters of Navajo history; and to the west, Sleeping Ute Mountain is the place where Ute stories say the Rain God gathered all the clouds in his pocket. And while Mesa Verde lies in the centre of present-day Ute territory, the ledges of this central plateau harbour a series of ancient cliff dwellings inhabited by the Anasazi.

The name Mesa Verde, Spanish for "green table," refers to the fertile soil and hunting conditions on the mesa tops that were densely populated from AD 900 to 1300. The Anasazi took advantage of nature and built their communities into the side of the cliff under the protection of sandstone overhangs. Of the five thousand ruins uncovered, the Cliff Palace is one of the most magnificent examples of how the Anasazi fitted their stone construction to the available space and contours of the land. Towers and three-storey dwellings surround circular structures called kivas, the Hopi name for underground rooms, which are still used for ceremonies and social gatherings.

Like Betatakin, which is believed to have been inhabited only between AD 1250 and 1286, the Cliff Palace was occupied for less than one hundred years. Possibly a climatic change forced the Anasazi to move to more fertile areas, leaving these structures empty for more than seven hundred years, like ghosts of an enchanted past.

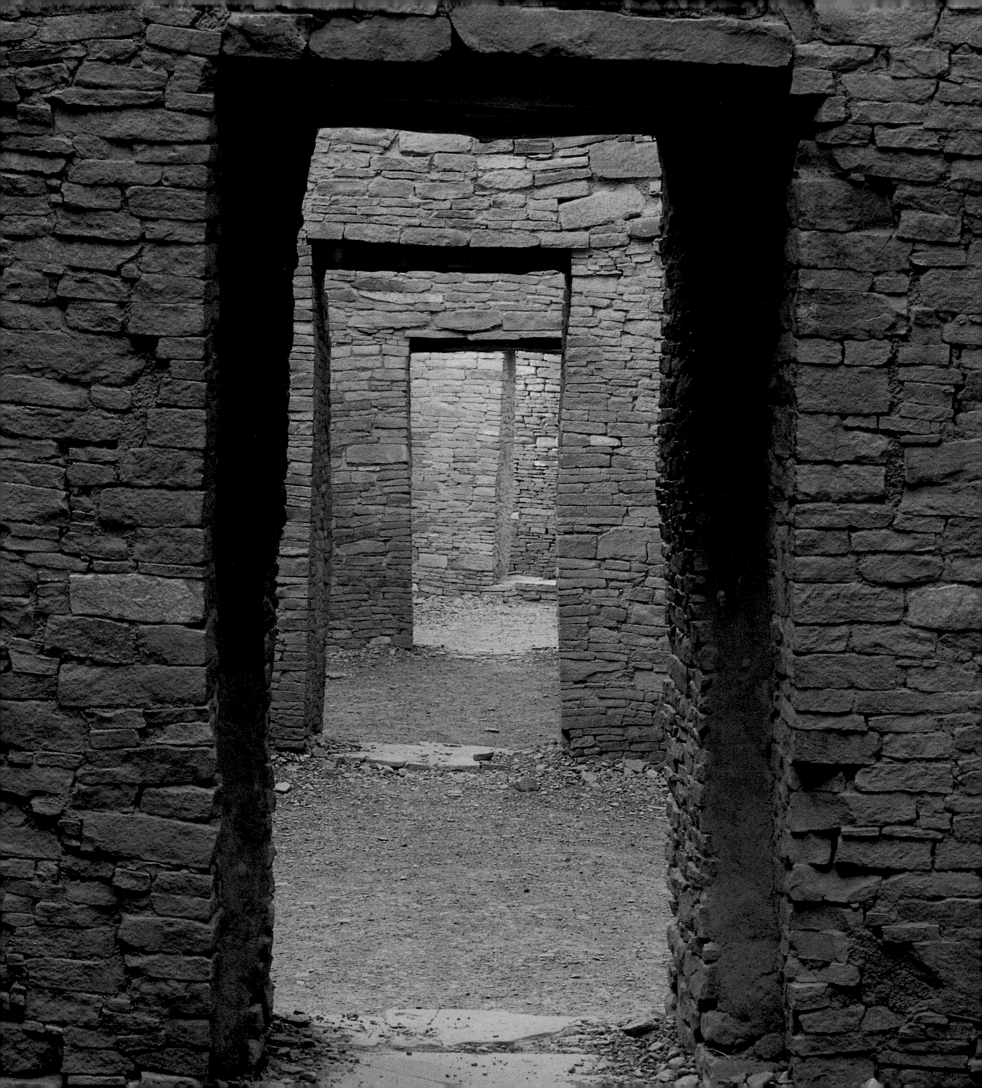

left: *"Doors," Pueblo Bonito, Chaco Culture National Historic Park, New Mexico, September 1990*

*Canyon rim, sunset light, Chaco Culture National Historic Park, New Mexico, September 1990*

# Chaco Canyon

## *Hub of the Anasazi Culture*

Chaco Canyon was perhaps the greatest seat of power of the Anasazi culture, which flourished here between AD 900 and 1300. Pueblo Bonito, a city complex of eight hundred rooms and thirty-two kivas, is nestled in the base of the eastern cliffs at a major crossroads in the canyon. Archeologists believe it was the centre of a large trade network comprising seventy or eighty surrounding villages, accessible by four hundred miles of well-built roadways. However, more recent investigations using aerial remote sensing techniques suggest that Pueblo Bonito may have been Chaco's major ceremonial centre – the legendary "Middle Place" of the Anasazi spiritual world – with more than a thousand miles of roads over an area of sixty thousand square miles.

This classic Anasazi period is identified by multistory villages that were sustained by irrigation and supported by a vast distribution network. Although each community had many kivas, the ritual functions of Chaco are believed to have taken place in Casa Rinconada, the largest kiva in the valley. For the Hopi, who believe their ancestors passed through here, this round, underground ceremonial room symbolizes the womb of the Earth Mother, where man emerged from the underworld. Today, Hopi communities continue to use kivas for ceremonies, often involving drumming and dancing. It seems certain this kiva was the Anasazi link with the cosmos; its two outer entrances are built on a north-south axis, directly in line with celestial north, and congruent with the four cardinal directions.

In Pueblo Bonito, the doorways align with each other, creating a feeling of transformation as you pass from room to room, like a rebirth into successive spiritual worlds. Navajo oral histories of Chaco Canyon say that it was here that the Holy People won back all their property from the Great Gambler, who was then exiled in the sky. Hopi stories identify Chaco as one of the stops their ancestors made on the long migration, following the footsteps of Maasaw to their home on the Three Mesas to the west. And although scientists suggest that a change in climate precipitated the Anasazi's departure, Navajo stories teach that the Ancient Ones were dispersed by a whirlwind because they had abandoned the ways of their ancestors.

101

*Pueblo Bonito, sunset light, Chaco Culture
National Historic Park, New Mexico,
September 1990*

*right: Pueblo Bonito from above, Chaco Culture
National Historic Park, New Mexico,
September 1990*

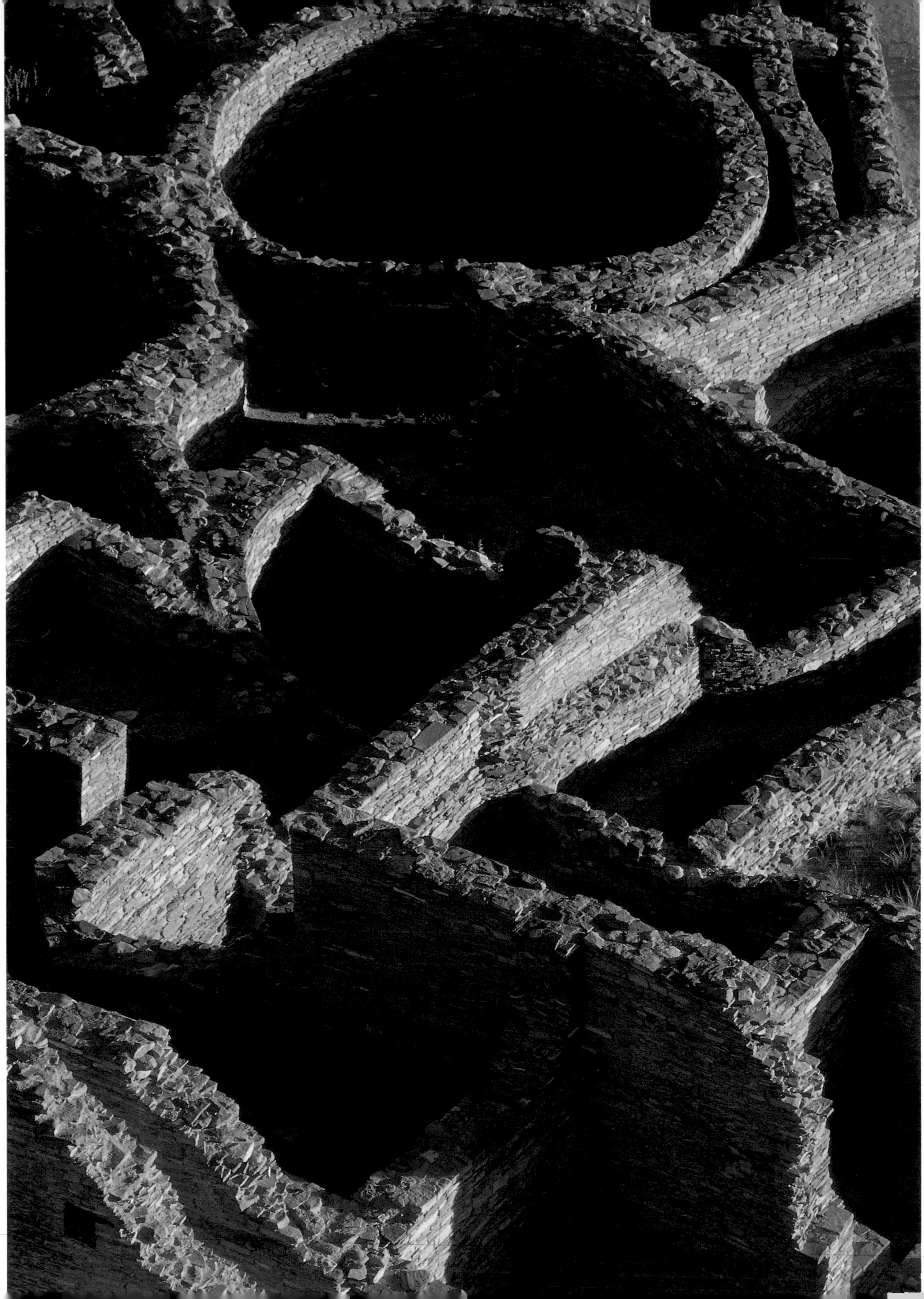

104

*Silhouette of Pueblo Bonito, Chaco Culture
National Historic Park, New Mexico,
September 1990*

*right: "Lunar Necklace," multiple exposure
of moon and Casa Rinconada (fisheye lens; see
Photographer's Notes, p.202), Chaco Culture
National Historic Park, September 1990*

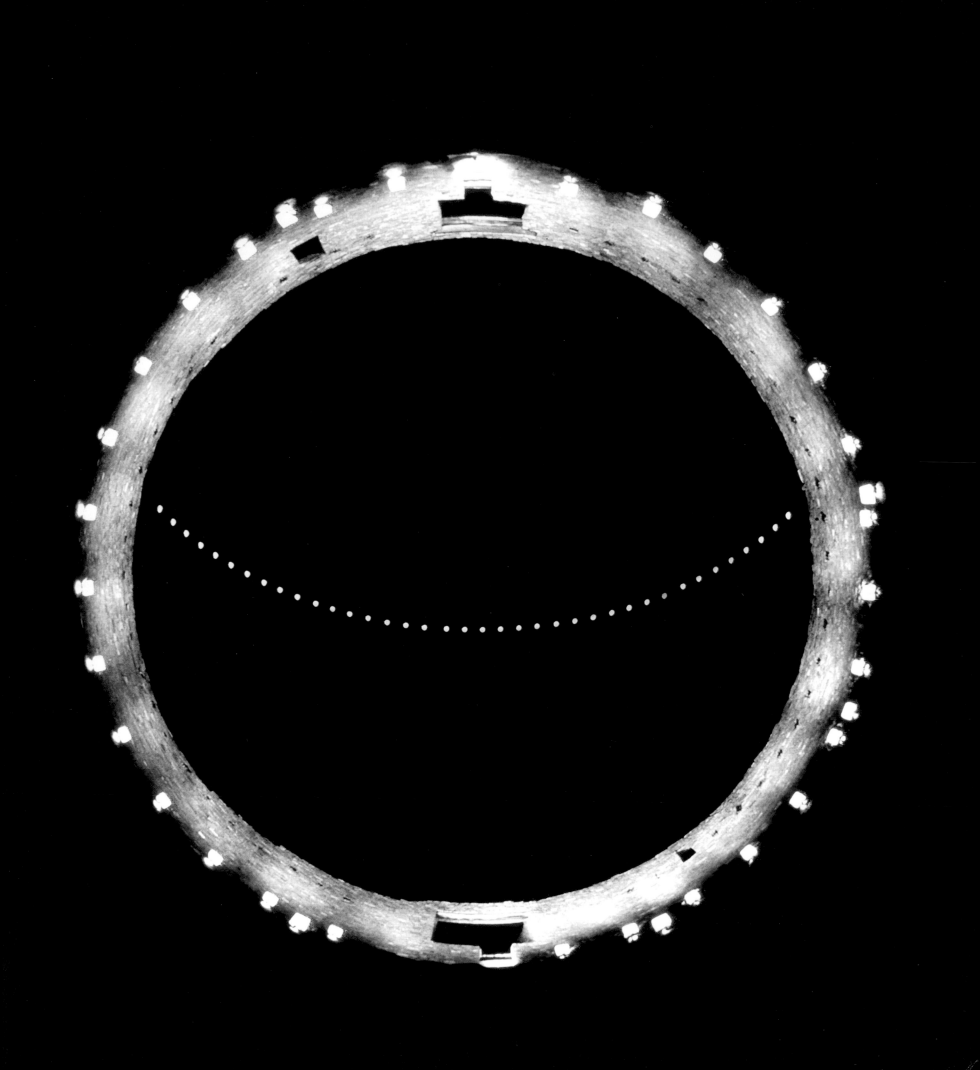

106

*Kiva at Chetro Ketl, Chaco Culture National*
*Historic Park, New Mexico, September 1990*

*Navajo Mountain and Lake Powell, Page, Arizona, September 1990*

# Navajo Mountain

## *Head of the Earth*

From the shores of Lake Powell, on the border of Utah and Arizona, Navajo Mountain emerges through the mist, forty miles to the east. Called Naatsis'aan in Navajo, the mountain is known as "the Head of Earth," the place that brings clouds from the heavens. A Navajo creation story speaks of Black Body and Blue Body, the first man and woman, who built the mountain with earth brought from the underworld. Geological evidence concurs: the mountain is made up of a lava core that would have turned black and blue as it solidified.

Navajo stories connect this cloud-making mountain to a rainbow in stone, the nearby sandstone arch called Rainbow Bridge, the earth's largest natural bridge. For the Navajo, this is the home of the Rainbow People, and a place of pilgrimage where correct rituals ensure the coming of life-giving rains. To pass under the bridge without chanting the correct songs is said to bring certain death.

The Navajo have many traditional chants, performed to restore physical and spiritual well-being. For example, when the Mountain Healing Song is sung over a person, that person's spirit makes the journey to a holy place beyond the sacred mountain, where he is blessed or healed by the Divine Ones who live there.

# Antelope Canyon

## *Rainbow of the Earth*

Near Page, Arizona, is a network of slot canyons that eventually empty into Lake Powell. The best known is Antelope Canyon. Peering down from ground level into a two-hundred-foot drop, all that is visible is a black fissure in the sandstone. But inside lies a rainbow of colour.

Centuries of flash floods have etched out the sweeping shapes of chambers, columns, corridors, sinkholes and caves. In the Navajo language, Tse'neh'na'eh'diz'sjaa means "where water has painted a picture of itself." Local Navajo people say that their ancestors, the Anasazi, used the canyons as refuge from the elements as well as from their enemies. The canyons have sacred significance because they represent the womb from which the Earth Mother gives birth and are believed to be monuments to the life force of the female energy of water. Some Navajo people continue to perform water purification ceremonies here.

Navajo stories warn that slot canyons are dangerous. This is the home of the chindi, wicked spirits who spend most of their time in the afterworld located below the earth. Here these dangerous spirits seek revenge for wrongs done to them during their life. They are barely visible, but sometimes they can be heard making noise while wandering through dark canyon recesses.

*Reflected sunlight on sandstone formations, Antelope Canyon, Page, Arizona, April 1992*

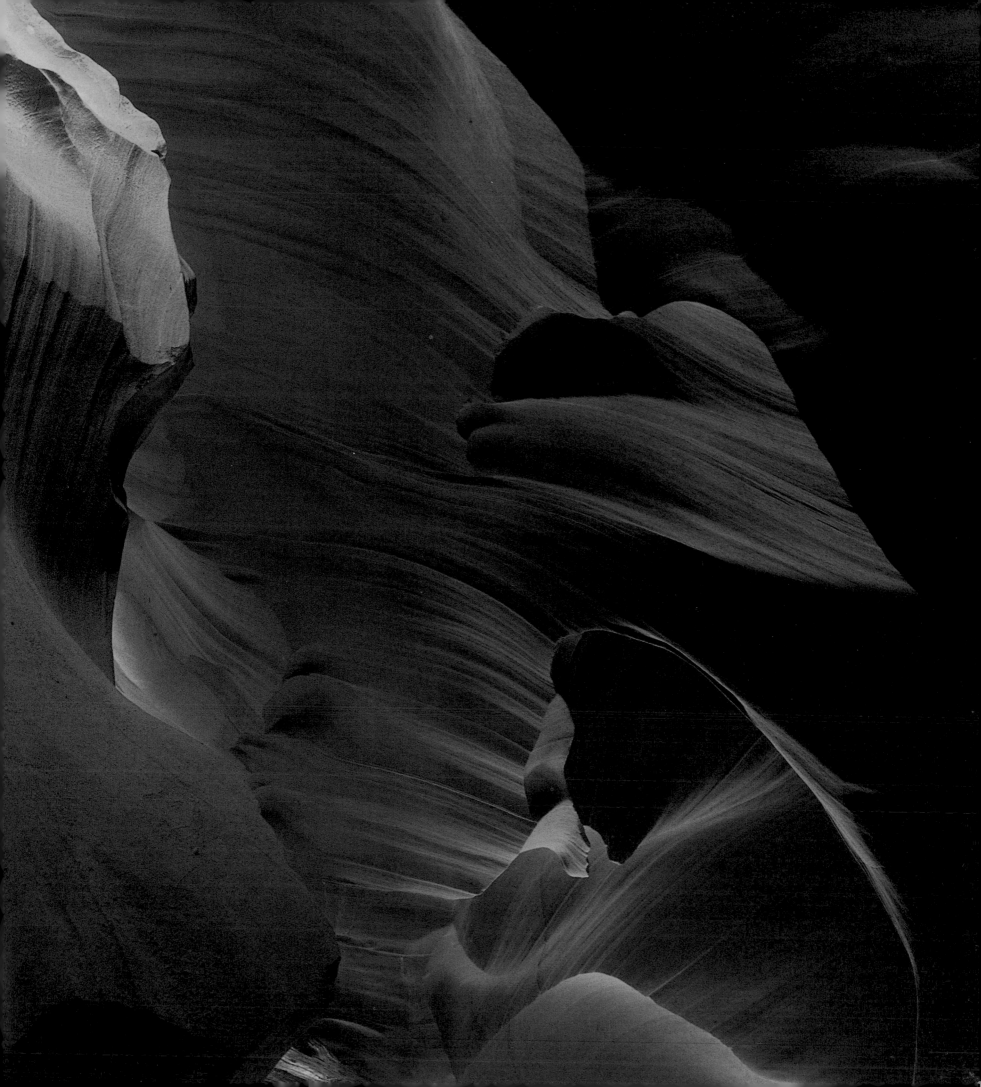

*Reflected sunlight on sandstone formations,*
*Antelope Canyon, Page, Arizona, April 1992*

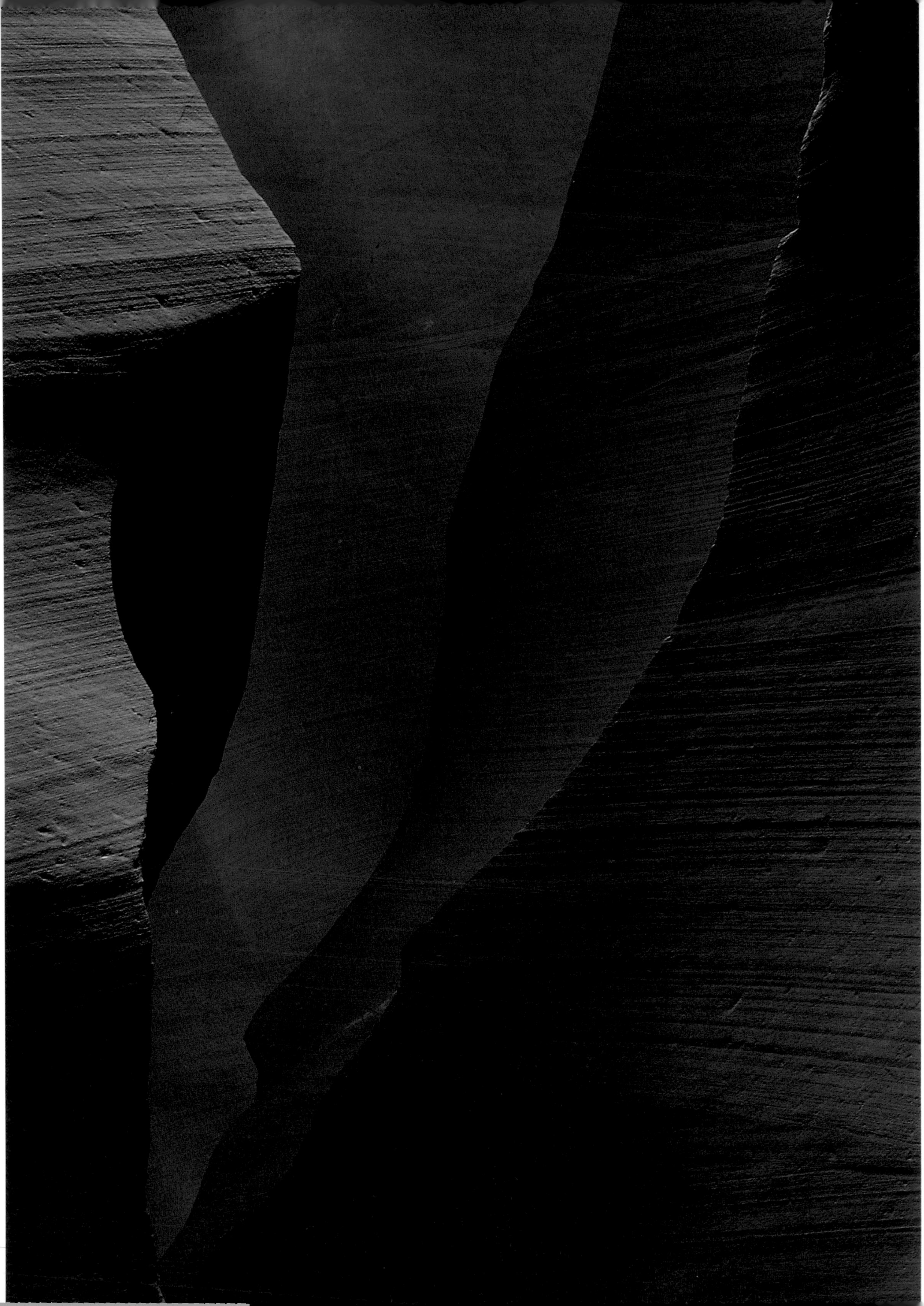

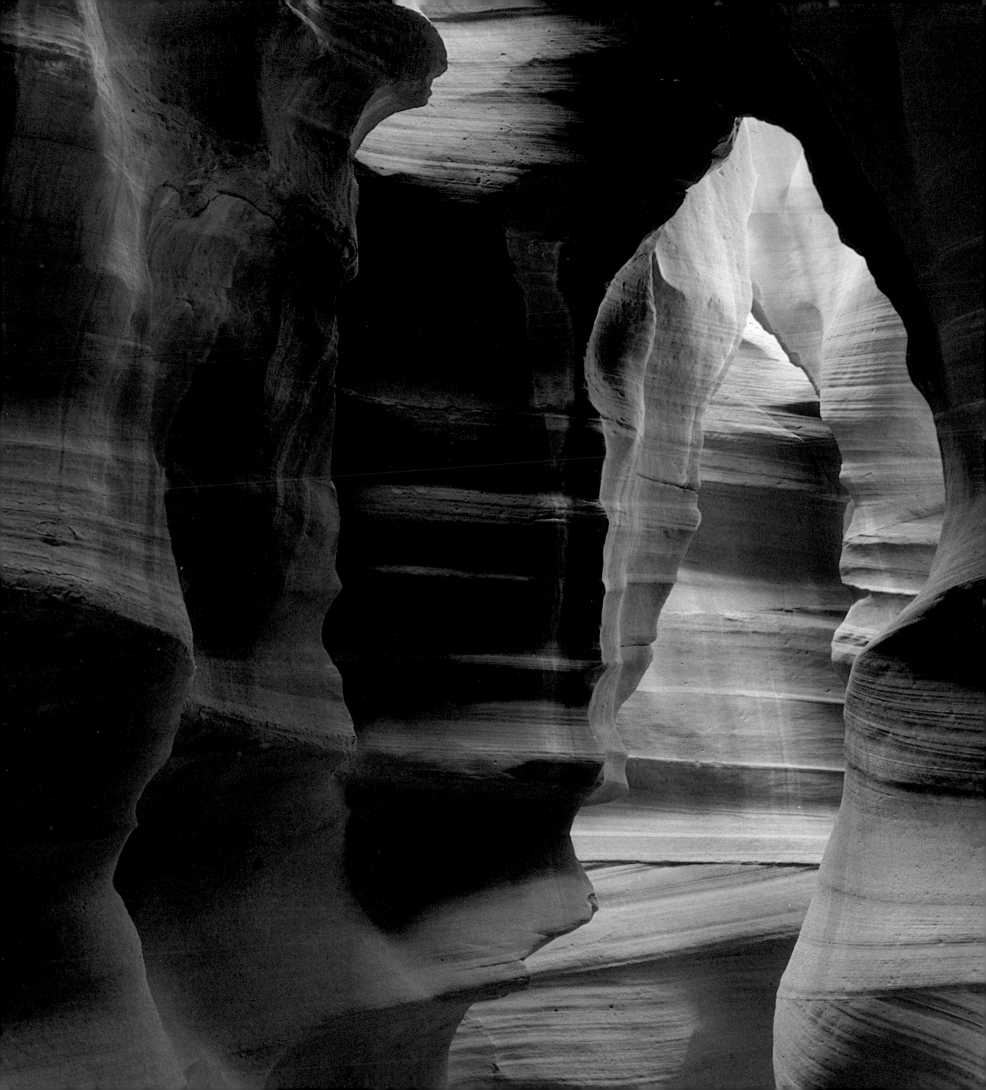

113

*Reflected sunlight on sandstone formations,*
*Antelope Canyon, Page, Arizona,*
*September 1990*

*Detail of canyon walls, Peach Canyon, Arizona, April 1992*

# Peach Canyon

## *Abode of the Chindi*

114 Peach Canyon is located on private Navajo land about thirty miles southeast of Antelope Canyon. Almost impassable in some places, it narrows to a slit with ledges too tenuous to walk across.

Many Navajo stories speak of beasts like tse do nahu nti, the impossible crevice monster, and tse aheeniditii, the crushing rock monster, who live in slot canyons. In one story, the sons of Changing Woman and Father Sun want to destroy the monsters, and seek their father to help them. Their journey takes them through the canyon that crushes, where Spider Woman advises them to chant special prayers. She also provides magic feathers that protect them from the crashing walls and allow them to escape and continue their quest.

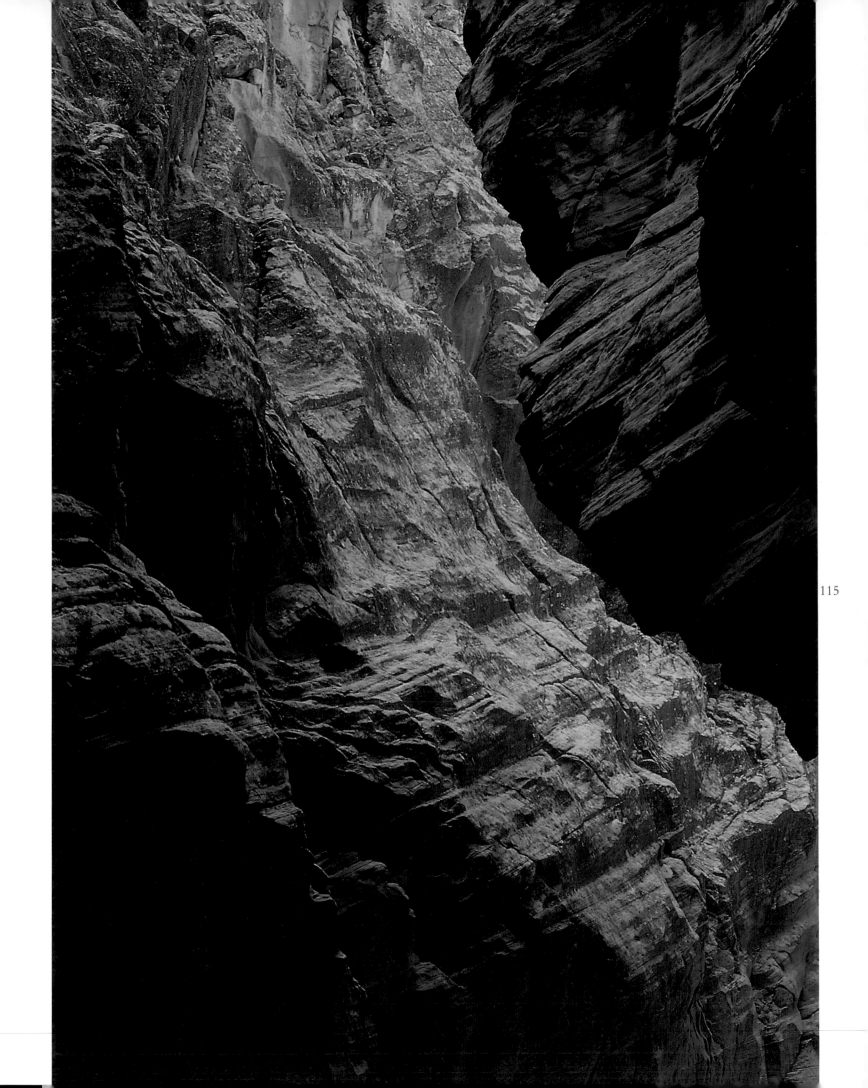

*Silhouette of Cathedral Rock and moon in predawn sky, Sedona, Arizona, September 1990*

*right: Lightning storm on Mund's Mountain, Sedona, Arizona, September 1990*

# Wipuk

## *Foot of the Rocks*

The Red Rock Country of Sedona was home to native people as early as ten thousand years ago. The Hohokam and Sinagua people were the ancestors of the Yavapai, the hunter-gatherers who came here in the sixteenth century and called it Wipuk, meaning "at the foot of the rocks." The Yavapai regarded the land with reverence and did not enter the canyons except for ceremonial purposes; in 1875 they were forced from the area, and many perished along the March of Tears to reservations in the east.

Today, Sedona resembles a huge magnet, attracting people from around the world who yearn to experience the strong earth energies reported here. The land is a catalyst for many emotions; some feel invigorated by the brilliantly burnished red rock, while others find it overpowering and enervating. The fantastical rock shapes inspire the imagination; the centre spires of Cathedral Rock suggest the profile of two hands together in prayer, or the figures of a bride and bridegroom. One Yavapai story tells that Sedona is the home of the goddess Kamalapukwia, or "grandmother of the supernatural," who lives in a cave. Her grandson, Sakarakaamche, the first man on earth, possesses great medicine power. Some say that it is he and his grandmother who stand back to back as the dual spires of Cathedral Rock.

According to their creation story, all Yavapai originated at Wipuk. Sakarakaamche taught them how to pray, to sing and to dance. Singing is a form of prayer, passed down through the generations; it connects people with the earth and maintains their vitality. One of Sakarakaamcha's songs describes how he descended to earth on flashes of lightning, sang as he knelt on the ground and caused medicine plants to sprout out of the earth when he lifted his hands. The Yavapai believe that if the songs are not sung and the stories are not told, the land will die.

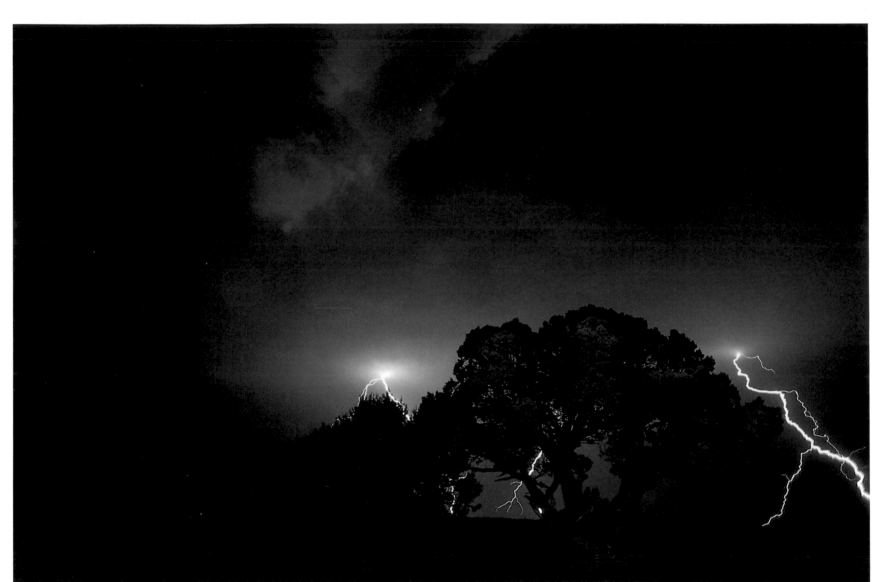

118

*Medicine wheel overlooking Long Canyon,*
*Sedona, Arizona, September 1990*

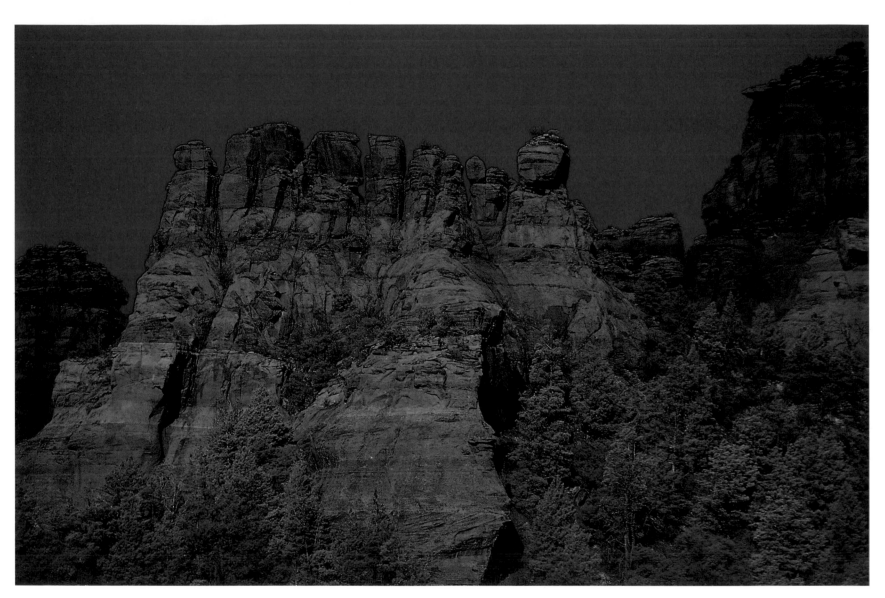

119

*Rock formation, Sedona, Arizona,*
*September 1990*

*"Moonrise Over Bryce," erosional formations, Bryce Canyon National Park, Utah, April 1992*

*right and following page: Erosional formations, Bryce Canyon National Park, Utah, April 1992*

# Bryce Canyon

*Place of the Legend People*

120   Bryce Canyon in south-central Utah cradles some of the most singular and startling geography in North America. Geologically it is the uppermost point of what is called the Grand Staircase, a series of cliffs that reflect steps in time, from the 60-million-year-old Pink Cliffs that form Bryce, to the 225-million-year-old Kaibab Plateau that shapes the north rim of the Grand Canyon, some hundred miles south.

For many, the spires, turrets, columns and cliffs at Bryce, which took an eternity to carve, are awe inspiring. Bryce is actually not a canyon at all, but a huge amphitheatre sculpted by rain, snow and ice. The Paiute Indians who lived here gave it a name that translates to "red rocks standing like men in a bowl-shaped canyon." According to a Paiute story, before there were any Indians, this place was inhabited by Legend People called To-when-an-ung-wa, who looked partly like people and partly like birds, animals or reptiles. For some reason, the Legend People in that place were bad, so Coyote turned them all into rocks. You can see them now, some standing in rows, some sitting down, some holding onto others, their faces painted just as they were before they became rocks.

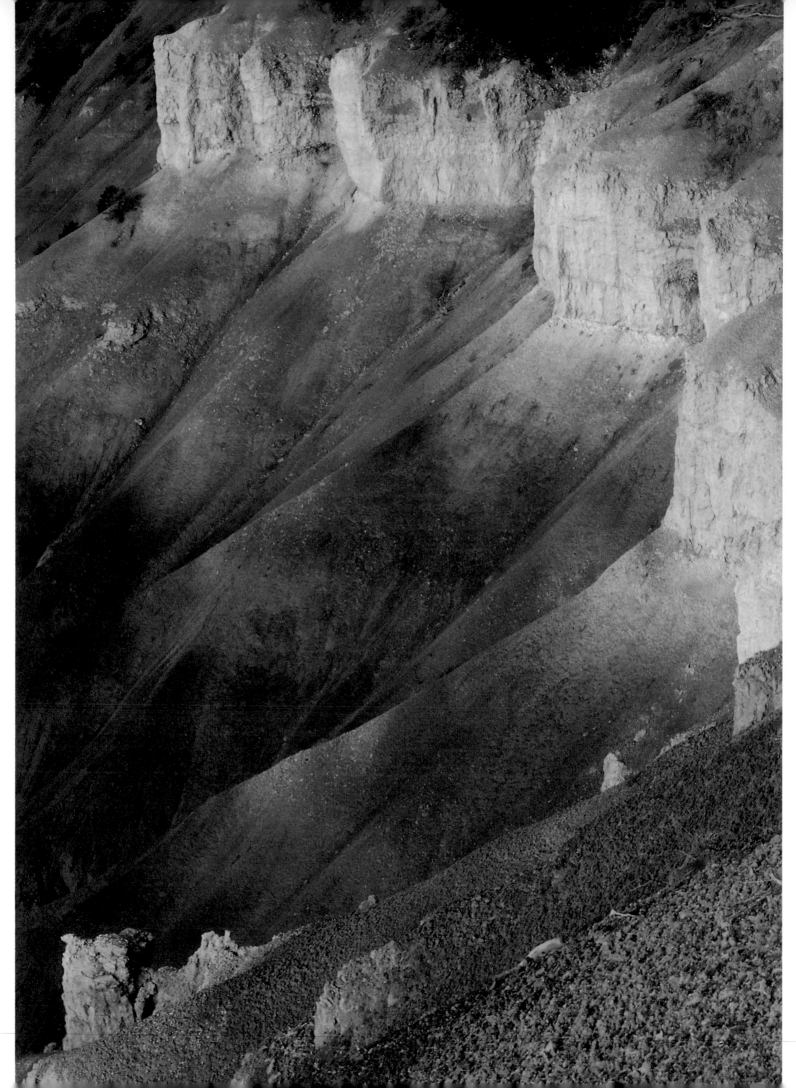

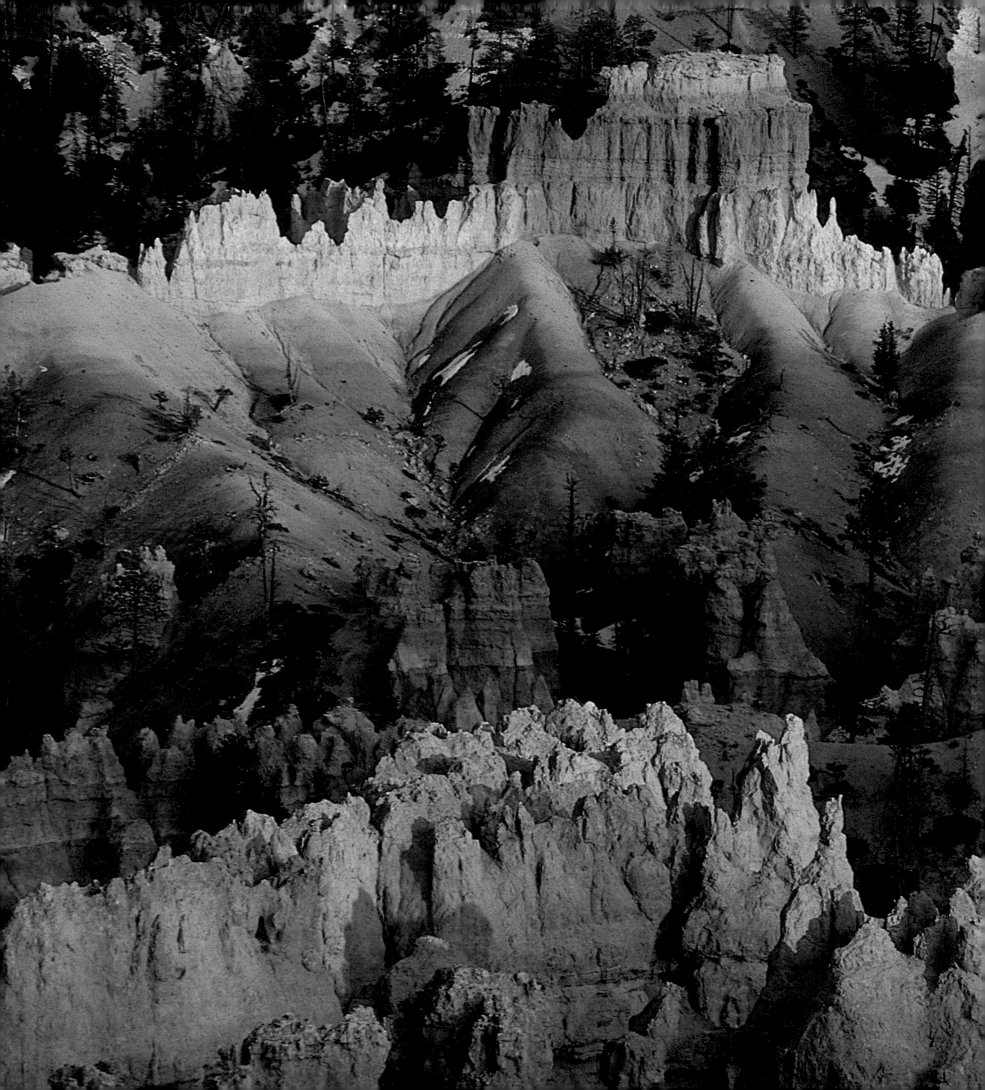

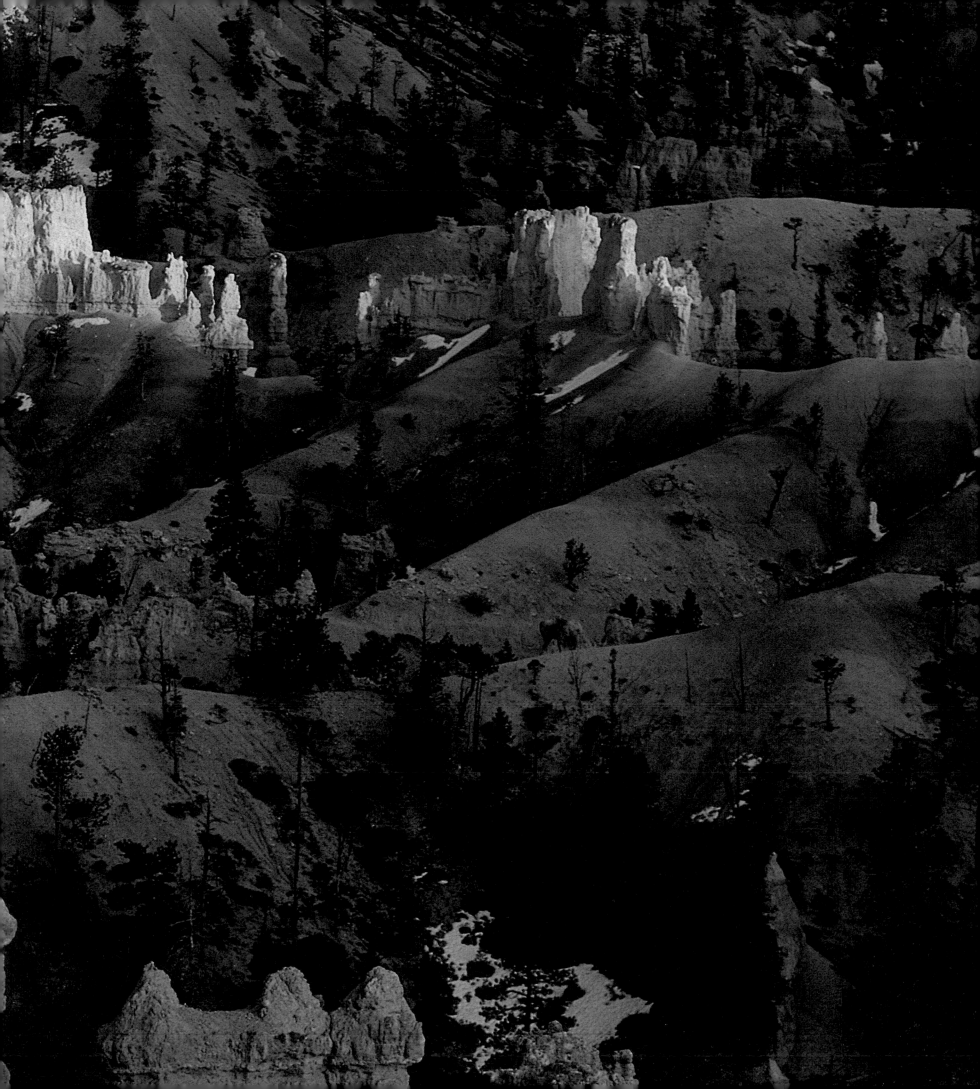

*Weeping Rock, Zion National Park,*
*Utah, April 1993*

*right: Echo Canyon, Zion National Park,*
*Utah, April 1992*

# Mukuntuweap

## *Place Where Spirits Lurk*

124   This land is steeped in human history. The early Basketmakers and Anasazi were followed by the Paiute, who feared and respected the powerful spirits of the land. More recently, the Ute and Navajo displaced the Paiute. In 1909 the area was proclaimed a National Monument and named Mukuntuweap, the Paiute word for "straight canyon," but it was renamed Zion only two years later, in reference to the early Mormon settlers who saw it as their Heavenly City of God.

In spring, the walls of Zion are festooned with greenery and flowers that entice one to the Temple of Sinawava at the head of the canyon. Here the Wolf God of the Paiute still triumphs in the natural amphitheatre named in his honour. But even though the Wolf God was a friendly deity, it is said that his power was not great enough to subdue the evil forces that lurk in The Narrows; this continuation of Zion Canyon is a dead-end chasm called I-oo-goon, meaning "arrow quiver" or "the place where one must come out the same way he went in." Consequently, the Paiute were careful not to be caught here at night.

Many of the other natural monuments at Zion have been endowed with names that reflect their inspirational qualities, such as Great White Throne, Angel's Landing and The Altar of Sacrifice, referring to the red wash of colour on the rocks. At Weeping Rock, a prominent landmark in Zion Canyon, an underground spring continuously feeds the cliff face with rivulets that fall like teardrops from the overhang.

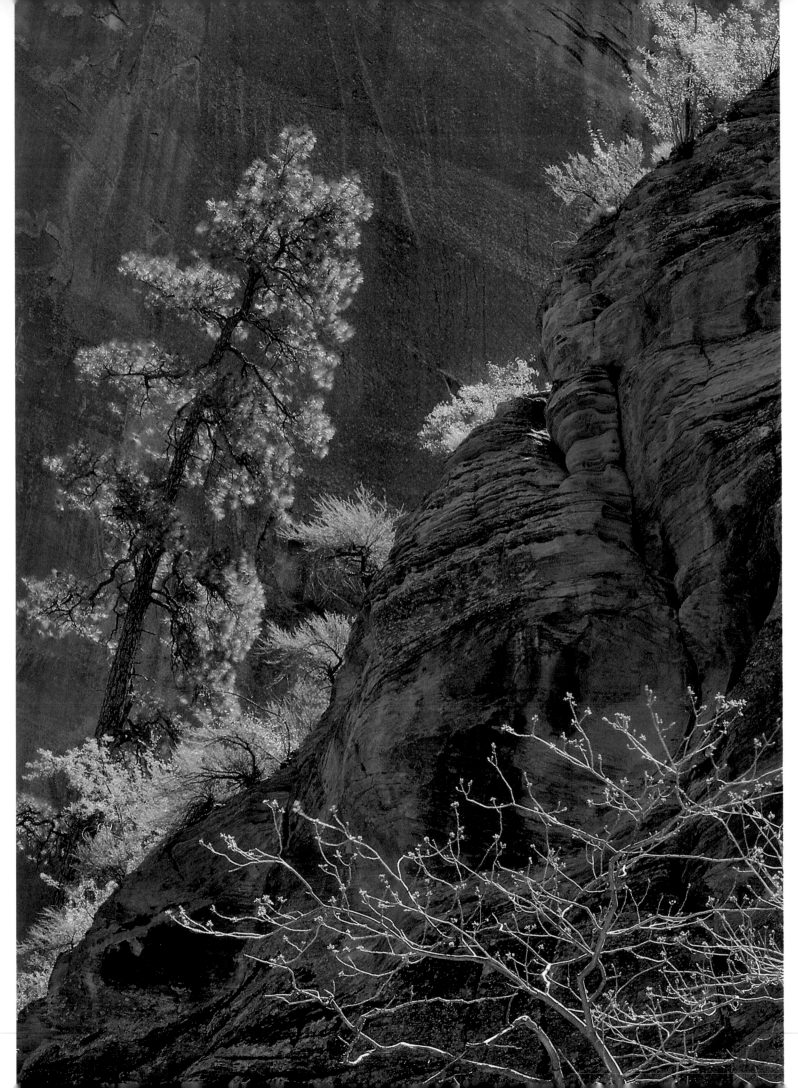

*Cliff face, Cable Mountain,*
*Zion National Park, Utah, April 1992*

127

*Rock debris, Temple of Sinawava,*
*Zion National Park, Utah, April 1993*

*Cove at Barker Dam,*
*Joshua Tree National Monument,*
*California, April 1993*

*right: Sunrise and Joshua trees,*
*Joshua Tree National Monument,*
*California, Easter Sunday, 1993*

# Twenty-Nine Palms

## *Oasis of Fertility*

128  California's Joshua Tree National Monument is an unusual desert area characterized most visibly by the many Joshua trees that grow here. The Joshua tree is actually a variety of the yucca plant and grows only in North America's southwestern deserts, sometimes living for hundreds of years. Since it is the only kind of tree that can survive on the open desert, it is an important source of life for a highly complex ecosystem that includes birds, insects, snakes and desert rodents. In the past, the Serrano, Cahuilla, and Chemehuevi people who lived here ate the flowers and the nutritious seeds of the Joshua tree. The Mormons who travelled in this region held it in high esteem because the limbs looked like the welcoming outstretched arms of the prophet Joshua, a sign to them that they were near their "promised land."

Because of the paucity of rain in the desert, oases are crucially important to its animal and human inhabitants. At Joshua Tree, there are four palm oases, each with a natural supply of underground water. One is Twenty-Nine Palms, whose name has been adopted by the town that has grown around it. The Serrano (Spanish for "highlander") Indians called it Marrah, the place of "little springs and much grass." One story tells that the Serrano people originally came from the San Bernadino Mountains, where the women gave birth mainly to female babies. The Medicine Man told them that in order to produce males they should go east to the desert, set up camp where there was water, and each time a male was born plant a tree. In the first year they planted twenty-nine palms.

To the Serrano Indians, the drooping fronds of the palm trees harbour evil spirits that can be heard at night in the rustling of the wind. In the past, they would set the palms on fire, hoping to drive the spirits away, and, in so doing, would burn away the dead fronds and underbrush, allowing a new cycle of life to begin at the oasis.

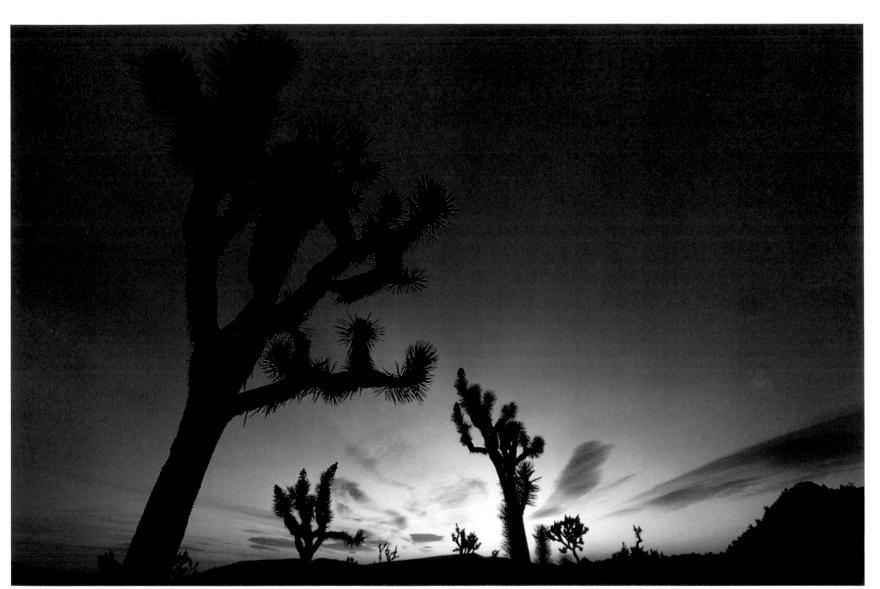

*Palm frond backlit by direct sunlight,*
*Cottonwood Spring, Joshua Tree National*
*Monument, California, April 1993*

# WEST

*To the West and the Thunder Bird*
*Who flies over the universe hidden in a cloak of*
*Rain clouds and cleanses the world of filth,*
*Cleanse our bodies and souls of all evil things.*

*Painted Rock, Carrizo Plain,*
*California, April 1993*

*right: Pictographs in unidentified cave,*
*southern California, April 1993*

# Painted Rock

## *Place of Warning*

132 Located in the San Joaquin Valley of southern California is a 180,000-acre wildlife reserve with a rich array of wildflowers, endangered species of plants and animals and a migratory bird sanctuary. In its midst lies a holy place called Painted Rock, a massive sandstone monolith that rises 150 feet above the plain.

In the past, the Chumash and Yokut people came to this valley for its game-rich grasslands, trading and tribal rituals. A corridor inside Painted Rock contains an amphitheatre of paintings that depict great cosmological events. To the contemporary Chumash people who live in the area, this rock is an important part of their spiritual life and culture, and continues to be used for sacred ceremonies.

In one local story that links this place with Mesoamerican traditions, the Dreamer, a High Priest of the Feathered Serpent, sent out word for all people to gather at this ceremonial site. He spoke to the assembly about love, charity and humility, then said that someday Quetzalcoatl, the great Messiah, would return to bring peace and prosperity to the land. Another story warns that a curse will fall upon anyone who wrongfully occupies the land.

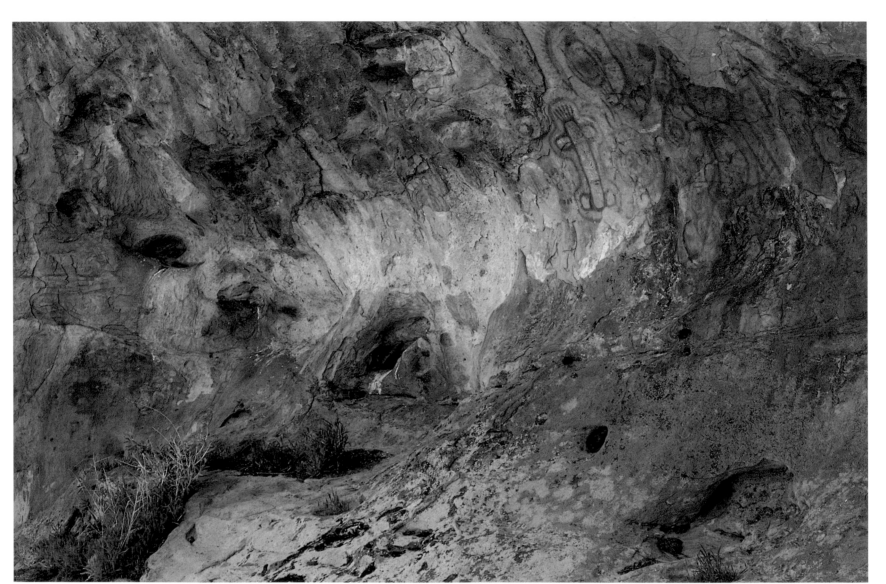

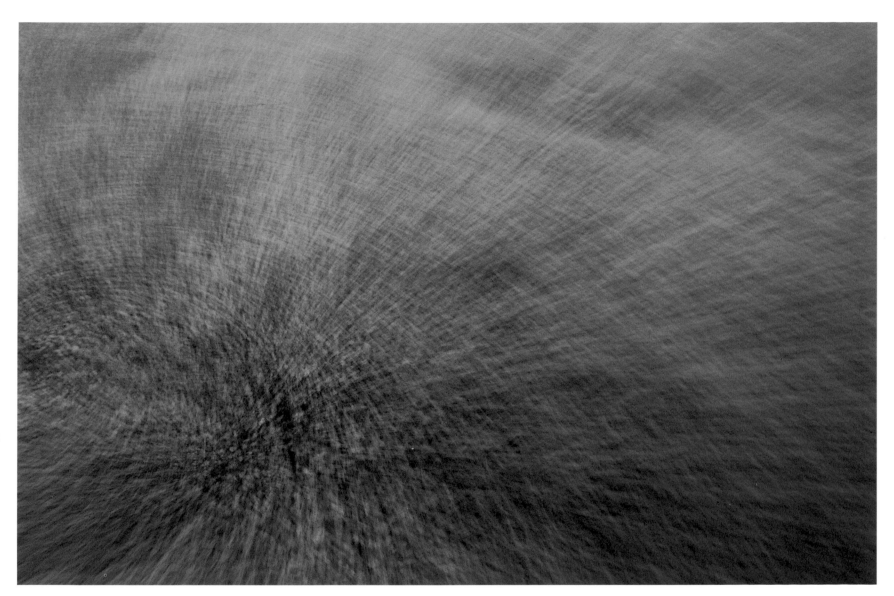

134

*Camera motion on field of wildflowers,*
*Carrizo Plain, California, April 1993*

135

*Sunflowers and hills at Painted Rock,*
*Carrizo Plain, California, April 1993*

*"Moonbite," cloud and moon during
lunar eclipse, California, August 1988*

*right: Pictographs on wall of Painted Cave,
San Marcos Pass, Santa Ynez Mountains,
California, April 1993*

# Painted Cave

## *Gallery of Rock Art*

136 Painted Cave lies twenty-six hundred feet above sea level in the rugged Santa Ynez Mountains of southern California. Although it seems well protected, the wind has eroded the sandstone surface, leaving only five feet remaining of the original twenty-one-foot panel. Human destruction has also caused great damage. Graffiti and gunshots have left their marks on what some consider the finest rock art in North America. A heavy metal grate now protects the paintings, which were made by Barbareno Chumash artists about one thousand years ago.

One of the paintings, a black circle outlined in white, is thought to depict the Nov. 24, 1677 solar eclipse that would have been visible to the Chumash people of this area, for whom the sun was the most important cosmological element. The paintings are believed to have been part of ritual ceremonies at sacred sites, performed by members of a powerful group of shamans who may have been inspired by using vision-inducing substances such as the white flowers of the datura plant. The rock art was created to link the Chumash with sacred events in their past, to maintain balance between supernatural forces in nature, and to manipulate supernatural power. Local Native historians have said that Indians in the past would avoid the cave because some of the paintings are thought to represent funerary boats carrying the dead to nearby island graves.

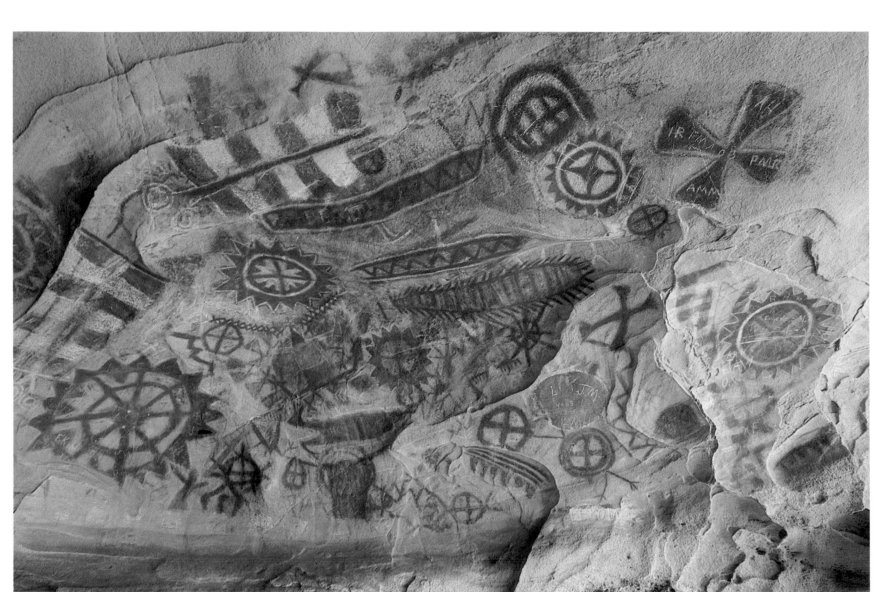

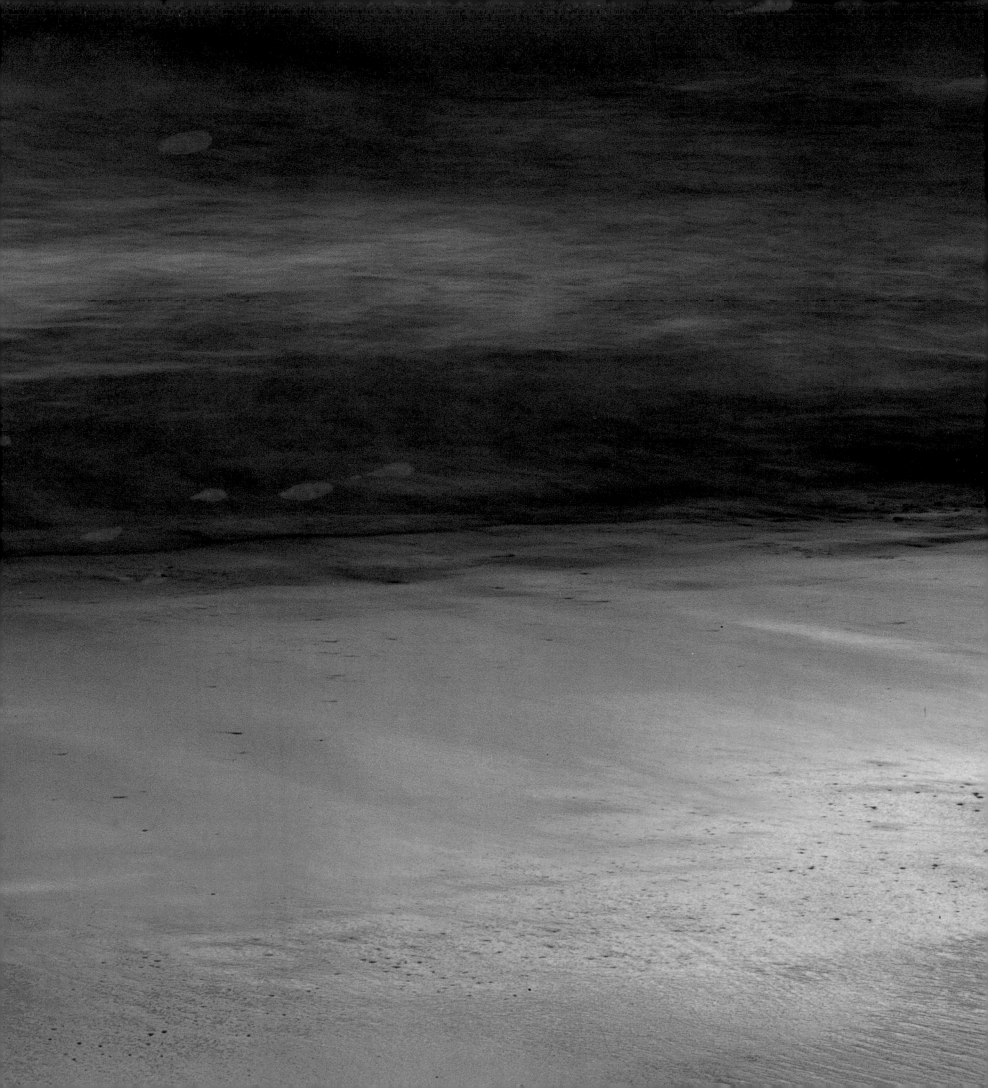

# Humqaq

## *Gateway to the Eternal*

Known to the Chumash Indians as Humqaq, "a wild and stormy place," Conception Point is the tip of an isthmus of land that extends into the Pacific Ocean, northwest of Santa Barbara, California. This site is considered the Western Gate of the continent, where souls enter and exit Earth.

The Chumash are the guardians of this gateway, and Humqaq is the legendary halfway house to which the soul of the deceased retreats before making the final journey on the bridge to Similaqsa, the afterworld. Chumash stories tell of the steep cliff at Humqaq, which can be reached only by rope, where there is a basin fed by fresh water. Here the spirit of the dead is said to paint itself in prepa-ration for the journey across the waters that separate this world from the next. When the spirit sees the light in the west, it is ready to make the transition.

The eloquent and detailed account of the transition includes a stage at which the soul travels through a ravine of clashing rocks and is confronted on either side by two birds called qaq, who peck out his eyes. He replaces them with poppies so that he can once again see, crosses the last bridge and is finally safe, living forever with abundance and perpetual youth. It is said that sometimes a soul can be seen on his journey, as a light with a blue trail, and that the gates of Similaqsa can be heard closing behind him, like the sound of a cannon.

*Detail of foothill woodlands, Juniper Canyon,*
*Pinnacles National Monument, California,*
*April 1993*

*right: Moon over Pinnacles, predawn light,*
*Pinnacles National Monument, California,*
*April 1993*

# Pinnacles

## *Place of the Great Divide*

140   The history of Pinnacles National Monument is as startling as its monolithic, seemingly endless peaks. The peaks were born 23 million years ago from the lava flow of a volcano positioned between two layers of the earth's crust known as the Pacific and the North American plates. As the volcanic mountain of Pinnacles was formed, the Pacific Plate started moving to the northwest, and over millions of years of drifting, left behind a portion of these rhyolitic spires 195 miles to the south. This same plate movement created the San Andreas Fault, a rift zone reaching north from the Mendocino coast of San Francisco and south to the Gulf of Mexico. It continues to produce substantial movements even today as the two underground plates of earth grind against each other.

For the past two thousand years, the Mutsun-speaking people lived to the east of these towering mounds, while the Chalon-speaking people occupied the area to the west. The land is a unique example of a chaparral ecosystem that supports four distinct plant communities and the animals and birds that are attracted to them. The lower level streams are a source of year-round water, while the upper rock and scree support ninety species of lichen and provide nesting sites for birds such as the endangered California condor. It is not hard to understand how the people of this area viewed the natural world, often referring to the eagle, coyote, falcon, hawk, condor, owl, fox, deer and raven as the "first people" in the history of their culture.

141

*Views of Gabilan Range from High Peaks Trail,*
*Pinnacles National Monument, California,*
*April 1993*

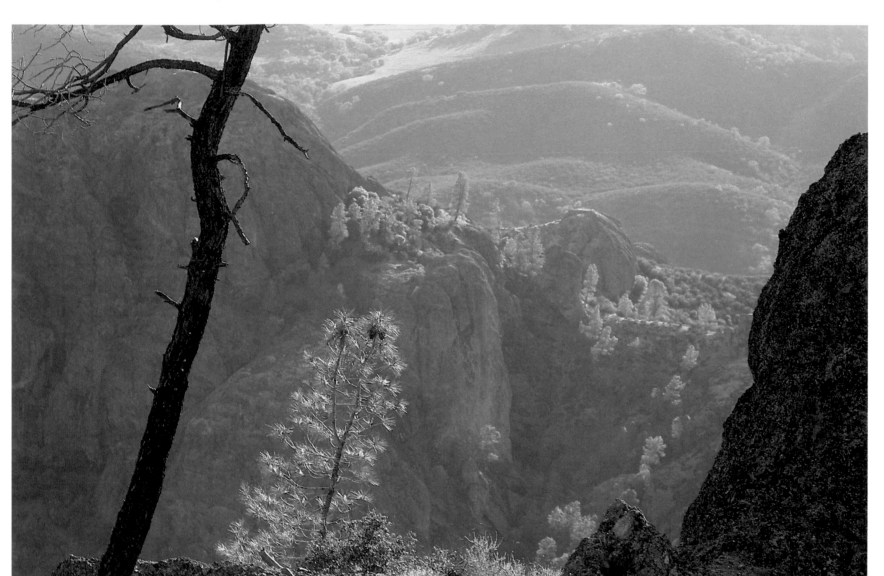

143

*Multiple exposure of moon setting at Goat Rock, Bodega Bay, California, August 1988*

*right: Shoreline at Goat Rock, Bodega Bay, California, August 1988*

# Bodega Bay

## *Where Moon Falls Down*

144  Time seems to stand still at Bodega Bay, California, where the morning mists, the sultry sun and the pounding surf lull one into a dream world. By night, the full moon casts a mystical glow on the rising tidal waters, silhouetting Goat Rock in stark relief.

To the Indians of many eastern tribes, the moon is seen as a woman. She has three faces: the crescent moon as a young maiden, the full moon as a mature mother and the new moon or dark moon as an old woman. By contrast, for many west-coast Native peoples, the moon is masculine. The Snoqualmie people in Washington have a story that the moon, called Snoqualm, or Chief of the Heavens, fell down and became a mountain. So important is the moon to all the Indians of North America that their traditional way of measuring time was by its cycles.

The Bodega tribe of the Coastal Miwok culture who lived here held ceremonies where spirits of bears and birds were impersonated, with special rituals for the condor and flicker. Birds were captured and reared in their camps to provide feathers for the chief to wear, after which they were released in a ceremony of song and dance.

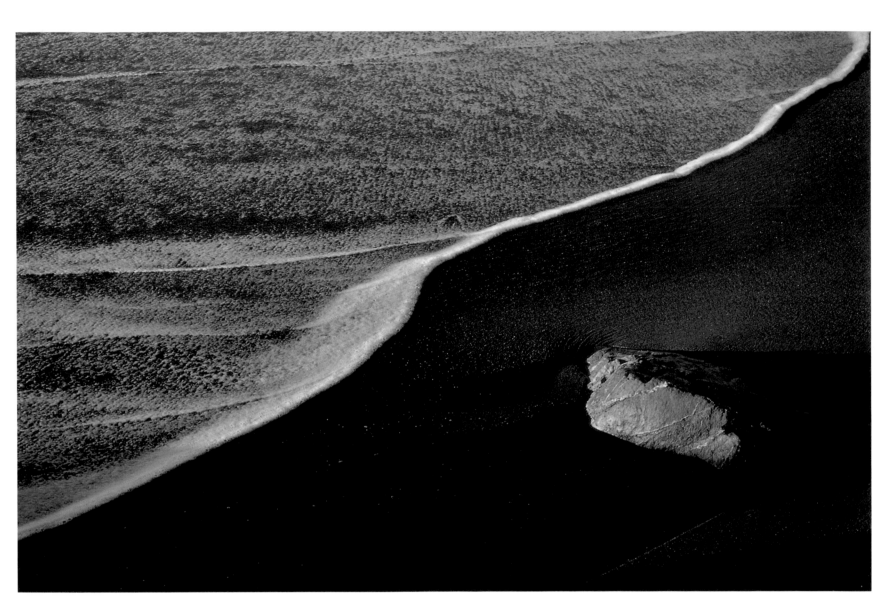

*Post-sunset light on western slope, Mount Shasta, California, November 1987*

*right: "SkyHole," one-hour exposure of stars (fisheye lens, see Photographer's Notes, p.203), Mount Shasta, California, August 1988*

# Mount Shasta

*Lodge of the Great Spirit*

146 Home to California's largest glaciers, Mount Shasta stands as a 14,162-foot beacon at the intersection of three mountain ranges: the Sierra Nevada to the southeast, the Cascades to the north and the Klamath to the west. This towering volcanic landmark is revered by the Shasta, Karok, Modok and Wintun tribes of northern California who recognize Mount Shasta as a spiritual centre. The blowing snows and swirling clouds at the summit of this immense mountain are seen as the smoke hole of the Great Spirit's lodge as well as the entrance to Earth from the Above World.

Many of the area's geographical landmarks are immortalized in stories. One relates how a Karok chief told his people to build a mountain high enough to see the sea. When they finished, they emptied their baskets of leftover earth onto the plains below. These are the hundreds of little hills in Shasta Valley. The Modoc tell of the Chief of the Sky Spirits who grew so weary of his icy home in the Above World that he carved a hole in the sky and emptied out all the ice and snow, forming an immense mound known today as Mount Shasta. This lengthy creation story goes on to explain how he formed the trees, rivers, animals and rocky paths, endowing all the features of the mountain with spiritual significance.

A Shasta story accounts for Thumb Rock, a projection at the eastern end of the Red Banks. It is thought to be the pointed thumb of an Indian princess who disobeyed her father, the chief, and ran away up the mountain, only to freeze to death there. The message of this story is that the mountain should never be climbed. Native people today still heed that warning and do not climb it, although some lower slopes, such as Panther Meadows, are used for spiritual ceremonies.

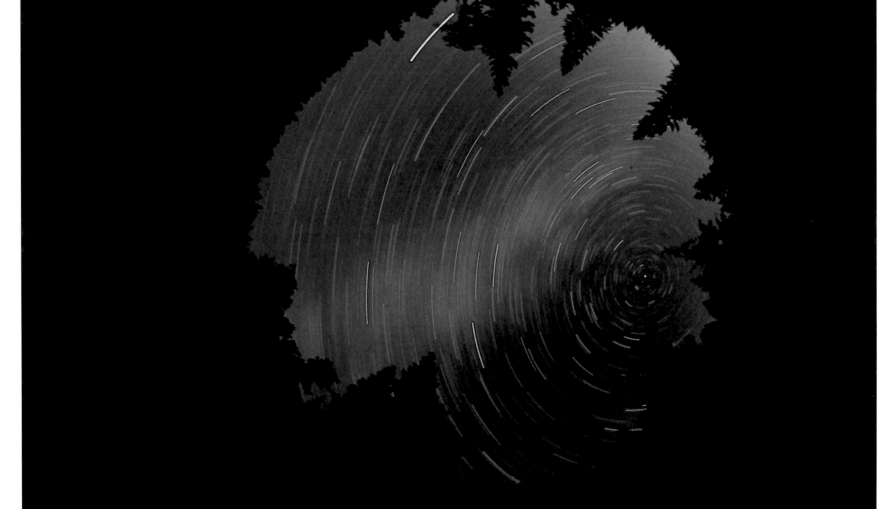

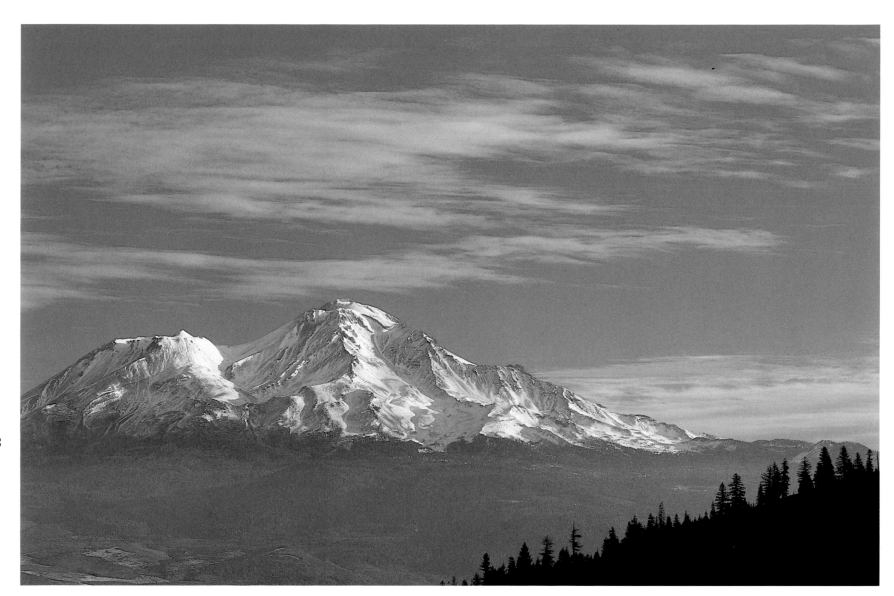

*View from the west, Mount Shasta,*
*California, November 1987*

149

*Panther Meadows, Mount Shasta,*
*California, November 1987*

150

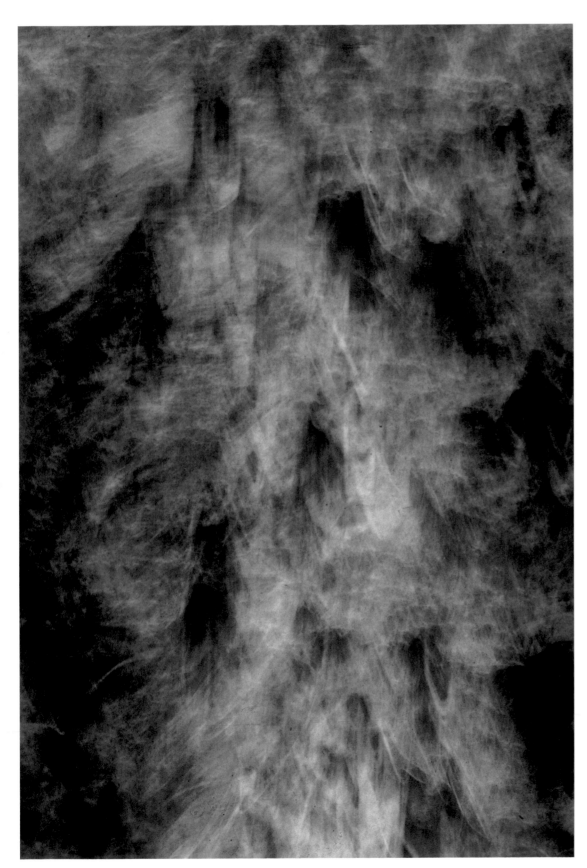

*Composite of camera movement on moss-clad spruce, western slope, Mount Shasta, California, August 1988*

*right: Triple exposure, wildflowers, Mount Shasta, California, August 1988*

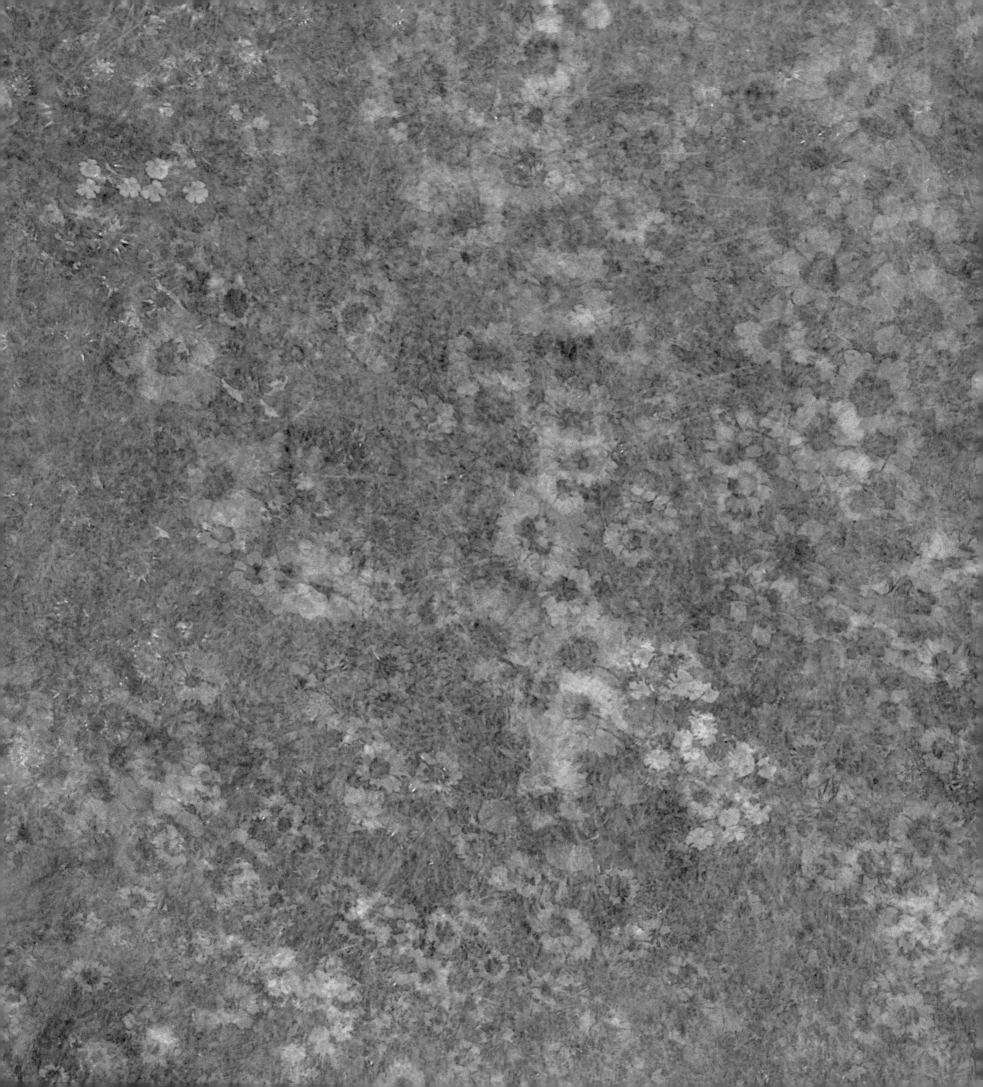

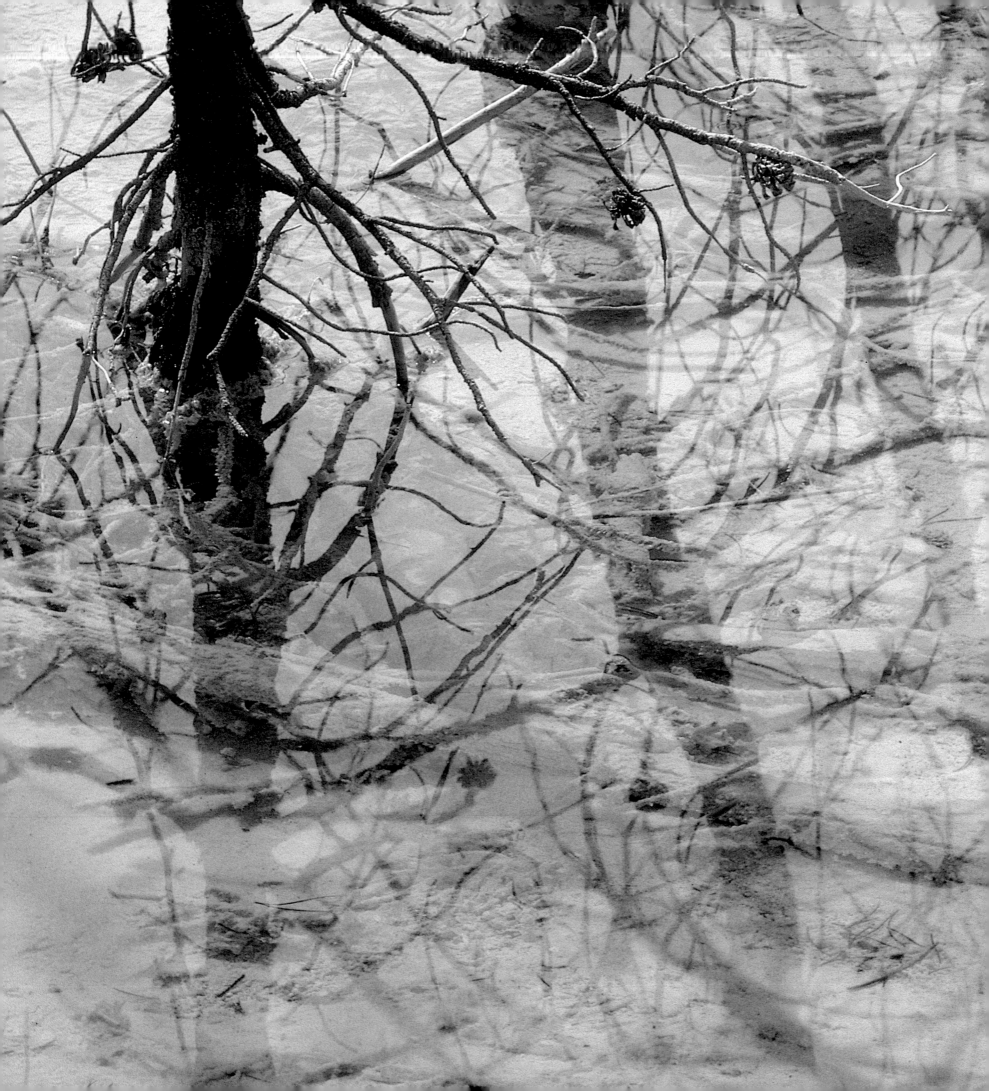

*left: Deadfall in thermal pool, Mammoth Hot Springs, Yellowstone National Park, Wyoming, April 1992*

*Bison and fire-swept slope, Yellowstone National Park, Wyoming, April 1992*

# Yellowstone

## *Land of the Great Fire*

Yellowstone National Park lies in the northwest corner of Wyoming, 120 miles west of Big Horn Medicine Wheel. Famous for its thermal springs painted with a rainbow of mineral hues, and for its diversity of wildlife, Yellowstone is a natural treasure.

Here is the land upon which the Great Spirit smiled, telling medicine man Spotted Bear and his people that the animals would provide everything they needed if they treated them like brothers. In particular, he instructed them to thank the buffalo and to kill them only if necessary. According to this Cheyenne creation story, the Great Spirit was angered by the needless waste of others who came to this land, fishing and hunting only for sport. Soon all the people were destroying the streams, forests and the buffalo. Angered, the Great Spirit allowed the smoke of their fires to choke them and brought rains upon the land. The people

escaped to higher altitudes, but as the rains continued, they were forced to the high peaks, where the Medicine Man exhorted that they should live in peace and return to the way of the buffalo. Here they found a white buffalo hide and stretched it above them and across the entire Yellowstone Valley. Spotted Bear stood in the Bridger Mountains and anchored the hide to peaks in all directions. Then he raised one end to allow the West Wind to lift it into a dome to protect the people, the animals and the valley from the devastating rains. As peace was once again restored to the land, the Great Spirit stopped the rains, the sun shone and the white hide gleamed in colours of red, white and blue. As the huge skin shrank, all that remained was a magnificent rainbow arch across the Yellowstone Valley.

153

*Detail of Canary Hot Springs, Mammoth Hot Springs, Yellowstone National Park, Wyoming, April 1992*

*Detail of Minerva Terrace, Mammoth
Hot Springs, Yellowstone National Park,
Wyoming, April 1992*

*West edge of lake, Crater Lake National Park, Oregon, June 1993*

*right: Approaching storm over Wizard Island, Crater Lake National Park, Oregon, June 1993*

# Crater Lake

*Triumph of the Above World*

156    At 1,932 feet, Oregon's Crater Lake is the deepest lake in North America, and some say it contains the purest water in the world. Although it lies at an altitude of nine thousand feet in the Cascade Range, the water rarely freezes because its large volume acts as a heat reservoir.

The creation story of this unique crater is told by the Maklaks, the ancestors of the present-day Klamath Indians. Almost eight thousand years ago, the Maklaks, known as the people of the marsh, witnessed the eruption of Mount Mazama; this volcanic mountain was the passageway to the kingdom of light for the spirit Llal, Chief of the Below World, who lived in the darkness deep inside. One time, Llal left the depths of Mount Mazama and came up onto earth, where he fell in love with the tribal chief's beautiful daughter and prom-ised her eternal life if she would return

with him to his lodge below the mountain. When she refused, he became angry and declared that he would destroy her people with fire. The mighty Chief of the Above World, Skell, took pity on the people and defended them from the top of Mount Shasta. From their mountain tops, the two chiefs waged a furious battle, hurling red-hot rocks as large as hills, causing earth tremors and great landslides of fire. While the people fled in terror to the waters of Klamath Lake, two old medicine men offered to sacrifice themselves and jumped into the pit of fire on top of the mountain. The Chief of the Above World was moved by their bravery and drove Llal back into Mount Mazama. When the sun rose, the great Mount Mazama was gone. It had fallen in on Llal, and all that remained was a large chasm. Torrential rains filled it with the clear water the Maklaks called Lake of

Blue Waters, a place where they came to bathe and to receive visions of the inner world of the spirit.

Rising majestically near the west shore of the lake is Wizard Island, home of the Spirit Chief who rules over the Land of the Dead. According to tradition, it is here that the ancestors emerged from deep in the earth, through a cave in Crater Lake; deceased spirits are also returned to the lake, with evil ones confined to the fire pit at the top of the cone known as Wizard Island. The Spirit Chief then decreed that only wise elders could approach his realm to commune with the ancestor spirits. Because this island is sacred to the con-temporary Klamath Indians, they do not reveal its Native name.

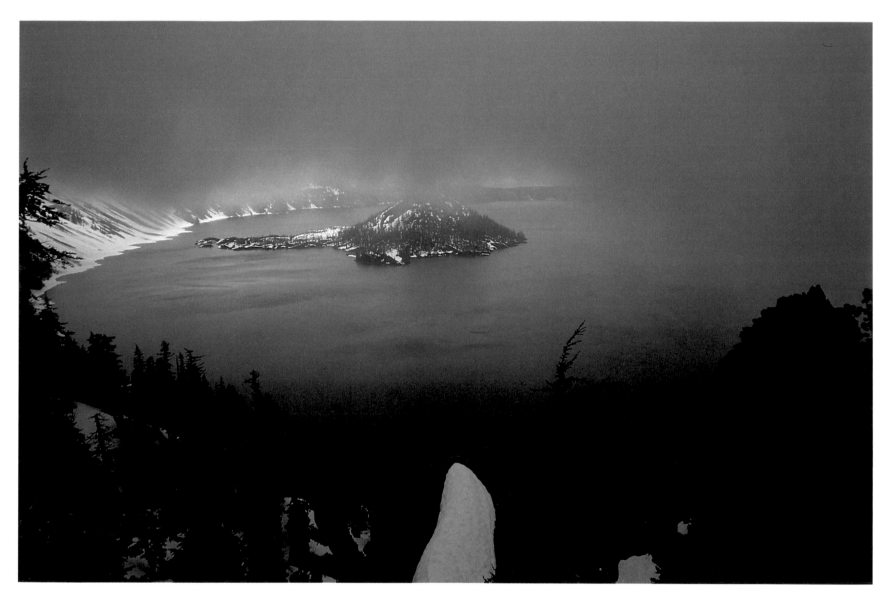

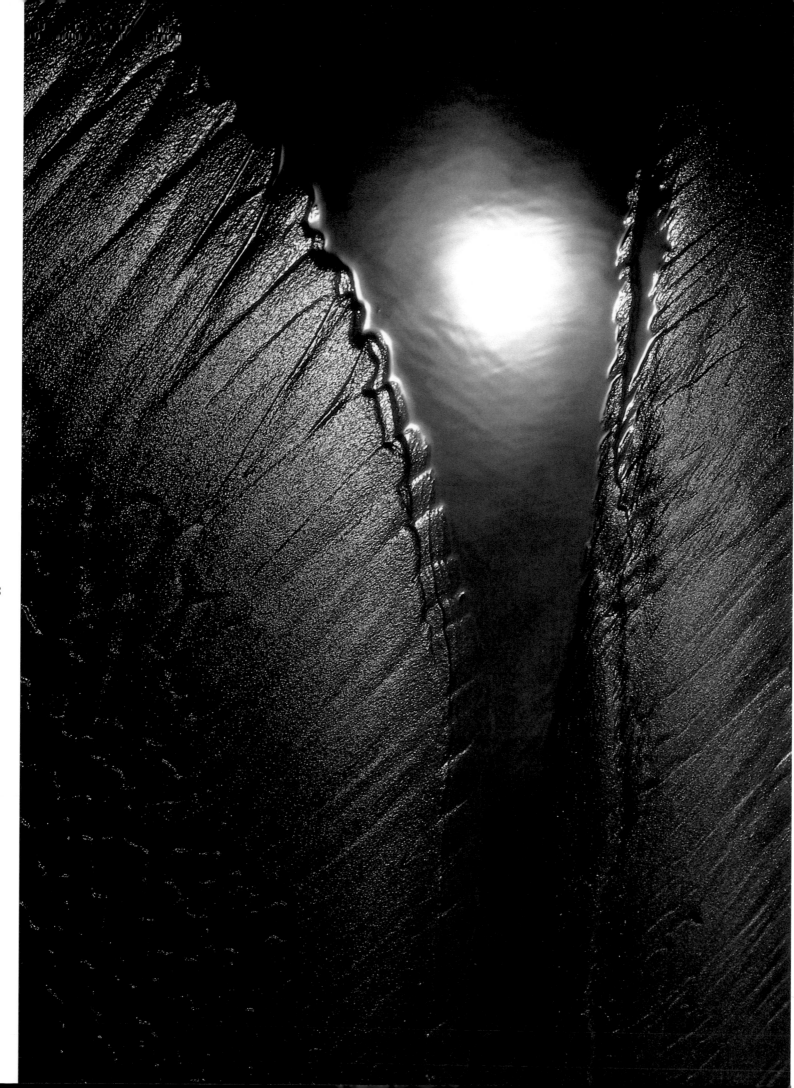

Driftwood on beach, Cape Flattery,
Washington, October 1987

# Strait of Juan de Fuca

## *Waters of Life*

The Strait of Juan de Fuca is a long and narrow channel that separates Washington's Olympic Peninsula from Vancouver Island, British Columbia. This is the land of the Nuu-chah-nulth (Nootka), with more than a dozen groups living on the west coast of the island, and one, the Makah, at the tip of the peninsula. The name Nootka comes from nu-tka, meaning "to go around"; when Captain James Cook arrived on the west coast of Vancouver Island in 1778, he thought this was part of the mainland. The native Mowachaht people directed him to explore around the island, and misunderstanding their words, he mistakenly gave them this as a name, which persists to the present.

The Nuu-chah-nulth believe they have lived here forever, and certainly there is evidence of human habitation since the last glacier receded eleven thousand years ago.

They moved from ocean-side summer encampments to wintering grounds in more sheltered villages on inland streams, making use of the rich seasonal resources in both the maritime and forest environments. The mighty spruce, hemlock and cedar provided planks for canoes, bent-box containers and totem poles. Nuu-chah-nulth stories tell of spirit beings and supernatural powers seen all around them, such as the salmon who lives in the house beneath the sea, and Thunderbird, who can beat his wings to make thunder, blink his eyes to cause lightning, and pick up a whale as easily as an eagle carries off a trout. Today, these creatures seem to appear silently and unexpectedly in the shape of a gnarled tree root or in the weathered contours of driftwood.

The reputation of the Nuu-chah-nulth as great whalers lives on, although this way

of life is now gone. Harpooning the whales from forty-foot dugout canoes was much more than a means of subsistence; it was a religious act of the highest order, a ritual hunt by the select who had earned the right to take part. For weeks the chief whaler, and later his crew, prepared by bathing in a secret prayer pool as the moon grew to fullness. In order to win the favours of the whale spirits, they did not eat meat or engage in sexual activity, and rubbed their bodies with hemlock branches to rid themselves of human odours. According to the Nuu-chah-nulth, women were directly linked to the whale spirit. Prior to the hunt, the wife of the chief whaler would lie on her bed like a docile whale in order to break the bond tying her to the animal, staying there until receiving word of a successful hunt. Then came a time of great

159

rejoicing. The whole village rushed to the beach to assist, and the women gave thanks to the great whale spirit.

As well as hunting, the Nuu-chah-nulth also relied on beached whales, performing special rituals and ceremonies to help the whales come ashore. In fact, an ancient whaler's shrine in Friendly Cove, on Nootka Sound, contained cedar-carved figures and the remains of children whose spirits were believed to call or attract animals to the hunter. One story tells of hunters who found a whale and were followed by a bounty of salmon as they brought it ashore. Afterward, they made their canoes in the shape of a whale with a special headdress.

160

*Autumn foliage near Port Angeles, Washington, October 1987*

*below: "Forest Canopy," Pacific Rim National Park, British Columbia, June 1990*

*right: Arbutus bark, Victoria, British Columbia, January 1987*

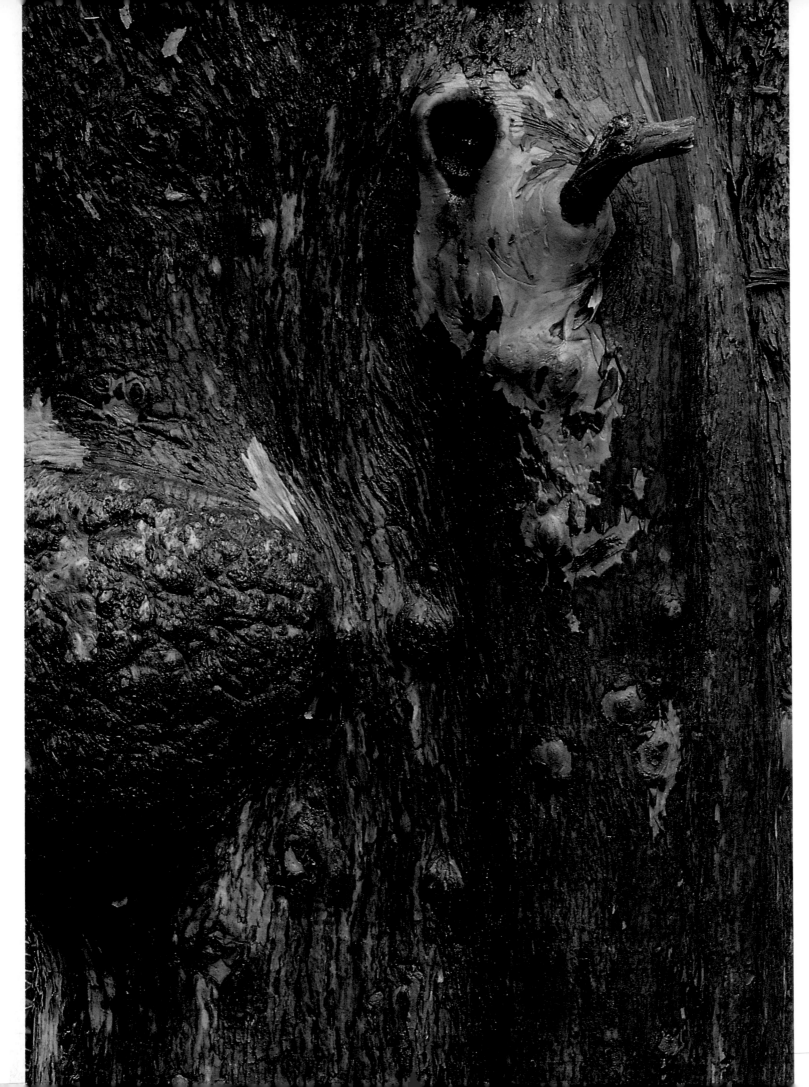

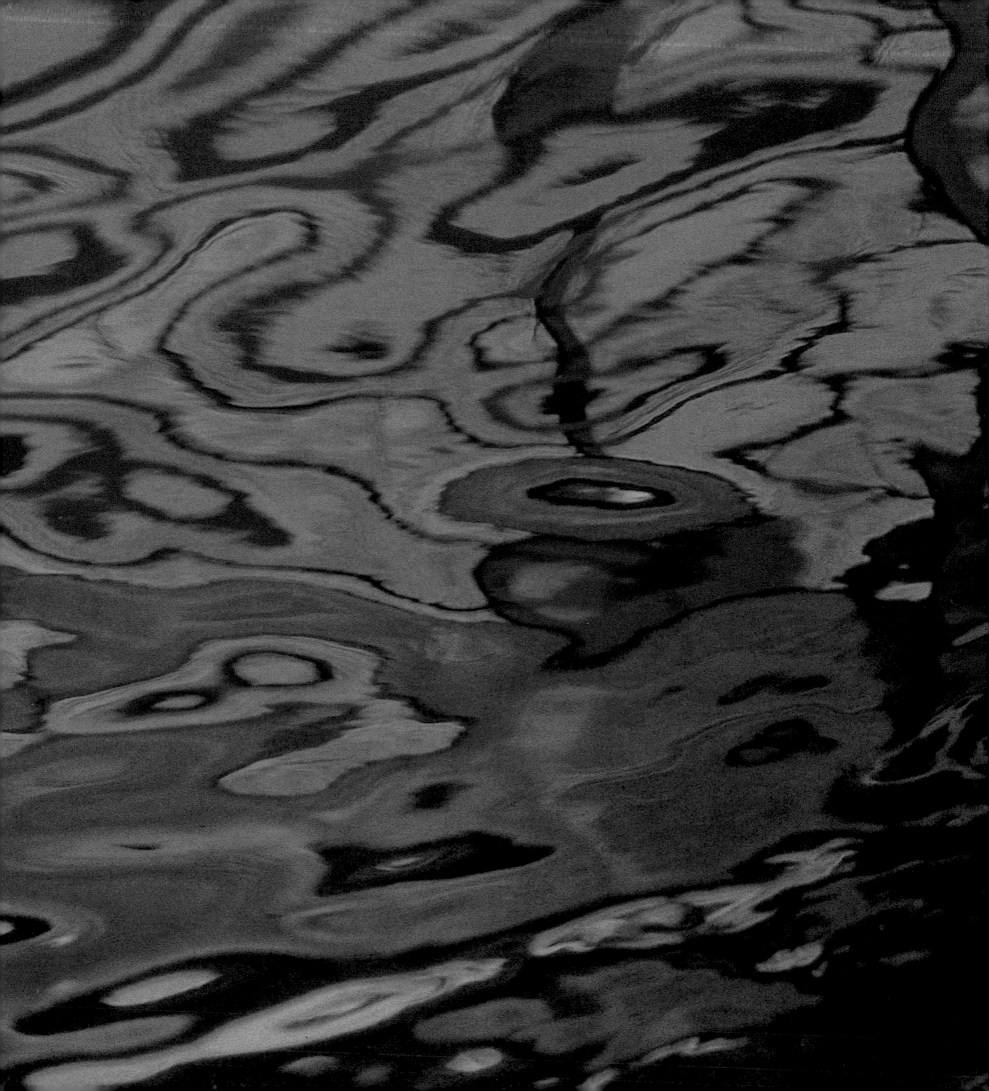

163

left: *"Spirit Waters," water reflection in*
*harbour, Victoria, British Columbia,*
*December 1980*

*Rainbow kelp in tidal pool, Lyle Island,*
*Pacific Rim National Park, British Columbia,*
*May 1985*

*"Cosmic Leap," composite of humpback whale and rainbow, Pacific Ocean, February 1987*

# NORTH

*To the North and its guard, the White Eagle*
*Keep us pure and clean of mind, thoughts as white as*
*Thy blanket, the snow. Make us hardy.*

*Unidentified stream, Fanny Bay,*
*South Moresby, Queen Charlotte Islands,*
*British Columbia, July 1982*

# Gwaii Haanas

## *Islands of Wonder*

166 The 154 islands that make up the Queen Charlottes, located fifty miles west of the British Columbia mainland, are the only part of Canada that escaped the last ice age. To the Haida people, who have thrived here for ten thousand years, they are known as Gwaii Haanas, Islands of Wonder.

Off the southwest coast of the large southern island called Moresby is Anthony Island. Here is the ancient village of Sgan Gwaii, or red cod island town. It is more popularly known as Ninstints, the European version of the word for the village head chief, Nan stins, or "He Who Is Two." Now designated a United Nations World Heritage Site, this ancient ceremonial village is distinguished by fifteen totem poles carved more than 150 years ago by Haida artists who were revered for their skill. Some are mortuary poles featur-

ing containers for the ashes of the dead. Others, known as frontal posts, identify great lodges; the moon and thunderbird, for example, signal the house of an early chief called Koyah, or Raven, who was the chief servant of Sha-lana, the Creator.

Uninhabited by humans since 1880 when its population was decimated by smallpox, the village today is home to the honoured spirits of the dead, and to the ancient carvings that are slowly being returned to the verdant mosses and thousand-year-old trees of the forest. But the Haida of Sgan Gwaii are not forgotten. Their tradition lives on in the work of contemporary artists who are known throughout the world for their exquisite designs in argillite and silver, as well as cedar.

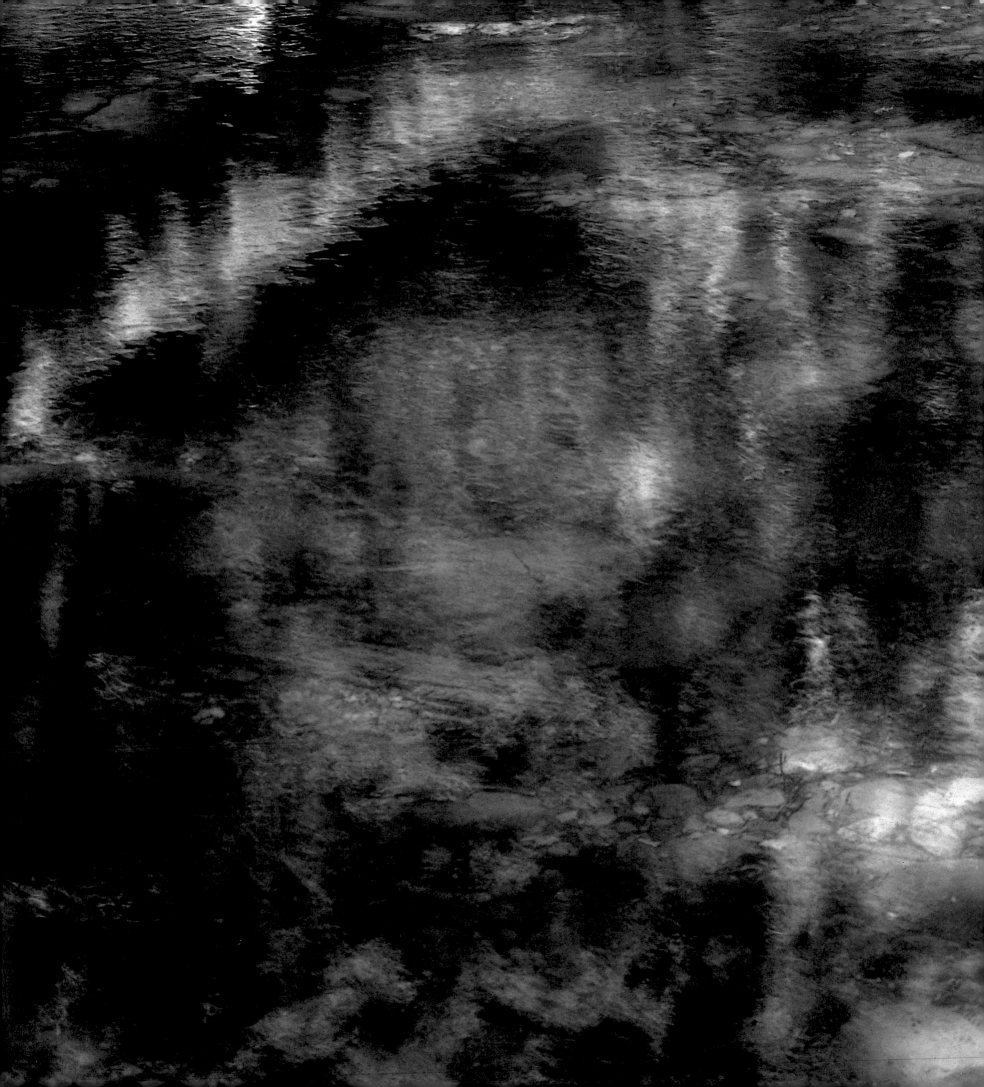

168

*Moss-clad forest, west coast, South Moresby,*
*Queen Charlotte Islands, British Columbia,*
*July 1982*

169

*Rock face, Ninstints, Anthony Island,*
*Queen Charlotte Islands, British Columbia,*
*July 1982*

*Mortuary poles, Ninstints, Anthony Island,*
*Queen Charlotte Islands, British Columbia,*
*July 1982*

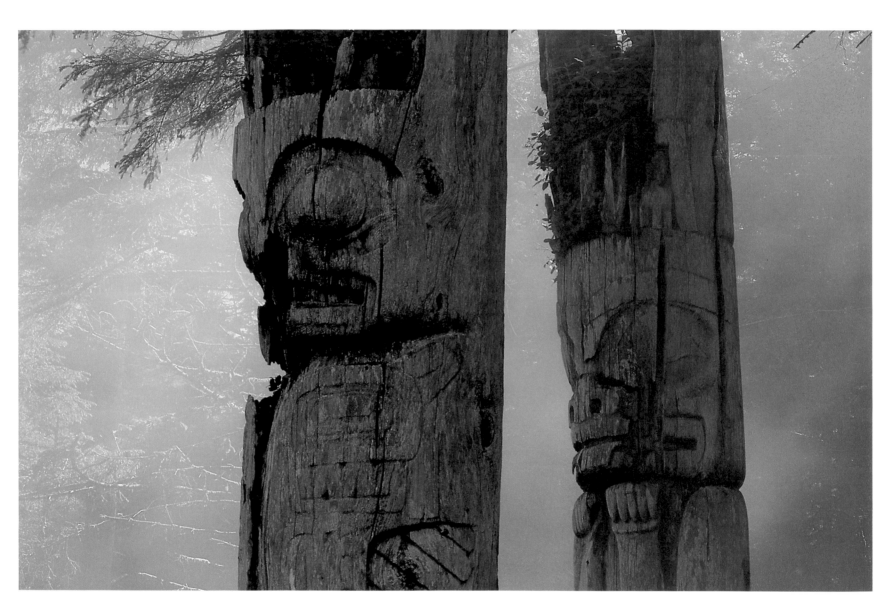

*Detail of totem poles, Sitka National Historic Park, Alaska, June 1993*

# Sitka

*Home of the Totem Spirits*

172 Sitka is situated on Tongass Island, which lies at the northern end of the chain of islands dotting the southeast coast of Alaska. Although it takes its name from Russian fur traders, Tlingit Indian stories tell how their ancestors migrated here ten thousand years ago as the glaciers started to retreat, coming to the temperate coast from inland homes in the Nass Valley.

The coastal rainforests produce straight, tall trees, ideal for totem carvings. One Tlingit story relates how a carved log washed up on the beach, inspiring them to record their history in cedar and to paint the carved stories with pigments made from hematite, graphite and copper.

The Tlingit universe abounds with spirits; it is said that omens can be heard in the hoot of an owl or the cry of a raven. In this world, the shaman mediates between humans and the kushtakas, the powerful Land Otter People who save those lost in the forest or at sea. Because those saved are then transformed into half-human, half-otter beings like their rescuers, it is the shaman's task to reclaim the lost spirit before the kushtaka can transform it. The stories of these legendary struggles were often recorded on totem poles.

The Tlingit are renowned as well for their ornamented woven baskets and Chilkat blankets, which are unique to this area. Created with fibres from the inner bark of cedar and mountain goat wool, the blankets incorporate traditional and semi-religious motifs designed by men, which are then woven by women. To achieve the customarily rich hues and elaborate designs, the wool used in these highly valued ceremonial blankets is soaked in dyes made from black hemlock bark, yellow tree moss and corroded copper, which produces blue-green tones.

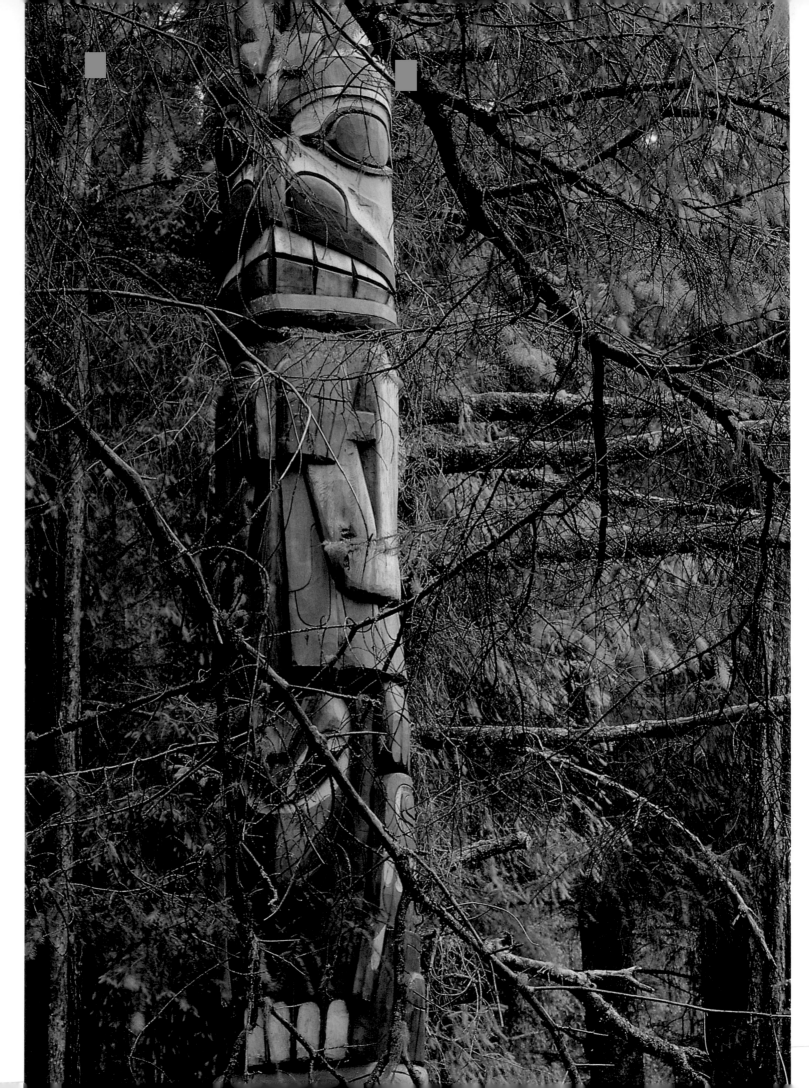

173

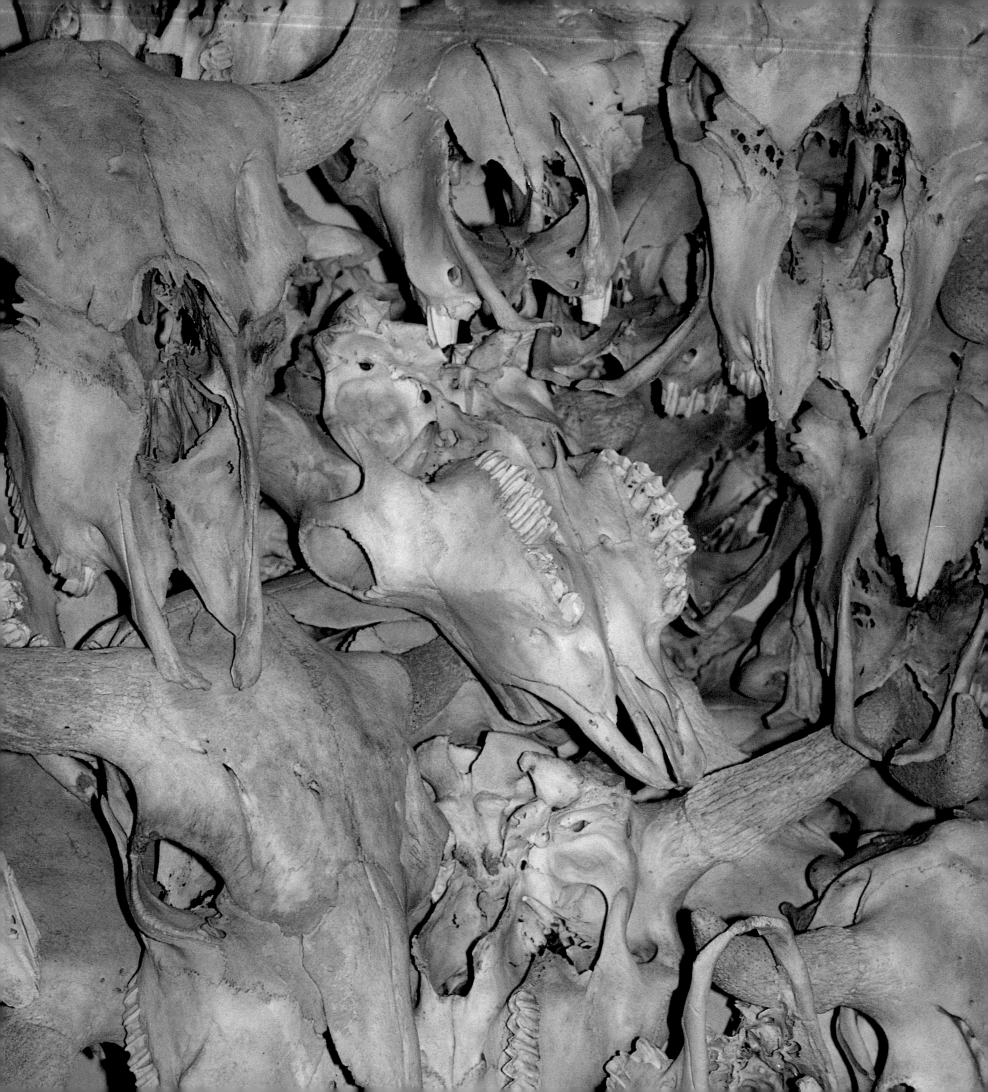

*left: Bison skulls, Head-Smashed-In Buffalo Jump, near Fort McLeod, Alberta, September 1993*

*"Prophecy," silhouettes of bison, unidentified prairie location, April 1982*

# Head-Smashed-In

## *Climax of the Hunt*

Head-Smashed-In is one of the oldest, largest and best-preserved buffalo jumps in North America. Located near present-day Fort Macleod, Alberta, where prairies and mountains meet, the thirty-three-foot cliff was used for hunts as early as 3700 BC. The Blackfoot Nation, or Nitsitapii (meaning "Real People"), believe they are the only ones to have made use of this jump, which was traditionally called Piskun. The name Head-Smashed-In comes from the Peigan tribe of the Blackfoot, from a story told about a young man who was mortally wounded as he hid below the overhang to watch the buffalo fall.

Prehunt rituals of dances and songs included prayers to call the buffalo, using a sacred Buffalo Stone called the Iniskim. Buffalo runners, who disguised themselves as animals and lured the buffalo over the cliff, fasted for days prior to the jump and prayed to the Great Buffalo Spirit to deliver a bountiful hunt; they also smudged themselves with sacred sweetgrass, and chewed it to increase their endurance. As many as five hundred people worked together, without the benefit of horses, to herd the buffalo and channel them into a drive lane. Buffalo that survived the impact of the jump were killed by hunters at the bottom to prevent them from warning other herds about the trap.

Within view of Head-Smashed-In is Chief Mountain, revered by a number of tribes in the region. Called Ukimazi by the Cree, and Ninaistuki by the Blackfoot, Chief Mountain is known as the home of the Wind Spirit and Thunderbird. A young man, seeking his life-guiding animal spirit in a vision quest, often choses a site where he can view sacred forms such as Chief Mountain, Crows Nest Mountain or the Sweetgrass Hills. This helps assure communion with the Great Spirit. Traditionally, the vision seeker tied a buffalo skull to thongs attached to skewers that pierced the skin on his chest and dragged the skull up the mountain.

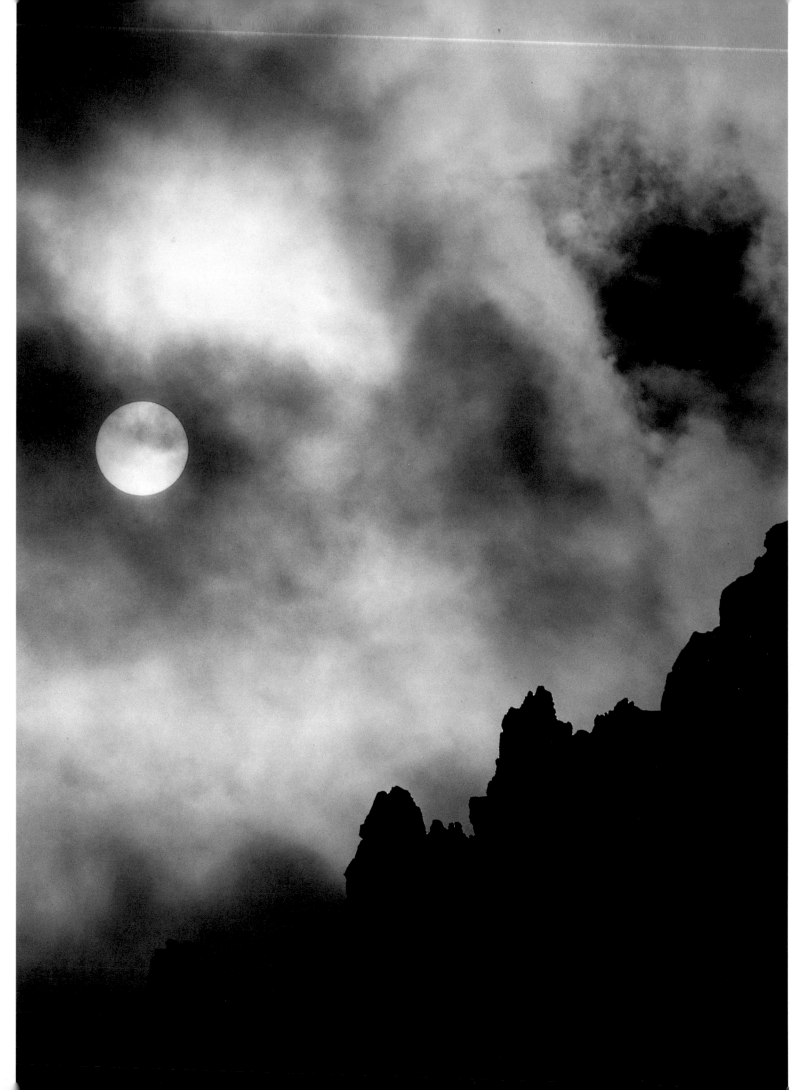

*left: Approaching storm and sun, mountain ridge, Rocky Mountains, Banff National Park, Alberta, September 1989*

*Snow pattern and reflection on slope at Sentinal Pass, Larch Valley, Rocky Mountains, Banff National Park, Alberta, August 1970*

# Shining Mountains

## *Backbone-of-the-World*

The earliest written historical records in the 1760s refer to Indian reports about the "mountains of crystals" in the far west. The Blackfoot (Nitsitapii) translated this to Mistukiz-Ikanaziaw, but also call the Rocky Mountains the "Backbone-of-the-World," and know this range as the home of spirit powers that include Wind Maker, Cold Maker and Thunder. They believe the Great Spirit is everywhere – in the waters, trees, birds and animals, as well as the mountains and sky. Natos, the Sun, is the creative power who is the source of life; he provides for the people as long as they revere all nature, and he warms the land that is filled with his presence.

The power of Natos is seen in the traditional Blackfoot story of Poia (Scarface), or Star Boy, who lived in the sky. He and his mother, Feather Woman, were banished to the earth for digging a sacred turnip. She dies of grief, leaving Star Boy alone. The object of a great deal of ridicule because of the scar on his face, Star Boy journeys to the mountains in search of Natos, following the path of the Sun to the Sun's lodge. Natos removes Star Boy's scar and appoints him his messenger. He is to tell the Blackfoot that Natos will cure their sick if they give a Sundance every year. So Star Boy learns the Sundance songs and prayers and returns to instruct the people. According to the Blackfoot, each step of Star Boy's sacred journey can be seen today in the mountains and hills of their nation.

Many other sacred signs are found in this land. Where the foothills meet the mountains, one can see Na'pi, the Keeper of Men, who rejected the Chief Woman because she was poorly dressed. When she reappeared in her finery, Na'pi chose her as his wife; she refused, and in retaliation, turned him into a lone pine tree. The beautiful setting where this took place is a reminder that appearances can deceive. On the steep scree slopes of Larch Valley, overlooking the Valley of the Ten Peaks in Banff National Park, the trail snakes around Sentinel Mountain (called Nitai-istuki or Lone Mountain by the Blackfoot), affording a commanding view before it descends into Paradise Valley. At these high points, concave "prayer seats" or "fasting beds" fashioned out of rock show where a young man would seek to make contact with the spirits during a vision quest.

*Approaching storm, unidentified mountain pass, St. Elias Mountains, Yukon, September 1983*

*right: Icy passage near Juneau, Alaska, June, 1993*

# St. Elias

*Father of the Peaks*

178 Mount St. Elias, which lies in the southwest corner of the Yukon bordering Alaska, is part of the Canadian Cordillera, which includes nearby Mount Logan, the highest point in Canada. Two hundred years ago, this region was in the last stages of a minor ice age in which a series of valley glaciers descended from the heights of Mount St. Elias, through the Alsek Pass and into the sea in Yakutat Bay. But the Yakutat tribe of the Coastal Tlingit culture speaks of a much earlier time, when all the world was covered in a deluge, with only the peaks of Mount St. Elias and two other summits to guide the ancestors and give them refuge on their journey from the north. The Tlingit have a traditional song that honours Mount St. Elias for opening the world with sunshine and bringing great happiness to the people.

Another Tlingit story recalls when Mount St. Elias married Mount Fairweather, visible today one hundred miles to the east. It was a turbulent relationship, resulting in Mount St. Elias moving west, leaving a trail of peaks in between as slaves to mark the way and retaining one slave as a go-between. The mountains to the east are identified as their children, who stayed with Fairweather, their mother.

Because the Tlingit believe that spirits inhabit mountains and glaciers, only shamans seeking supernatural powers would climb up to the higher slopes. The rest of the tribe were careful not to offend the spirits, addressing these landforms with respect by wearing proper dress, avoiding eye contact and covering their faces with pitch so as not to appear to be staring at the mountains. Retreating glaciers, with moraines that resemble long braided hair, are believed to be female, while male glaciers are considered more dangerous and more easily provoked to anger. Many attendant taboos were in effect to prevent disasters. Several glaciers along the flanks of Mount St. Elias are said to harbour mysterious but harmless spirits that look like giant worms.

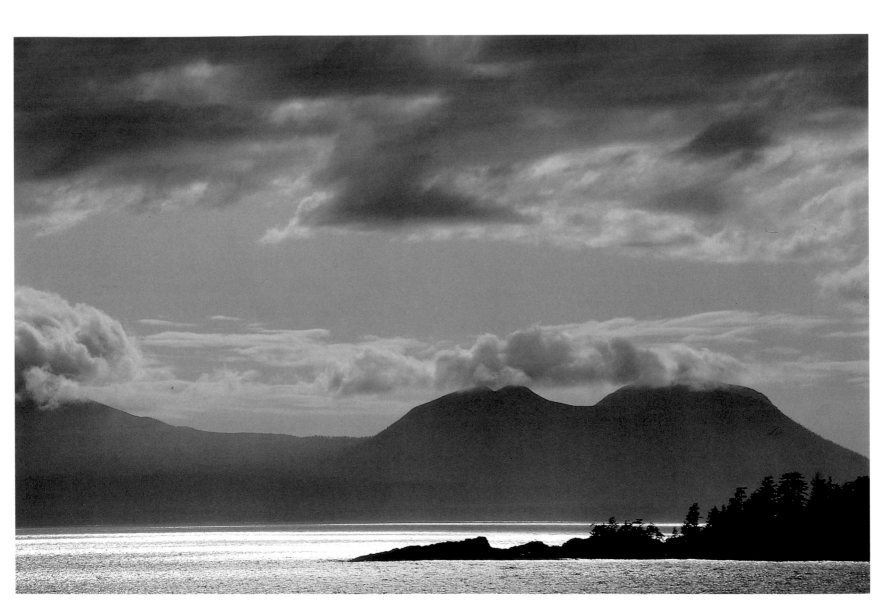

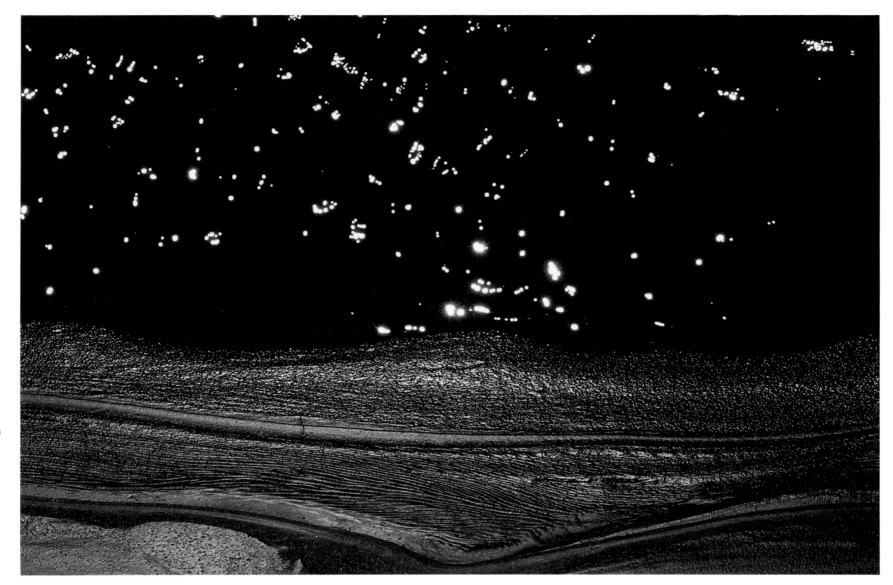

180

"Night Mystery," wet sand and sunlight on water, Mendenhall Glacier, Juneau, Alaska, June 1993

# Shishmaref

## *Place of the Great Whale Spirit*

The Inupiat village of Shishmaref lies just below the Arctic Circle on the Bering Strait, which divides Alaska and Russia. The peninsula on which it sits is believed to be a remnant of the ancient land bridge called Beringia, which allowed early Asian people to journey to North America.

The tradition of mask carving among the Inupiat people is a religious art, learned from and practised on behalf of the spirits by the shaman. Carving a mask enabled a shaman to intercede in the interest of his people and maintain harmony and balance with the spirit embodied in the mask. The spirit in the mask is thought to contain the vital force not only of the animal depicted, but of the whole chain of individual spirits of that genus.

Using large, open boats called umiaks, made from the skins of bearded seals, the traditional Inupiat community hunted whales and other large marine mammals. Preparatory feasts were held before the spring hunt; at this festival of renewal, all remaining whale meat from the previous year was distributed to indicate that only what was required would be taken, and to demonstrate to the whale that the village was worthy of the hunt. To ensure that spirit forms of the whale would be regenerated, special rituals included offering the whale a drink of water and opening a skull to release its spirit.

*Inupiat whale bone mask carved by Edwin J. Weyiouanna, Shishmaref, Alaska, June 1993*

181

*Cave of the Elders, Pictograph Caves State Park, Montana, May 1992*

*right: Pictograph Cave, Pictograph Caves State Park, Montana, May 1992*

# Pictograph Caves

## *Amphitheatre of Mystery*

182  At Pictograph Caves State Park near Billings, Montana, three caves are tucked high into the steep sandstone cliff that forms a large amphitheatre exposed to the southwest. Originally carved by the meanderings of the Yellowstone River, they were further enlarged by wind erosion and moisture seepage.

Pictograph Cave is by far the largest. Its walls display a blend of mineral stains and red ochre images of animals, birds and human figures painted some fifteen hundred years ago. At the western end of the cliff is a grotto called Ghost Cave, so named because the remains of three early inhabitants were found here around 1940. The marvellously sculpted wall of the middle cave, aptly known as the Cave of the Elders, was formed over millions of years by the hardening of mineral compounds left by ocean plants and shellfish when this area was covered by a primordial sea.

In the sixteenth century, the caves were inhabited by the Crow (Absaroka) people. The memory of their great Chief, Plenty Coups, who was renowned for his peace efforts and attempts to find a balance between ancestral and modern ways, is honoured by a nearby park that bears his name.

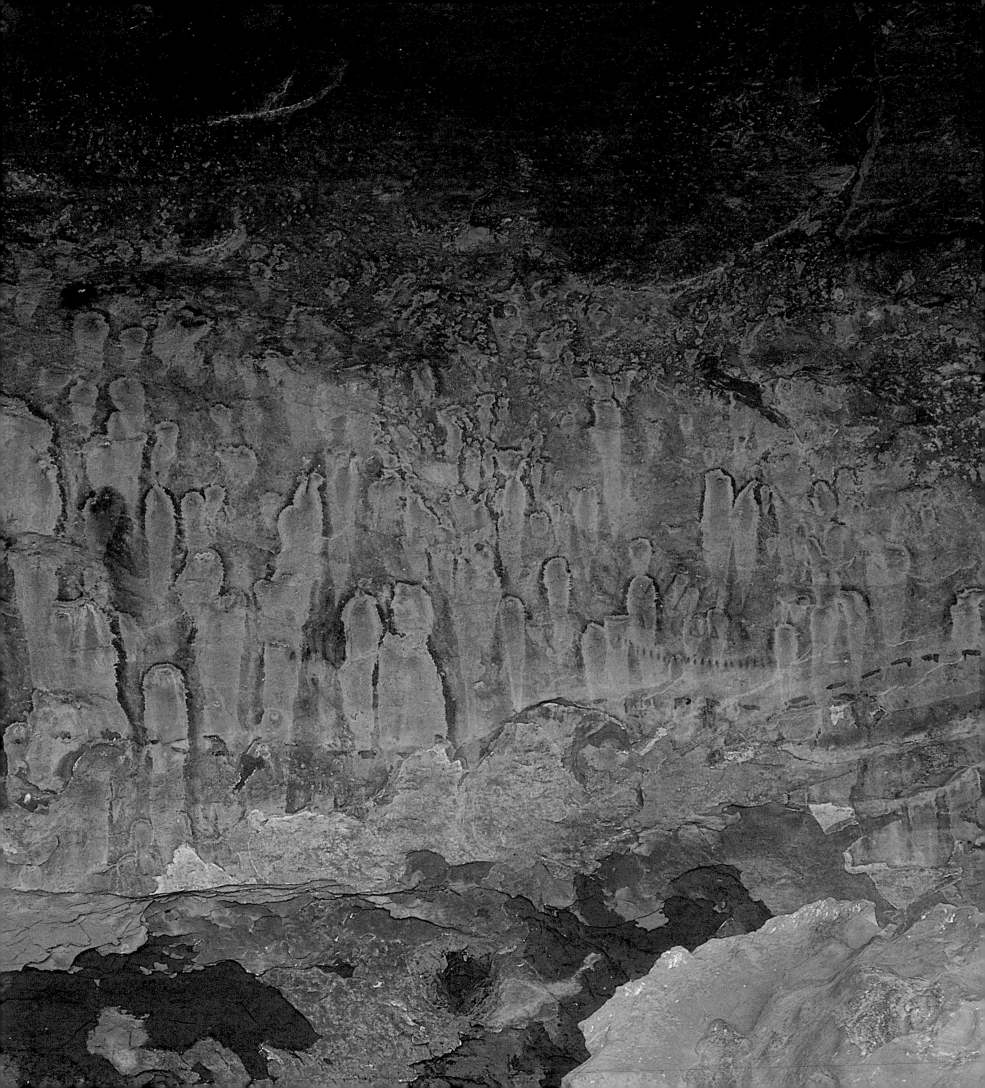

*Hoodoos, Red Deer River Valley, Drumheller, Alberta, July 1986*

*right: Erosional markings on sandstone, Dinosaur Provincial Park, Brooks, Alberta, September 1984*

# The Badlands

## *Valley of the Spirits*

184   The recent history of the badlands is not well known; most of our knowledge is focused on the period 65 million years ago when the region was a swamp inhabited by flesh-eating tyrannosaurs and plant-eating hadrosaurs. Canada's largest tract of badlands stretches south from Drumheller, Alberta, to the Montana border. The area between Dinosaur Provincial Park and Brooks contains one of the world's richest fossil beds making the soil ideal for the sacred sagebrush, whose greenery is burned to smudge or purify. The Blackfoot identify this as the place where the first Buffalo Stone was found more than one thousand years ago. These ammonite and baculite fossils, known as Iniskim, carry the animate power of the bull, and are part of the sacred bundle used in the Buffalo Calling Ceremony. They are a source of personal sacred power that can appear

in human form or in a dream, and are used in other ceremonies such as planting the sacred tobacco garden.

The southern edge of the badlands includes high sandstone cliffs and enigmatic rock formations that seem to echo and moan with the wind. To the Shoshone and Blackfoot, this is a special place, the hoodoo formations and rock carvings along the Milk River mirroring the spirit presence. Some archaeologists believe the petroglyphs were made by the Shoshone Tribe, ancestors of the Great Basin people. Blackfoot or Nitsitapii traditions, on the other hand, tell us that the markings such as those at Writing-on-Stone (called Masinasin by the Cree) were created by the spirits.

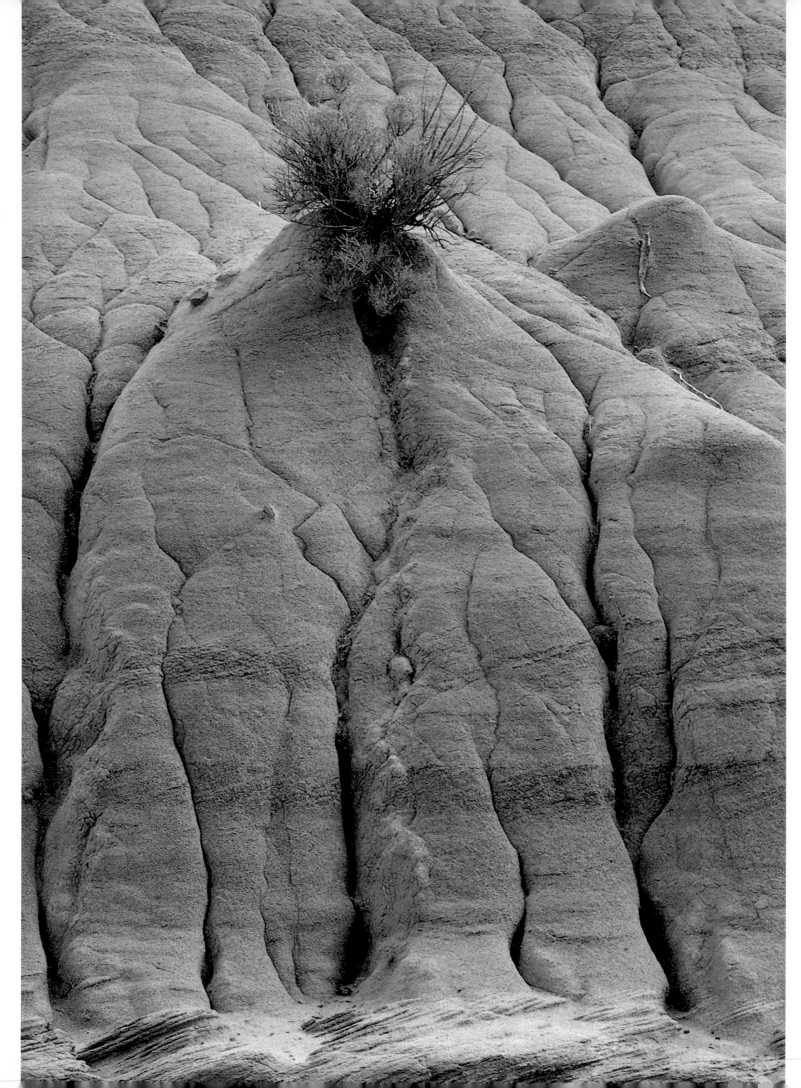

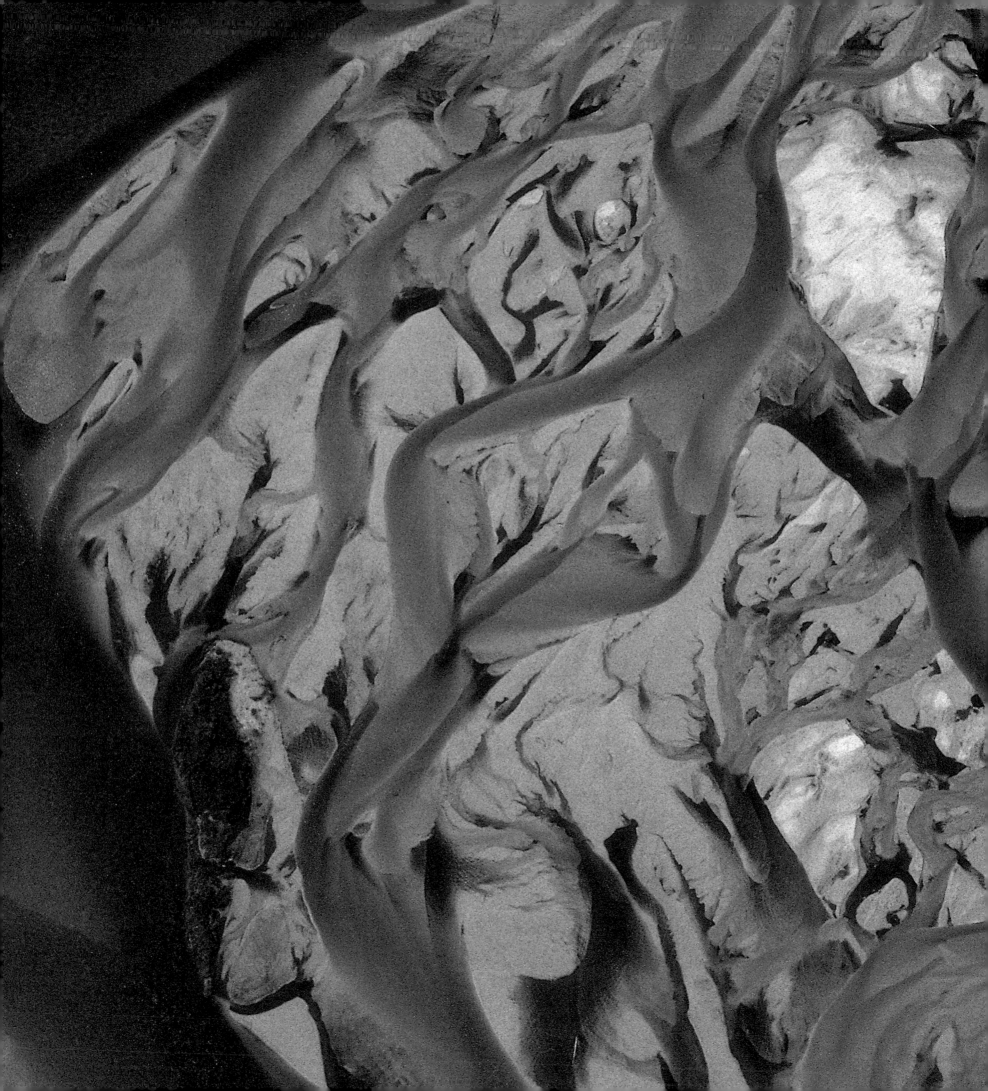

*Aerial view of bottom sand patterns,*
*William River, Athabasca Sand Dunes Park*
*Land Reserve, Saskatchewan, June 1991*

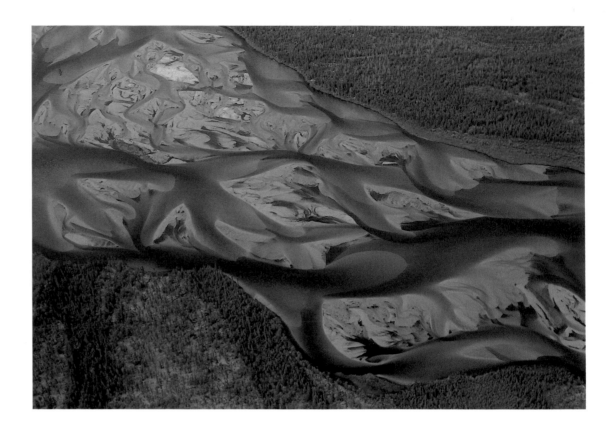

# William River

## *Braids of Fantasy*

Located at the edge of the boreal forest in northern Saskatchewan, the waters of Lake Athabasca eventually drain into the Beaufort Sea in the western Arctic. The world's largest sand dunes at this latitude are here, formed more than ten thousand years ago and continuously in motion for the past six thousand years. Here the William River carves its way northward through the Athabasca Sand Dunes, carrying millions of tons of sand and emptying them into a broad V-shaped delta on the southern shore of Lake Athabasca. From the air, the patterns created by the river's flow seem magical; the sandy bottom is visible through the pure, clear current, the deepest sections revealing the darker shapes and the shallower areas creating the brighter tones.

Eight thousand years ago, the Paleo-Indians followed the caribou migrations from their summer range on the open tundra into this winter range in the boreal forest. More recently, the two-thousand-year-old Taltheilei culture were forebears to the ancestors of the present-day Chipewyan tribe of the Dene Nation. The Chipewyan origin story tells of the union of primeval woman with a dog that was transformed into a man at night. Many Dene traditions deal with the relationship between humans and nature, including the belief that spirit-animal beings come in dreams, giving humans power to control the migration of game and other natural phenomena. One Dene story tells of how Hottah, the moose, directs a young man named Caribou-footed to help the chief of the Sky Country to find his stolen medicine belt. The northern lights are messages from him, telling his brothers on earth about the great home beyond the sky.

188

*Detail of fallen log, Athabasca Sand Dunes Park*
*Land Reserve, Saskatchewan, June 1991*

189

*"Enchanted Forest," Beaver Point, Athabasca
Sand Dunes Park Land Reserve, Saskatchewan,
June 1991*

*Camera motion on poplar grove in sunset light, Great Sandhills, Saskatchewan, July 1981*

*right: Dawn light on sand ridge, Great Sandhills, Saskatchewan, June 1986*

# The Great Sandhills

*Place of the Little People*

190  The Great Sandhills in southwest Saskatchewan are a 300,000 acre post-glacial desert surrounded by prairie. This unique island of sand encloses some stable dunes that rise several hundred feet, as well as others that constantly shift in the wind, removing the tracks of mule deer, antelope and rabbits that take refuge here.

This fragile environment shelters a rare and diverse selection of native grasses and protects the Memekweciwak, the "little people" of Plains Cree oral history. These dwarfs, who are responsible for making chipped-flint arrowheads, live in sandy riverbanks and in the sandhills. They can grant powers and are highly desired as spirit guides.

The Nitsitapii or Blackfoot people also believe the spirits of their ancestors reside here in the Great Sandhills.

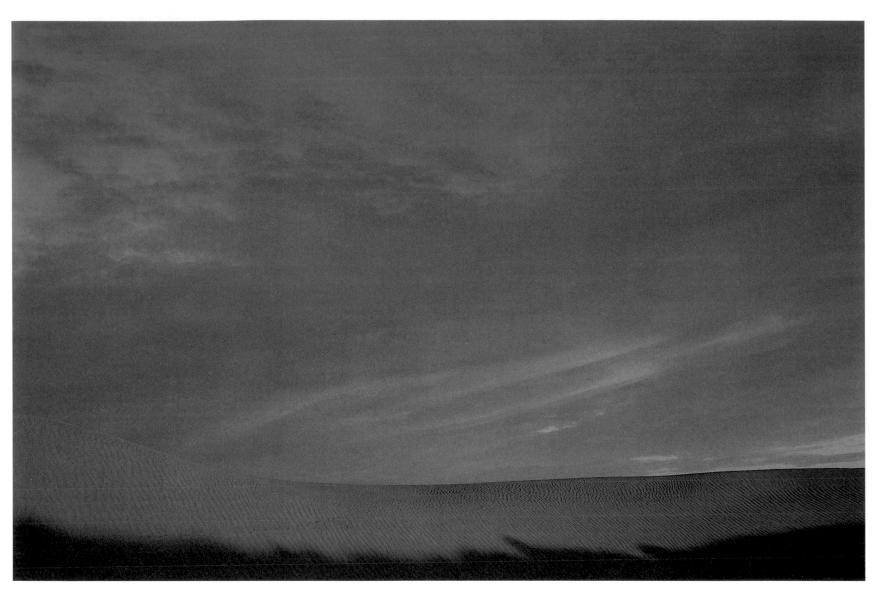

*Cattails backlit by morning sun, Wanuskewin Heritage Park, Saskatoon, Saskatchewan, September 1992*

*right: Autumn foliage backlit by morning sun, Wanuskewin Heritage Park, Saskatoon, Saskatchewan, September 1992*

# Wanuskewin

## *Valley of Peace*

192    The valley that opens onto the South Saskatchewan River just three miles north of Saskatoon is named Wanuskewin, Cree for "seeking peace of mind" or "living in harmony." The name Saskatoon comes from Mis-sask-quah-too-min, the Cree word meaning "red willow berry." Not only does this tranquil valley provide a spiritual retreat for those seeking peace of mind, but it also stands as a magnificent example of harmony among people. Five Indian nations, three levels of government and local corporations cooperated in the development and protection of this area as a heritage site.

An hour's walk through the valley leads to two buffalo jumps, numerous tipi rings, a medicine wheel and nineteen archaeological sites that attest to more than six thousand years of habitation by the Plains Indians. Today, Wanuskewin continues to be used for sweat lodge ceremonies. Wes Fineday, a Cree guide at Wanuskewin, says that although all the earth is sacred, this valley is a special place, a haven of neutrality where tribes laid down their arms. Wanuskewin draws people to learn, to partake in ceremony, to fast and to attain help from spirit powers.

According to Fineday, Wanuskewin is one of many extraordinary places where it is possible to achieve an understanding of one's position in the world. This understanding comes by going to a place of knowledge deep inside, and leads to a sense of harmony that allows one to form a connection with the "land beyond the mist ... the land in the memory." Fineday hopes that visitors here will be touched by the essence, and start to know their own spirit, fulfilling the invitation of Wanuskewin to "see nature like an eagle."

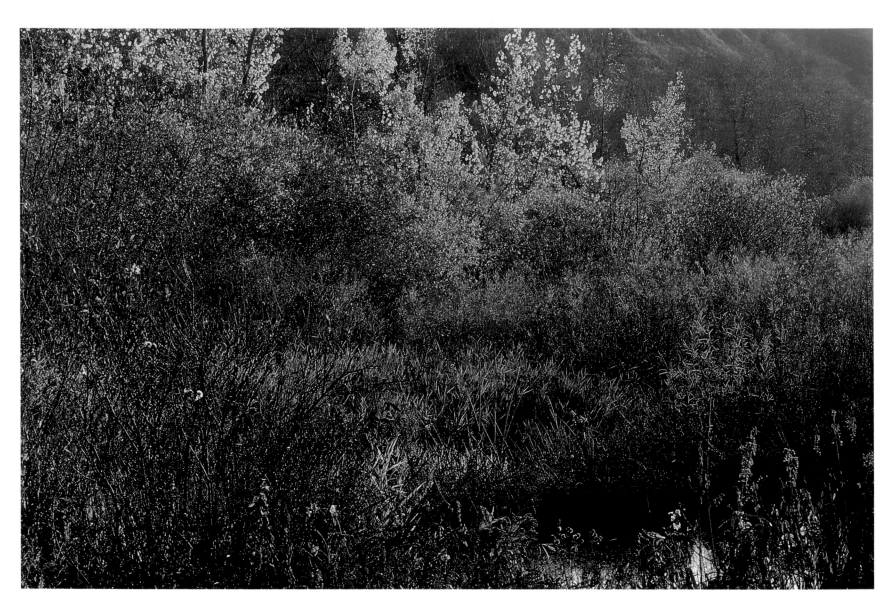

194

*Early morning frost at Opamihaw Creek,*
*Wanuskewin Heritage Park, Saskatoon,*
*Saskatchewan, October 1992*

195

*First snowfall of the season, Wanuskewin
Heritage Park, Saskatoon, Saskatchewan,
November 1992*

*Detail of beached iceberg, Eskimo Point, Manitoba, June 1985*

*right: "White Canoe," detail of beached iceberg, Eskimo Point, Manitoba, June 1985*

# Eskimo Point

## *Land of the Inuit*

196   Inuit settlements on the west coast of Hudson Bay date back at least four thousand years. Eskimo Point, near Churchill, Manitoba, is a twentieth-century village, but Eskimo Point in the Northwest Territories has been an Inuit summer camp for more than five hundred years. It has recently reverted to its original name, Arviat, meaning "place of the bowhead whale."

The Inuit have traditionally constructed figures of rock on the vast expanses of tundra. These structures are called inukshuks, meaning "acting in the capacity of a human." They function as the visual language of the people, serving as personal message centres to hunters, as "caribou drives" or "drift fences" to guide game, and even as indicators to kayakers in sight of land. Some are revered as locations of power, never to be touched or approached. Others are believed to bring good fortune and are venerated and given gifts. Perhaps the best way to describe the significance of these landmarks is in the words of an Inuit hunter who, pointing to one, said, "This attaches me to my ancestors and to the land." In English we have no word for the Inuit "unganaqtuq nyna," meaning a deep and total attachment to the earth.

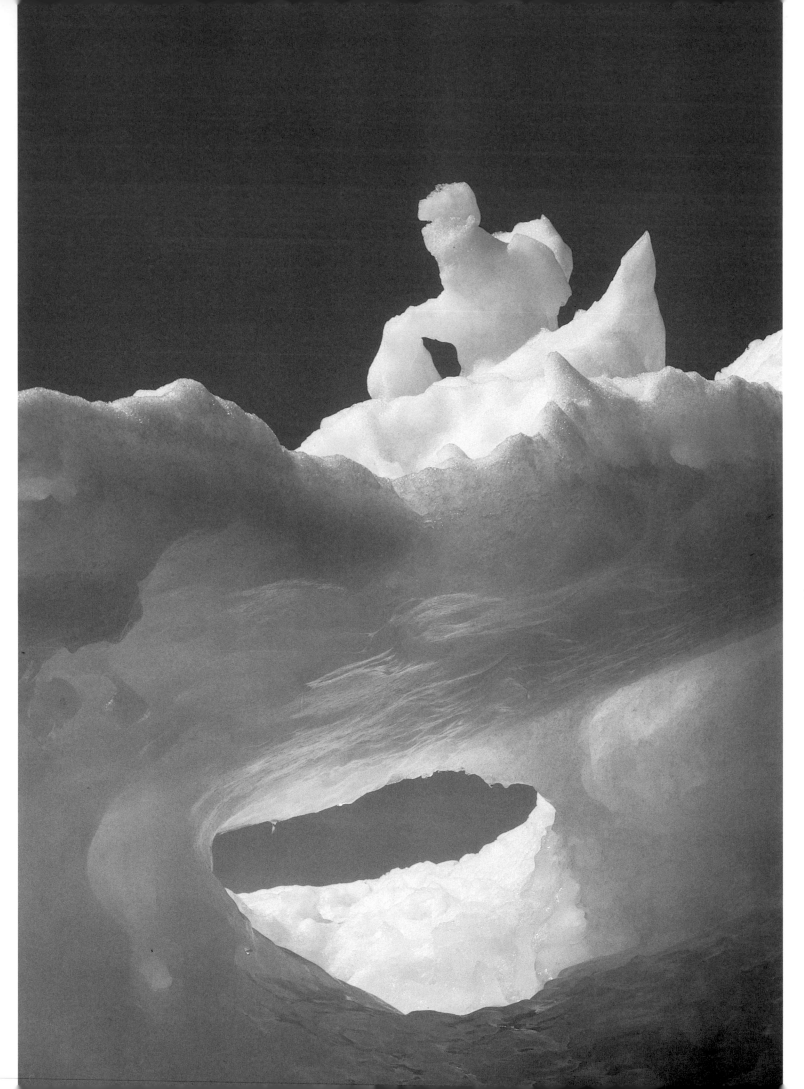

*View from summit, sunset light,*
*Moose Mountain Medicine Wheel,*
*Saskatchewan, June 1990*

*right: Lichen on rock, Moose Mountain*
*Medicine Wheel, Saskatchewan, June 1990*

*overleaf: "Full Circle," central cairn*
*(fisheye lens: see Photographer's Notes, p.202),*
*Moose Mountain Medicine Wheel,*
*Saskatchewan, June 1990*

# Moose Mountain

## Circle Without End

198 At the summit of a 560-foot treeless hill called Moose Mountain in south-east Saskatchewan lies a medicine wheel with five lines of stones radiating from a central cairn. In this area dominated by plains, the mountainous setting is unusual, overlooking lush undulating hills rolling down to the relatively flat prairie landscape in the distance. A multitude of tipi rings in the area indicates this was the home of Cree and Assiniboine encampments for untold generations who thrived on the bounty of the game and the shelter provided by nearby groves. The wheel is located on land that is now privately owned, and is protected by the Cree family that lives here.

No one really knows why or when this medicine wheel was built. Archaeologists who have studied the eighty major medicine wheels in North America – of which nearly sixty are found in the Canadian Prairies – suggest this one may have been used for animal divination; others believe it portrays astronomical alignments that could have been seen either two thousand years ago or three hundred years ago. Some current opinions dispute this theory because the nomadic hunting cultures of the Plains Indians did not follow the stars, and their stories do not contain astronomical themes. It is known that Plains Indian people named prominent hills, using their features for navigation, and that stone cairns found on outlying hills appear to align with the spokes of this wheel. One investigator has compared these to inukshuks (stone cairns) of the Arctic, which were used as message centres and directional aids for travel in the tundra.

Still others suggest this wheel is a good example of a Thirst Dance site, the annual Cree ceremony similar to the Sundance, which was often held in the hills to pray for rains to nourish grasslands and buffalo. Perhaps the most important explanation comes from Cree elders who say that medicine wheels belong to another creation time; they were made for ceremonies by their ancestors and are sacred grounds that should not be disturbed.

The Moose Mountain Medicine Wheel is the culmination of our journey, a final stone in the circular path we have followed around North America. The round symbol speaks of infinity and of continuity in life; everything in the natural world operates in cycles that are repeated over and over, giving us the opportunity to enter into this never-ending path. The circle also speaks of the interconnectedness of all things, the equality of all life, and suggests that by living in harmony with the world around us, we too can experience a deep and abiding peace.

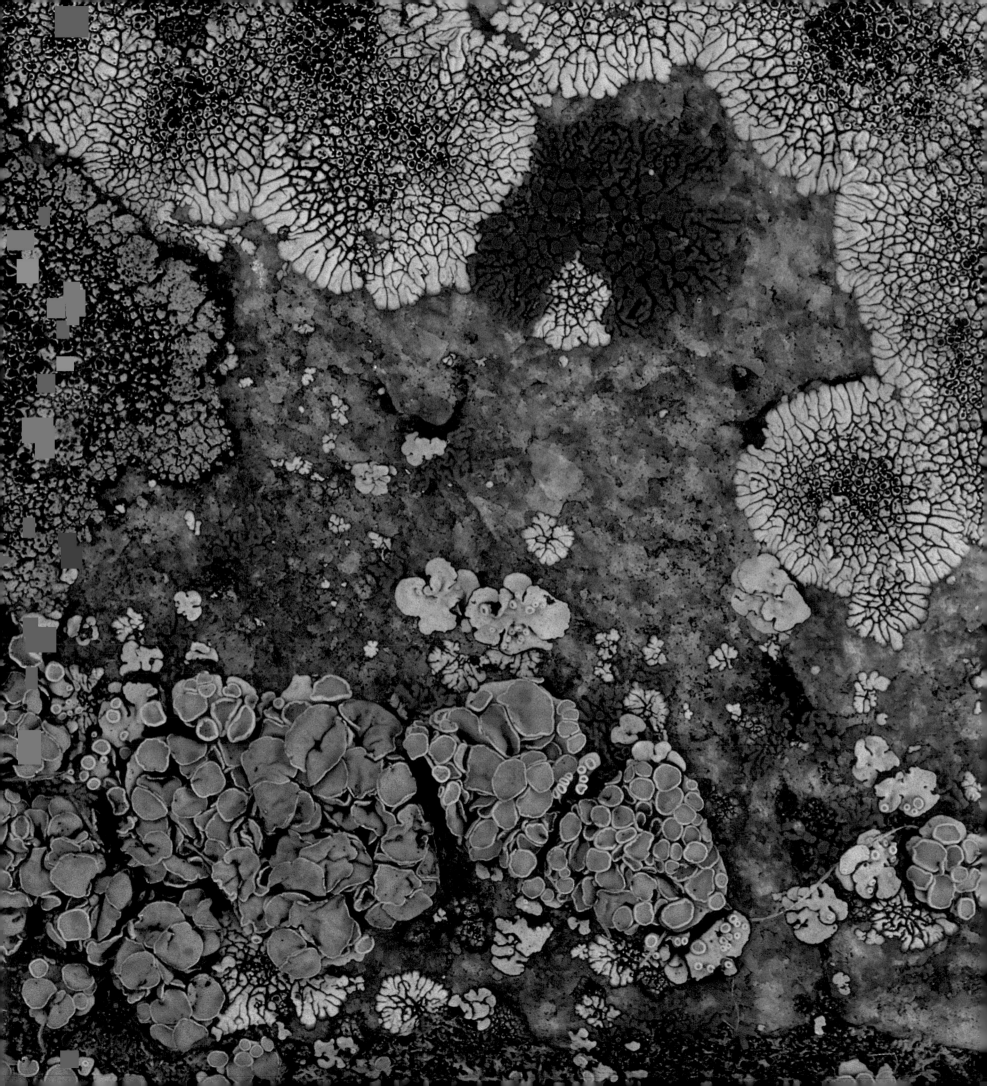

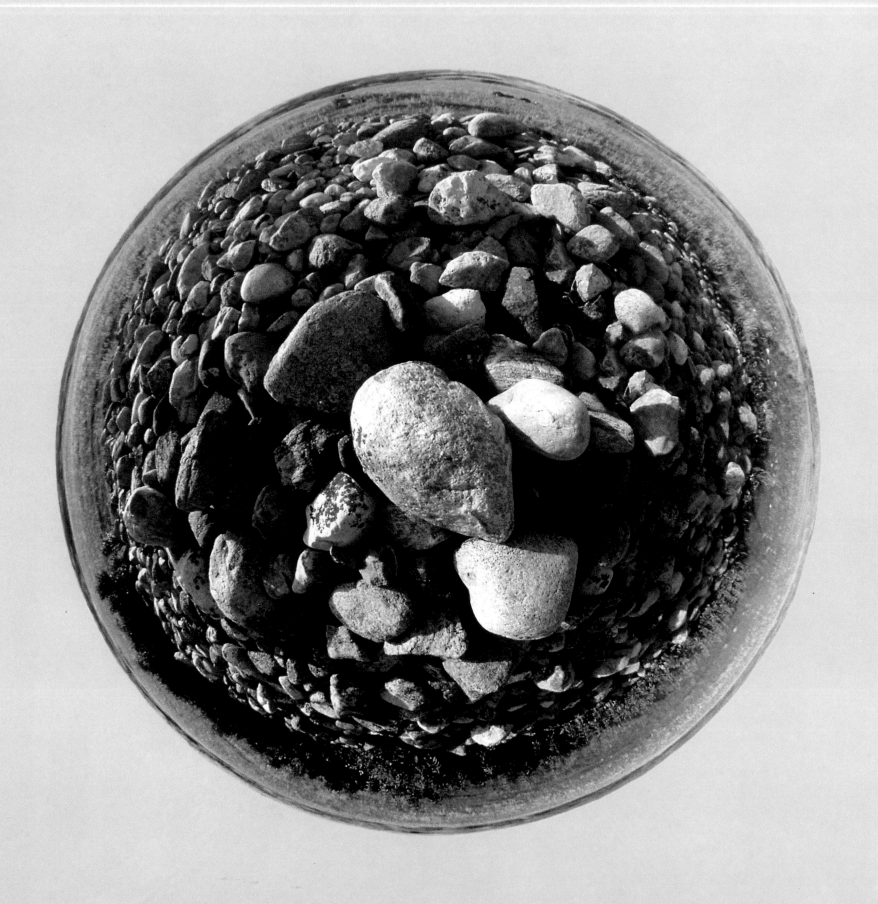

As I sat down to complete the writing for the final site, the phone rang with news that my aging mother was failing quickly. I left the work and went to be at her side. Her eyes were open but she seemed to be in another world. I placed my hand on her brow, gave her assurance of my love, and gently drew down her eyelids. Without further words, she quietly slipped away.

I have no doubt that she has gone to a better place where she will continue her journey. Like the eternal circle, the last leg of the journey is not an end, but the stepping stone to a new beginning.

*To Mother Earth we come from thee and*
*will return to thee,*
*Keep us in plenty that our days may be*
*long with thee,*

*Great Spirit we thank thee and appreciate*
*all these wonderful gifts to us.*
*Have pity on us.*

# PHOTOGRAPHER'S NOTES

Though my journey into Native North America has been a profoundly personal one, it was originally presented to me as a photographic assignment. As such, my purpose, direction and motivation throughout the project was always to make photographs, and virtually every facet of my travel was oriented to that end.

As the dates of the photographs indicate, my journey to the twenty-eight spokes of the medicine wheel did not occur in the order in which they are presented here. My visits to the fifty-four locations began with a 1971 hike over Sentinal Pass in Banff National Park (see Shining Mountains, p. 177) and ended with an exploration of the Rock Eagle Effigy near Atlanta, Georgia in October of 1993 (p. 58), just prior to the completion of this book. Much of my travel was by Volkswagen camper (1961, 1966, 1972, and 1986 models successively), which provided not only transportation but also an office, equipment storage space, library, kitchen, and sleeping quarters. I like to think of these excursions as borrowing from the lifestyle of the turtle: although the pace was relatively slow, particularly during uphill hauls and stretches into the wind, I carried my house with me, and thus could camp in remote locations, ready for an early morning shoot. Other modes of conveyance included a cruise ship, a hot air balloon, a motorized rubber raft, a canoe, small aircraft, a 4-wheel drive jeep, kayaks, a train, and numerous motorboats and rental cars.

I work exclusively with 35mm colour slide films, and the photographs in Spirit of the Land were made with a variety of brands: Ektachrome, Kodachrome, Fujichrome, Fujichrome Velvia and Agfachrome. My choice of film is determined by the effect I wish to achieve, the quality of light, the time of day and the desired colour intensity. Generally I shoot Kodachrome in low contrast light and when subtlety or a pastel effect is called for; Ektachrome when a greater latitude of tones is present in the scene; Fujichrome for brilliance and for the greatest variation of nature's green tones; Fujichrome Velvia for the ultimate in colour saturation and sharpness; and Agfachrome for a rustic portrayal of earth tones.

For camera stability and precise composition, I use a Manfrotto model 055 tripod (marketed as Bogan in the United States), and either an Amplis or Manfrotto ball and socket head, for virtually all my work. The 35mm format is ideal for portability of cameras, film and lenses – a crucial consideration when photographing in remote locales – and allows for convenient storage of mounted slides. By 1985 I was using eighteen lenses ranging from an 8mm fisheye to a 4200mm telephoto, but my workhorse lens has been my Nikkor 80-200mm f2.8 zoom. I rarely use filters but occasionally add a polarizer for added definition, or a colour enhancer to give emphasis to warmer tones.

On long trips I carry several camera bodies, my favourite being the Nikon F3 which I usually leave on the automatic exposure mode, manipulating the manual override as required. I often work with two cameras so that a second one is ready immediately after I finish a roll of film. Sometimes I load each camera with different film so I can compare the results or achieve a contrasting effect.

On the journeys I made for this book, I almost never stayed as long as I would have liked at any one place, but usually planned on three to five days per site. As a general rule, I organized my time so that I was on location before dawn, relaxing during the midday light, then returning for more photography an hour or two prior to sunset. Often I continued photographing into the night, sometimes lighting my foregrounds artifically or using long exposure times for special results. My favourite example of the multiple flash technique is "Lunar Necklace" (p.105). Casa Rinconada is a large circular stone structure, its roof open to the sky. I obtained special permission to be there after dark; prior to the rising of the full moon, I set my camera in the center with a fisheye lens (180 degree angle of view) pointing straight up and focussed on infinity, the stone perimeter showing in the viewfinder as a complete circle. Then at a distance of a few feet inside the wall, I circled the structure, lighting the wall with about twenty-five equidistant flashes, finishing with a strobe into each of the thirty-five portals before ending the exposure. Then I waited twenty minutes for the full

moon to rise above the east wall, and made a second exposure on the same frame. Every fifteen minutes thereafter, I tripped the shutter, thus tracing the orbit of the moon across the sky. A sleeping bag, lawn chair, and alarm clock allowed me to doze in comfort between exposures.

I made "Sky Hole" (p. 146) also using a fisheye lens pointing upwards, but this time leaving the shutter open for a complete hour to record the star trails around Polaris. Using Fujichrome 50, the resulting image took on a distinctly green tone. Working with a photography lab, I made a duplicate slide, adding a cyan filter in order to provide a more pleasing hue.

The circular image of the Moose Mountain Medicine Wheel (page 200) was also made with a fisheye lens. In this case I stood over the central cairn, pointing the camera downwards so that the complete horizon, as well as my feet and legs, were visible in the viewfinder. Later I worked with the photo lab to electronically remove the feet and legs from the image and to extend the blue sky in every direction. Computer technology was also used to combine parts of three photographs to achieve the effect of the moon rising over the human effigy at Manito Ahbee (p.23).

Sometimes I find that special effects allow me to convey the essence of a site more readily than would a documentary image, and I have identified composites and multiple or long exposures in the picture captions. But the vast majority of my photographs are straight-forward images that need no manipulation to convey the spirit of the place. "Totem Landscape" (shown here) is a classic example. To me, its special strength lies not in its colours and textures, but rather in its ability to introduce a different reality. By rotating the image a quarter turn, as I've done here, the shoreline and its accompanying reflection take on the appearance of a totem pole, with spirit faces that bear a startling resemblance to some of those carved by people of the Northwest Coast. The moral for me is that the spirit world manifested in nature is available to anyone who takes the time to explore it.

This book is a collection of images expressing my personal responses to these sacred landscapes, rather than an attempt to portray in some objective way what a visitor might see. Sometimes it took me several days just to get the feeling of a place, to discover the stories, and then to interpret my response photographically. I made about a thousand photographs per site — sometimes two or three thousand — knowing that on the average only three or four images would be selected for the book. Choosing the photographs involved several waves of "honing down," as I worked in a team that included the editor, book designer and researcher. We always asked first whether the photograph caught the spirit of the place, and second whether it worked with the overall flow of the book.

Because the images I made and the images we chose are an expression of my own way of seeing, the creation of this book has been a deeply personal experience. Perhaps the greatest lessons for a photographer are not in learning to master camera technique, but in learning the true meaning of humility and how to dance in a spirit of cooperation.

203

*"Totem Landscape," rocky shoreline and reflection (image rotated a quarter turn), Manitoulin Island, April 1993*

# References

Allen, D. Totem Poles of the Northwest. Surrey BC: Hancock House Publishers, 1977.

Allen, Paula Gunn. The Sacred Hoop: Recovering the Feminine in American Indian Traditions. Boston, MASS: Beacon Press, 1986.

Angel, Myron. The Painted Rock of California, A Legend (1910). San Luis Obispo, CA: Padre Productions, 1979.

Anishnaabe Kinoomagewin, Curriculum Development. Espanola, ONT: Anishnabe Spiritual Center, 1992.

Ashwell, Reg. Indian Tribes of the Northwest. Surrey, BC: Hancock House Publishers, 1977.

Atkinson, Richard. White Sands, wind, sand and time. Tucson, AZ: Southwest Parks and Monuments Association, 1977.

Beck, Mary Giraudo. Shamans and Kushtakas, North Coast Tales of the Supernatural. Bothell, WA: Alaska Northwest Books, 1991.

Beck, Peggy V., Anna Lee Walters, and Nia Francisco. The Sacred, Ways of Knowledge, Sources of Life. Tsaile, AZ: Navajo Community College Press, 1990.

Benzinger, Charles. Chaco Journey: Remembrance and Awakening. Sante Fe, NM: Timewindow Publications, 1988.

Berenholtz, Jim. Journey to the Four Directions. Sante Fe, NM: Bear & Co, 1993.

Bernbaum, Edwin. Sacred Mountains of the World. San Francisco: Sierra Club, 1990.

Berry, Thomas. The Dream of the Earth. San Francisco: Sierra Club, 1988.

Bierhorst, John. The Mythology of North America. New York: William Morrow and Co., 1985.

Bierhorst, John, ed. The Sacred Path; Spells, Prayers and Power Songs of the American Indians. New York: Quill, 1984.

Blackburn, Thomas C. December's Child, A Book of Chumash Oral Narratives. Berkeley, CA: University of California Press, 1975.

Black Elk, Wallace, and William S. Lyon. Black Elk, The Sacred Ways of a Lakota. New York: HarperCollins, 1990.

Brace, Ian. Boulder Monuments of Saskatchewan. Masters Thesis, University of Alberta, Edmonton, 1987.

Brown, Joseph Epes, ed. The Sacred Pipe, Black Elk's Account of the Seven Rites of the Oglala Sioux. Norman, OK: University of Oklahoma Press, 1984.

Brown, Joseph Epes. The Spiritual Legacy of the American Indian. New York: Crossroad Publishing, 1992.

Brown, Vinson. Voices of Earth and Sky. Happy Camp, CA: Naturegraph, 1974.

Bruchac, Joseph, and Diana Landau. Singing of Earth, A Native American Anthology. Berkeley, CA: The Nature Company, 1993.

Burger, Julian. The Gaia Atlas of First Peoples: A Future for the Indigenous World. New York: Anchor Books/Doubleday, 1990.

Burland, Cottie, Irene Nicholson, and Harold Osborne. Mythology of the Americas. London: Hamlyn, 1975.

Buswa, Ernestine, and Jean Shawana, eds. Teachings of the Medicine Wheel (Nishnaabe Bimaadziwin Kinoomaadwinan). West Bay, ONT: Ojibwe Cultural Foundation, 1992.

Caduto, Michael J., and Joseph Bruchac. Keepers of the Earth: Native Stories and Environmental Activities for Children. Saskatoon: Fifth House Publishers, 1989.

Caldwell, Joseph R., and Robert Hall, eds. Hopewellian Studies. Scientific Papers, Vol. X11. Illinois State Museum, Springfield, IL, 1977.

Campbell, Elizabeth W. Crozer. An Archeological Survey of the Twenty Nine Palms Region. Los Angeles, CA: Southwest Museum Papers Number Seven, 1931, 1963.

Campbell, Joseph. The Inner Reaches of Outer Space: Metaphor as Myth and as Religion. New York: Harper and Row, 1986.

Campbell, Joseph. The Mythic Image. Princeton: Princeton University Press, 1974.

Cantor, George. North American Indian Landmarks, A Traveller's Guide. Detroit, MI: Visible Ink Press, 1993.

Carter, Anthony. This is Haida. Vancouver: Agency Press Ltd., 1968.

Charging Eagle, Tom, and Ron Zeilinger. Black Hills: Sacred Hills. Chamberlain, SD: Tipi Press, 1987.

Chetwynd, Tom. Dictionary of Sacred Myth. Unwin Paperbacks, 1986.

Clark, Ella Elizabeth. Indian Legends of Canada. Toronto; McClelland and Stewart, 1960, 1983.

Coe, Michael, Dean Snow, and Elizabeth Benson. Atlas of Ancient America. New York: Facts on File.

Complete Guide to America's National Parks. Washington DC: National Park Foundation, 1992-93

Corbett, Cynthia. Power Trips: Journeys to Sacred Sites as a Way of Transformation. Sante Fe, NM: Timewindow Publications, 1988.

Cotta Vaz, Mark. Spirit in the Land. New York: Signet Paperback, 1988.

Cornett, James W. Desert Palm Oasis. Palm Springs Desert Museum, 1989.

Crawford, J.L. Zion National Park, Towers of Stone. Santa Barbara, CA: Sequoia Communications, 1988.

Damas, David, ed. Handbook of North American Indians, Vol. 5, Arctic. Washington, DC: Smithsonian, 1984.

Davis, Wade. Shadows in the Sun, Essays on the Spirit of Place. Edmonton, ALTA: Lone Pine Publishing, 1992.

Debassige, Blake, and Stephen Hogbin, curators. Political Landscapes #Two: Sacred and Secular Sites. Owen Sound, ONT: Tom Thomson Memorial Art Gallery, 1991.

Douglas, Marjory Stoneman. The Everglades: River of Grass. Georgia, Mockingbird Books, 1974, 1984.

Dragoo, Don W. Mounds for the Dead. Pittsburg, PA: Carnegie Museum of Natural History, 1963.

Edmonds, Margot, and Ella E. Clark. Voices of the Winds, Native American Legends. New York: Facts on File, 1989.

Erdoes, Richard, and Alfonson Ortiz, eds. American Indian Myths and Legends. New York: Pantheon Books, 1984.

Everhart, Ronald E. Glen Canyon-Lake Powell, The Story Behind the Scenery. K.C. Publications, 1984.

Fell, Barry. America B.C. New York: Pocket Books, Simon and Schuster, 1976, 1989.

Fidler, J. Havelock. Earth Energy: A Dowser's Investigation of Ley Lines. Wellingborough, England: Aquarian Press, 1983, 1988.

Fortney, David L. Mysterious Places -- Ancient Sites and Lost Cultures. New York: Random House/Crescent Books, 1992.

Fox, Matthew. The Coming of the Cosmic Christ. San Francisco: Harper and Row, 1988.

Frick, Thomas, ed. Sacred Theory of the Earth. Berkeley, CA: North Atlantic Books, 1986.

Furst, Peter T. "Roots and Continuities of Shamanism", in Stones, bones & skin: Ritual and Shamanic Art. Toronto: artscanada, Dec.1973-Jan.1974

Garfield, Viola E., and Linn A. Forrest. The Wolf and the Raven, Totem Poles of Southeastern Alaska. Seattle, WA: University of Washington Press, 1948, 1961-93.

George, Chief Dan. My Spirit Soars. Surrey, BC: Hancock House Publishers, 1982.

Golia, Jack de. Everglades: The Story Behind the Scenery. Las Vegas: KC Publications, 1978

Gonzales, Magda Weck (Star-Spider Woman), and J.A. Gonzales (Rattling Bear). Star-Spider Speaks: The Teachings of the Native American Tarot. Stamford, CT: U.S. Games, Inc., 1990.

Grande, John K. Art and Environment. Toronto, ONT: The Friendly Chameleon, 1993.

Grant, Campbell. Rock Art of the American Indian. Dillon, CO: Vistabooks, 1992.

Halifax, Joan. Shaman, The wounded healer. London: Thames and Hudson, 1982.

Halpin, Marjorie M. Totem Poles: An Illustrated Guide. Vancouver: University of British Columbia Press, 1981.

Hallendy, Norman. "Places of Power and Objects of Veneration in the Canadian Arctic." Unpublished manuscript, presented to the World Archaelogical Congress, Venezuela, 1990

Hamilton, Virginia, and Barry Moses. In the Beginning. Orlando, FL: Harcourt Brace Jovanovich, 1988.

Harpur, James, and Jennifer Westwood. The Atlas of Legendary Places. New York: Weidenfeld and Nicolson, 1989.

Helm, Jane, ed. Handbook of North American Indians, Vol. 6, Subarctic. Washington, DC: Smithsonian, 1987.

Hillerman, Tony. Indian Country, America's Sacred Land. Weston, MASS: Yearout Editions, 1987.

Hillerman, Tony. Talking God. New York: HarperCollins, 1989.

Holsinger, Rosemary, and P.I. Piemme. Shasta Indian Tales. Happy Camp, CA: Naturegraph Publishers, 1982.

Hudson, Travis. Guide to Painted Cave. Santa Barbara, CA: McNally & Loftin, 1982.

Hungry Wolf, Adolph. A Good Medicine Collection, Life in Harmony with Nature. Summertown, TN: Book Publishing Co., 1990.

Jackson, Victor L. Zion, the continuing story in pictures. Las Vegas, NV: KC Publications, 1989.

Jilek, Wolfgang. Indian Healing: Shamanic Ceremonialism in the Pacific Northwest Today. Surrey BC: Hancock House Publishers, 1982.

Jonker, Peter, ed. Saskatchewan's Endangered Spaces. Saskatoon, SASK: Extension Dept., University of Saskatchewan, 1992.

Joseph, Frank, ed. Sacred Sites, A Guidebook to Sacred Centers and Mysterious Places in the United States. St. Paul, MINN: Lewellyn Publications, 1992.

Kelemen, Pal. Art of the Americas: Ancient and Hispanic. New York: Thomas Crowell, 1969.

Kew, Della, and P.E. Goddard. Indian Art and Culture of the Northwest Coast. Surrey, BC: Hancock House Publishers, 1974.

Lame Deer, John (Fire), and Richard Erdoes. Lame Deer, Seeker of Visions. New York: Washington Square Press, 1972.

Langdon, Steve J. The Native People of Alaska. Anchorage, Al: Greatland Graphics, 1993.

Lankford, George E., ed. Native American Legends. Little Rock, AK: August House, 1987.

Leeming, David Adams. The World of Myth. New York: Oxford University Press, 1990.

Lehrman, Fredric. The Sacred Landscape. Berkeley, CA: Celestial Arts Publishing, 1988.

Leonard, George. The Silent Pulse. New York: E.P. Dutton, 1986.

Lister, Robert H. and Florence C. Those Who Came Before. Globe, AZ: Southwest Parks and Monuments, 1983.

Lombardi, Frances G. and Gerald Scott. Circle Without End. London: Thames and Hudson, 1979

Lopez, Barry. Arctic Dreams: Imagination and Desire in a Northern Landscape. New York, Charles Scribner's Sons, 1986.

Lopez, Barry. Crossing Open Ground. London, England: Pan Books, 1989.

Lothson, Gordon Allan. The Jeffers Petroglyphs Site, A Survey and Analysis of the Carvings. St. Paul, MINN: Minnesota Historical Society, 1976.

Lowie, Robert H. Indians of the Plains. Lincoln, NB: University of Nebraska Press, 1982.

Maclagan, David. Creation Myths: Man's Introduction to the World. London: Thames and Hudson, 1977.

Mails, Thomas E. Secret Native American Pathways, A Guide to Inner Peace. Tulsa, OK: Council Oak Books, 1988.

Mails, Thomas E. Fools Crow. Lincoln NB: University of Nebraska Press, 1979.

Mails, Thomas E. The Mystic Warriors of the Plains. New York: Mallard Press, 1972, 1991.

Manitopyes, Alvin, and Dave Courchene Jr. Voice of the Eagle. Calgary, ALTA: Aboriginal Awareness Society, 1992.

Mander, Jerry. In the Absence of the Sacred; The Failure of Technology and the Survival of the Indian Nations. San Francisco, CA: Sierra Club, 1991.

Mann, Nicholas. Sedona, Sacred Earth. Prescott, AZ. Zivah Publishers, 1991.

Marriott, Alice, and Carol Rachlin. Plains Indian Mythology. New York: New American Library, 1975.

Matlock, Gary, and Warren Scott. Enemy Ancestors -- The Anasazi World with a Guide to Sites. Northland Press, 1988.

Maud, Ralph. A Guide to B.C. Indian Myth and Legend. Vancouver: Talon Books, 1982.

Maybury-Lewis, David. Millennium -- Tribal Wisdom and the Modern World. New York: Viking Penguin, 1992.

McCall, Lynne, and Rosalind Perry. California's Chumash Indians. Santa Barbara Museum of Natural History, 1986.

McClellan, Catherine. Part of the Land, Part of the Water: A History of the Yukon Indians. Vancouver: Douglas and McIntyre, 1987.

McDonald, George F. Ninstints: Haida World Heritage Site. Vancouver: University of British Columbia Press, 1983.

McGaa, Ed, Eagle Man. Mother Earth Spirituality, Native American Paths to Healing Ourselves and Our World. San Francisco, CA: HarperCollins, 1989, 1990.

McGaa, Ed, Eagle Man. Rainbow Tribe, Ordinary People Journeying on the Red Road. San Francisco, CA: HarperCollins, 1992.

McGhee, Robert. Ancient Canada. Ottawa: Canadian Museum of Civilization, 1989.

Merz, Blanche. Points of Cosmic Energy. Essex, England: C.W. Daniel Co. Ltd, 1987.

Michell, John. The Earth Spirit: Its Ways, Shrines and Mysteries. London: Thames and Hudson, 1975.

Melville, J. McKim, and Claudia Putnam. Prehistoric Astronomy in the Southwest.

Boulder, CO: Johnson Books, 1989.

Miller, Jay. Earthmaker, Tribal Stories from Native North America. New York: Perigee Books, 1992.

Miller, Sherrill. The Pilgrim's Guide to The Sacred Earth. Distributed by Penguin Books, Toronto, 1992.

Milne, Courtney. The Sacred Earth. Saskatoon: Western Producer Prairie Books, 1991. Toronto: Penguin Books, 1992.

Mystic Places. Alexandria, VA: Time Life, 1987.

Nabokov, Peter. Native American Testimony, A Chronicle of Indian-White Relations from Prophecy to the Present, 1492-1992. New York: Penguin (Viking), 1992.

Natural Wonders of the World. Montreal: Reader's Digest Association Inc., 1980.

Newcomb, W.W. Jr. The Indians of Texas, From Prehistoric to Modern Times. Austin: University of Texas Press, 1961-1990.

Niehardt, John G. Black Elk Speaks. Lincoln, NB: University of Nebraska Press, 1988.

Noble, David Grant. Ancient Ruins of the Southwest. Flagstaff, AZ: Northland Publishing, 1981, 1991.

Nu-tka-, Captain Cook and the Spanish Explorers on the Coast. Sound Heritage, Vol V11, Number 1. Victoria, BC: Aural History Provincial Archives, 1978.

Nu-tka-, The History and Survival of Nootkan Culture. Sound Heritage, Volume V11, No. 2. Victoria, BC: Aural History Provincial Archives, 1978.

Ortiz, Alfonso, ed. Handbook of North American Indians, Vol. 9, Southwest. Washington, DC: Smithsonian Institute, 1979.

Patterson, Alex. A Field Guide to Rock Art Symbols of the Greater Southwest, Boulder, CO: Johnson Books, 1992.

Pearen, Shelley J. Exploring Manitoulin. University of Toronto Press, 1992.

Pennick, Nigel. Earth Harmony. London: Century, 1987.

Pennick, Nigel. Geomancy: The Ancient Science of Man in Harmony with the Earth. London: Thames and Hudson, 1979.

People of the Desert. Alexandria, VA: Time Life, 1993.

Peterson, Natasha. Sacred Sites: A Traveler's Guide to North America's Most Powerful, Mystical Landmarks. Chicago: Contemporary Books Inc., 1988.

Pike, Donald G. and David Muench. Anasazi: Ancient People of the Rock. New York: Harmony Books, 1974.

Place, Chuck. Ancient Walls, Indian Ruins of the Southwest.Golden, CO: Fulcrum Publishing, 1992.

Price, Joan Ellen. Sacred Mountains: Ways of Knowledge. Unpublished manuscript.

Ray, Dorothy Jean. Eskimo Masks: Art and Ceremony. University of Washington Press, 1967.

Realm of the Iroquois. Alexandria, VA: Time Life, 1993.

Reeves, Brian O.K., and Margaret Kennedy. Kunaitupii, Coming Together on Native Sacred Sites. Calgary, ALTA: Archeological Society of Alberta, 1993.

Reid, Bill, and Robert Bringhurst. The Raven Steals the Light. Vancouver: Douglas and McIntyre, 1984.

Roberts, Elizabeth, and Elias Amidon. Earth Prayers From Around the World. San Francisco, CA: HarperCollins, 1991.

Roseau River Three Fires Society. The Creek Study, An Anishanabe Understanding of the Petroforms. Winnipeg, MAN: Parks Branch, Manitoba Dept. of Natural Resources, 1990.

Ross, Dr. Allen C. Mitakuye Oyasin, "We are all related". Kyle, SD: Bear, 1989.

Roszak, Theodore. The Voice of the Earth. New York: Simon Schuster, 1992.

Sabo, George. Paths of Our Children. Fayetteville, AR: Arkansas Archeological Survey, 1992.

Sams, Jamie, and David Carson. Medicine Cards: The Discovery of Power Through the Ways of Animals. Sante Fe, NM: Bear and Co., 1988.

Schaafsma, Polly. Indian Rock Art of the Southwest. Albuquerque: University of New Mexico Press, 1980.

Sherman, Josepha. Indian Tribes of North America. New York, Portland House, 1990.

Silko, Leslie. Storyteller. New York: Little Brown and Co., 1981.

Silverberg, Robert. The Mound Builders. Athens, OH: Ohio University Press, 1989.

South Dakota Writers' Project, and Oscar Howe. Legends of the Mighty Sioux. Interior, SD: Badlands Natural History Association, 1987.

Sproule, Barbara C. Primal Myths: Creating the World. New York: Harper and Row, 1979.

Steiger, Brad. Indian Medicine Power. Westchester, PENN: Schiffer Publishing, 1984.

Storm, Hyemeyohsts. Seven Arrows. New York, Ballantyne Books, 1972.

Stuart, Gene S. America's Ancient Cities. Washington, D.C., National Geographic Society, 1988.

Sun Bear, and Wabun. The Medicine Wheel, Earth Astrology. New York: Prentice Hall, 1980.

Sun Bear, Wabun Wind, and Crysalis Mulligan. Dancing With the Wheel. The Medicine Wheel Workbook. New York, Simon and Shuster, 1991.

Sutphen, Dick. Sedona: Psychic Energy Vortexes. Malibu, CA: Valley of the Sun Printing Co., 1986.

Suttles, Wayne, ed. Handbook of North American Indians, Vol. 7, Northwest Coast. Washington, DC: Smithsonian, 1990.

Swan, James. Sacred Places: How the Living Earth Seeks Our Friendship. Sante Fe, NM: Bear and Co., 1990.

Swan, James, ed. The Power of Place and Human Environments. Wheaton, ILL: Quest Books, 1991.

Swinton, George. Eskimo Sculpture. Toronto: McClelland & Stewart, 1965.

The Mighty Chieftains. Alexandria, VA: Time Life, 1993.

The Buffalo Hunters. Alexandria, VA: Time Life, 1993.

The Spirit World. Alexandria, VA: Time Life, 1992.

The European Challenge. Alexandria, VA: Time Life, 1992.

The Sacred Tree. Lethbridge, ALTA: Four Worlds Development Press, 1984.

The First Americans. Alexandria, VA: Time Life, 1992.

Trigger, Buce C., ed. Handbook of North American Indians, Vol. 15, Northeast. Washington, DC: Smithsonian, 1978.

Viele, Catherine W. Voices in the Canyon. Southwest Parks and Monuments, 1990.

Wabun, and Barry Weinstock. Sun Bear, The Path of Power. Spokane, WA: Bear Tribe Publishing, 1983.

Wall, Steve, and Harvey Arden. Wisdomkeepers, Meetings with Native American Spiritual Elders. Hillsboro, OR: Beyond Words Publishing, 1990.

Waters, Frank. Masked Gods. Athens, OH: Ohio University Press, 1984.

Waters, Frank. Book of the Hopi. New York: Penguin (Viking), 1963, 1972-1977.

Westwood, Jennifer, ed. The Atlas of Mysterious Places. New York: Weidenfeld and Nicolson, 1987.

Wicklein, John. "Spirit Paths of the Anasazi", from Archeology, Jan/Feb. 1994, p. 36-41. NY: Archeological Institute.

Williamson, Ray. Living the Sky: The Cosmos of the American Indian. University of Oklahoma Press, 1984.

Wosien, Maria Gabriele. Sacred Dance: Encounter with the Gods. Avon, 1974.

Wright, Ronald. Stolen Continents -- The "New World" Through Indian Eyes Since 1492. Toronto: Penguin (Viking), 1992.

Young, Dudley. Origins of the Sacred. New York: HarperCollins, 1991.

Zambucka, Kristin. The Keepers of the Earth, Honolulu: Harrane Publishing, 1985.

Zanger, Michael. Mt. Shasta, History, Legend and Lore. Berkeley, CA: Celestial Arts, 1992.

Zeilinger, Ron. Sacred Ground, Reflections on Lakota Spirituality and the Gospel. Chamberlain, SD: Tipi Press, 1987.

205

# Index

207

ON THE MAKING OF THE BOOK

Jacket and interior designed by V. John Lee

Map designed and drawn by James Loates

Edited by Jackie Kaiser

Copy edited by Rosalyn Steiner

Production edited by Lori Ledingham

Production direction by Dianne Craig

Printed and bound by New Interlitho Italia S.p.A.


The text of *Spirit of the Land* is set in Stemple
Garamond, a traditional oldstyle typeface.
Headings are set in Neworder, a contemporary
display typeface.
Layout and Typesetting have been produced on
an IBM 486 in Aldus Pagemaker, Version 5.0

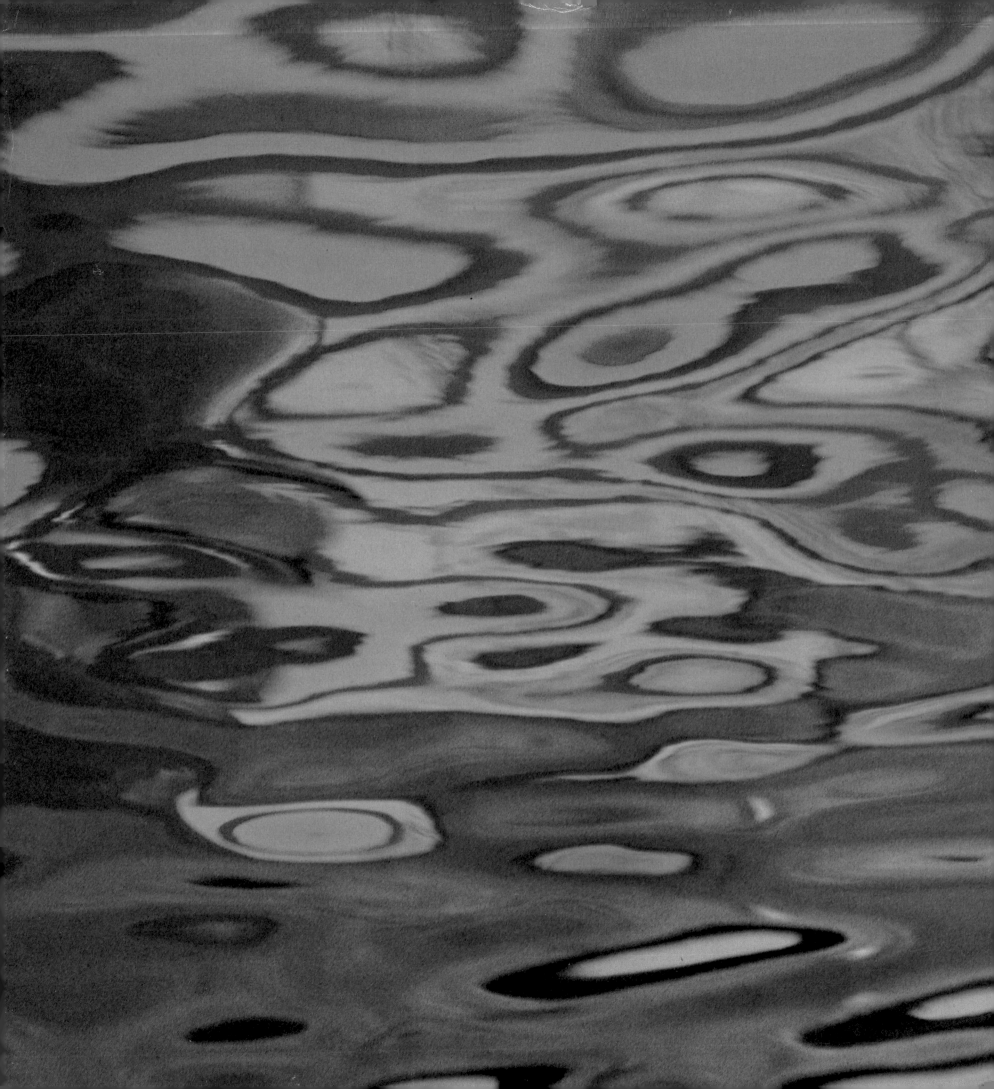

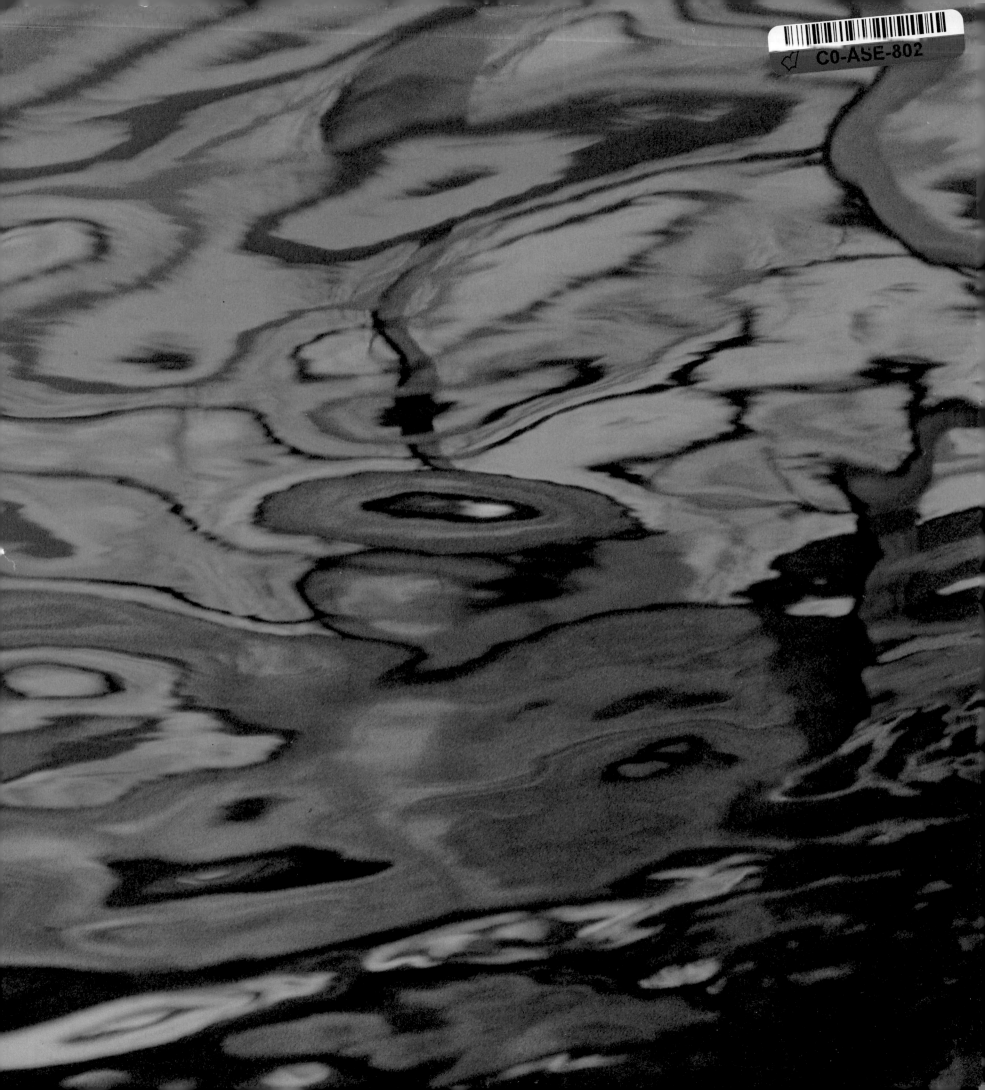

Miller, Jay. Earthmaker: Tribal Stories from Native North America. New York: Perigee Books, 1992.

Miller, Sherrill. The Pilgrim's Guide to The Sacred Earth. Distributed by Penguin Books, Boulder, CO: Johnson Books, 1989.

Milne, Courtney. The Sacred Earth. Saskatoon: Western Producer Prairie Books, 1991. Toronto, 1992.

Mystic Places. Alexandria, VA: Time Life, 1987.

Naboko, Peter. Native American Testimony, A Chronicle of Indian-White Relations from Prophecy to the Present, 1492-1992. New York: Penguin (Viking), 1992.

Natural Wonders of the World. Montreal: Reader's Digest Association Inc., 1980.

Newcomb, W.W. Jr. The Indians of Texas, From Prehistoric to Modern Times. Austin: University of Texas Press, 1961-1990.

Niehardt, John G. Black Elk Speaks. Lincoln, NB: University of Nebraska Press, 1988.

Noble, David Grant. Ancient Ruins of the Southwest. Flagstaff, AZ: Northland Publishing, 1981, 1991.

Nu-tka-. Captain Cook and the Spanish Explorers on the Coast, Sound Heritage, Vol VII, Number 1. Victoria, BC: Aural History Provincial Archives, 1978.

Nu-tka-. The History and Survival of Nootkan Culture. Sound Heritage, Volume VII, No. 2. Victoria, BC: Aural History Provincial Archives, 1978.

Ortiz, Alfonso, ed. Handbook of North American Indians, Vol. 9, Southwest. Washington, DC: Smithsonian Institute, 1979.

Patterson, Alex. A Field Guide to Rock Art Symbols of the Greater Southwest. Boulder, CO: Johnson Books, 1992.

Pearen, Shelley J. Exploring Manitoulin. University of Toronto Press, 1992.

Pennick, Nigel. Earth Harmony. London: Century, 1987.

Pennick, Nigel. Geomancy: The Ancient Science of Man in Harmony with the Earth. London: Thames and Hudson, 1979.

People of the Desert. Alexandria, VA: Time Life, 1993.

Peterson, Natasha. Sacred Sites: A Traveler's Guide to North America's Most Powerful, Mystical Landmarks. Chicago: Contemporary Books Inc., 1988.

Pike, Donald G. and David Muench. Anasazi: Ancient People of the Rock. New York: Harmony Books, 1974.

Place, Chuck. Ancient Walls, Indian Ruins of the Southwest. Golden, CO: Fulcrum Publishing, 1992.

Price, Joan Ellen. Sacred Mountains: Ways of Knowledge. Unpublished manuscript.

Ray, Dorothy Jean. Eskimo Masks: Art and Ceremony. University of Washington Press, 1967.

Realm of the Iroquois. Alexandria, VA: Time Life, 1993.

Reeves, Brian O.K., and Margaret Kennedy. Kunanupip, Coming Together on Native Sacred Sites. Calgary, ALTA: Archeological Society of Alberta, 1993.

Reid, Bill, and Robert Bringhurst. The Raven Steals the Light. Vancouver: Douglas and McIntyre, 1984.

Roberts, Elizabeth, and Elias Amidon. Earth Prayers from Around the World. San Francisco, CA: HarperCollins, 1991.

Roseau River Three Fires Society. The Creek Study, An Anishanabe Understanding of the Petroforms. Winnipeg, MAN: Parks Branch, Manitoba Dept. of Natural Resources, 1990.

Ross, Dr. Allen C. Mitakuye Oyasin, "We are all related". Kyle, SD: Bear, 1989.

Roszak, Theodore. The Voice of the Earth. New York: Simon Schuster, 1992.

Sabo, George. Paths of Our Children. Fayetteville, AR: Arkansas Archeological Survey, 1992.

Sams, Jamie, and David Carson. Medicine Cards: The Discovery of Power Through the Ways of Animals. Sante Fe, NM: Bear and Co., 1988.

Schaafsma, Polly. Indian Rock Art of the Southwest. Albuquerque: University of New Mexico Press, 1980.

Sherman, Josepha. Indian Tribes of North America. New York, Portland House, 1990.

Silko, Leslie. Storyteller. New York: Little Brown and Co., 1981.

Silverberg, Robert. The Mound Builders. Athens, OH: Ohio University Press, 1989.

Sproule, Barbara C. Primal Myths: Creating the World. New York: Harper and Row, 1979.

Steiger, Brad. Indian Medicine Power. Westchester, PENN: Schiffer Publishing, 1984.

Storm, Hyemeyohsts. Seven Arrows. New York, Ballantye Books, 1972.

Stuart, Gene S. America's Ancient Cities. Washington, D.C., National Geographic Society, 1988.

Sun Bear, and Wabun. The Medicine Wheel. Earth Astrology. New York: Prentice Hall, 1980.

Sun Bear, Wabun Wind, and Crysalis Mulligan. Dancing With the Wheel, The Medicine Wheel Workbook. New York, Simon and Shuster, 1991.

Sutphen, Dick. Sedona: Psychic Energy Vortexes. Malibu, CA: Valley of the Sun Prining Co., 1986.

Suttles, Wayne, ed. Handbook of North American Indians, Vol. 7, Northwest Coast. Washington, DC: Smithsonian, 1990.

Swan, James. Sacred Places: How the Living Earth Seeks Our Friendship. Sante Fe, NM: Bear and Co., 1990.

Swan, James, ed. The Power of Place and Human Environments. Wheaton, ILL: Quest Books, 1991.

Swinton, George. Eskimo Sculpture. Toronto: McClelland & Stewart, 1965.

The Mighty Chieftains. Alexandria, VA: Time Life, 1993.

The Buffalo Hunters. Alexandria, VA: Time Life, 1993.

The Spirit World. Alexandria, VA: Time Life, 1992.

The European Challenge. Alexandria, VA: Time Life, 1992.

The Sacred Tree. Lethbridge, ALTA: Four Worlds Development Press, 1984.

The First Americans. Alexandria, VA: Time Life, 1992.

Trigger, Buce C., ed. Handbook of North American Indians, Vol. 15, Northeast. Washington, DC: Smithsonian, 1978.

Viele, Catherine W. Voices in the Canyon. Southwest Parks and Monuments, 1990.

Wabun, and Barry Weinstock. Sun Bear, The Path of Power. Spokane, WA: Bear Tribe Publishing, 1983.

Wall, Steve, and Harvey Arden. Wisdomkeepers: Meetings with Native American Spiritual Elders. Hillsboro, OR: Beyond Words Publishing, 1990.

Waters, Frank. Masked Gods. Athens, OH: Ohio University Press, 1984.

Waters, Frank. Book of the Hopi. New York: Penguin (Viking), 1963, 1972-1977.

Westwood, Jennifer, ed. The Atlas of Mysterious Places. New York: Weidenfeld and Nicolson, 1987.

Wicklein, John. "Spirit Paths of the Anasazi", from Archeology, Jan/Feb. 1994, p. 36-41.

Williamson, Ray. Living the Sky: The Cosmos of the American Indian. University of Oklahoma Press, 1984.

Wosien, Maria Gabriele. Sacred Dance: Encounter with the Gods. Avon, 1974

Wright, Ronald. Stolen Continents -- The "New World" Through Indian Eyes Since 1492. Toronto: Penguin (Viking), 1992.

Young, Dudley. Origins of the Sacred. New York: HarperCollins, 1991.

Zambucka, Kristin. The Keepers of the Earth. Honolulu: Harrane Publishing, 1985.

Zanger, Michael. Mt. Shasta, History, Legend and Lore. Berkeley, CA: Celestial Arts, 1992.

Zeilinger, Ron. Sacred Ground, Reflections on Lakota Spirituality and the Gospel. Chamberlain, SD: Tipi Press, 1987.

# Index

206

# ON THE MAKING OF THE BOOK

Jacket and interior designed by V. John Lee

Map designed and drawn by James Loates

Edited by Jackie Kaiser

Copy edited by Rosalyn Steiner

Production edited by Lori Ledingham

Production direction by Dianne Craig

Printed and bound by New Interlitho Italia S.p.A.

The text of *Spirit of the Land* is set in Stempel Garamond, a traditional oldstyle typeface. Headings are set in Neworder, a contemporary display typeface. Layout and Typesetting have been produced on an IBM 486 in Aldus Pagemaker, Version 5.0

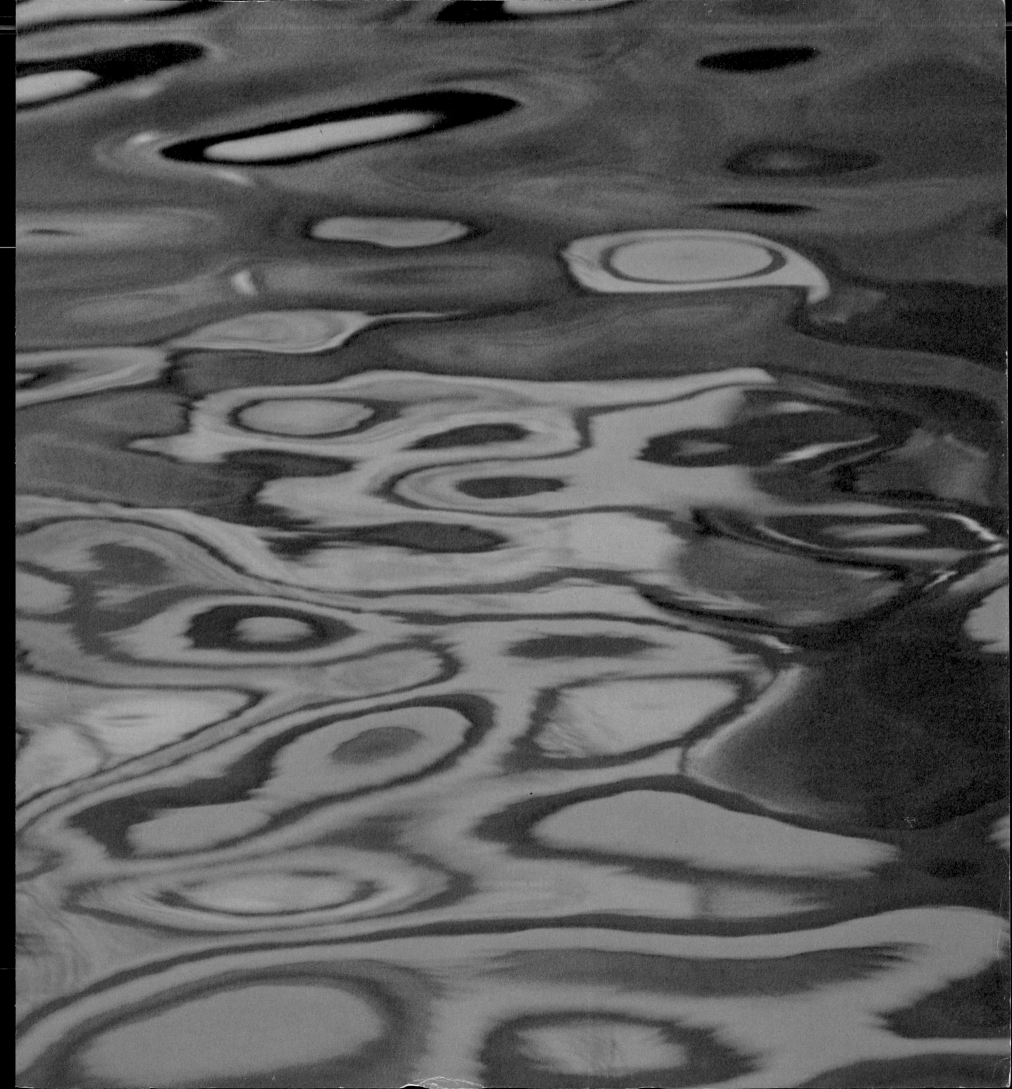

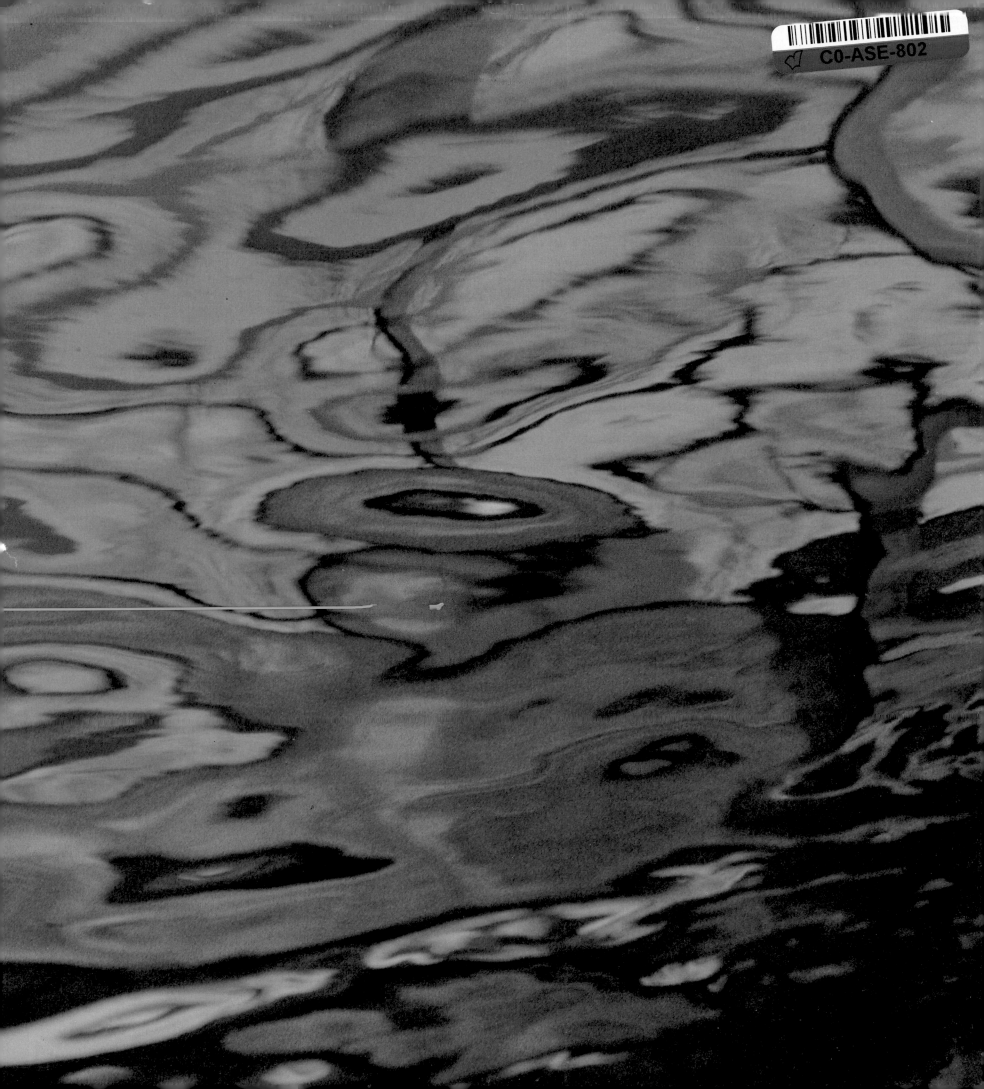